Praise for Cloaked in Shadow

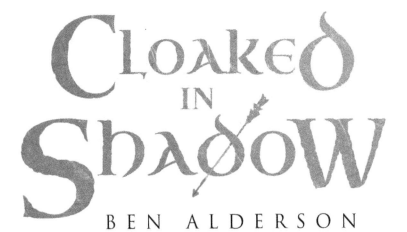

CLOAKED
IN
Shadow

BEN ALDERSON

OFTOMES PUBLISHING
UNITED KINGDOM

Cover Art by Gwenn Danae

Cover design by Eight Little Pages

Interior book design by Eight Little Pages

FOR HARRY, MY HADRIAN.

FOR JASMINE, MY NYAH.

In the beginning, the Goddess blessed the world with her breath. She blew life across a once barren land until beasts, creatures, and elves blossomed. With the life she bestowed came death, which crept into existence against her will.

He came for her children until they became his.

CHAPTER
ONE

I REACHED MY hand outside of the wagon, allowing the wind to stream through my fingers.

My magick stirred, aching for a release. The winds tussled playfully at my hair. It wanted me to answer, it begged me to.

If it wasn't for Mam's worried mutterings that echoed through my mind, I might have risked using it. It might even help pass the time. But as my mind toyed with the idea, I could almost feel her like a ghost leaning into my ear, *Keep it hidden, Zacriah; don't let it out.*

It was second nature to leave my power locked in its onyx cage. I could understand their concerns that someone would catch me and use my magick against me. But in quiet moments, I revelled in the thought.

So, I resisted, keeping my hands in my lap as the wagon bumped across the dirt path, leading away from home. Away from comfort. To take my mind off the ache within my chest, I lost myself in the clouds of dust the wagons wheels tussled up. I watched it dance and spin in torrents of wind, elegantly shifting into shapes and patterns.

I marvelled at the sights ahead of me. Thessolina was beautiful during the springtime, evident from the rolling emerald hills and fields of red blossom. Spring was my favourite of the four seasons; it had been since I was a youngling. I loved when the air was full of the fresh scents of bloomed flowers, sweet daffodils and tulips. And the unpredictable down pours of rain only a weather witch would sense. It was also the season I spent most of my time alone, hunting. Not sitting amongst elves whom I didn't enjoy the company of, like today. But that was out of my hands.

I shifted in my seat, trying to regain feeling that had long ago left my behind. I would've stretched, but the close proximity prevented me from doing so. Between the sack jammed beneath my legs and the two elves pressed on either side of me, there wasn't much room to breathe, let alone move around. Somehow, the guards had managed to squeeze fifteen of us into the wagon, like a school of fish clustered into a moving, wooden coffin. The stench of the stocky, red headed boy sitting next to me only added to the discomfort of the journey.

The smell I could fix, it wouldn't take much. But it was not worth the risk; so, again, I resisted the urge to use my magick and turned my attention back to the dancing dust.

～

THE SUN HAD begun to set behind the distant mountains of Karlf, giving room for the waned moon to take its place. Shivers ran down my spine as I yawned, exhaustion flickering behind my eyes. We had left in the morning and night was now upon us. It seemed that I was the only one bored by the journey, for most of those around me were too preoccupied conversing about what to expect when we arrived in Olderim. I wanted nothing more than to leave this god-awful space, return home and help Fa with the day's hunt. The thought of Fa hunting alone twisted within my stomach, tightening the knot of worry. He would need me; hunting was my skill, not his.

I looked over the sea of muted colours, clothing of muddy greys and faded greens— another reminder of home. Horith was not a town built on riches, but one driven by the need to work to survive. I couldn't help but think of how we would stand out in the capital. If the guard's uniforms were anything to go by, the fashion in Olderim was much different.

Leading the wagon on armoured Elks sat the two royal guards who'd not uttered a word since we departed, only staring ahead, refusing to enter conversation with the many attempting to ask questions.

I didn't blame their silence.

They were both clothed in the grand uniform of the King's royal legion, a vast difference to what we wore. A deep violet leather undershirt lay beneath scaled, rose gold chainmail. Their long sandy hair hung loose and tumbled behind them, woven with plaits and braids. Horned helms covered their heads, two slits on either side to allow their ears to roam free without the constraints of metal. It was common practice by all elves to have our ears on display; wearing them like badges of honour. But it was not the only reason they stood free. I'd seen them twitch every so often, shifting as they followed far off noises, searching for possible threats beyond the skyline.

I wondered if the reason they seemed so tense had anything to do with the recent rumours of ransacked villages and towns. Although that was all they were, rumours. Nothing had been confirmed. I was certain it was only gossip, nothing more than mutated whispers passed from neighbouring villages. I'd seen no proof of these remarks, nor believed them possible.

I ran a hand over the shaved sides of my head, feeling the coarse hair brush underneath my fingers, a style much different than the guards. My bun had been thrown together moments before I left. Mam had created a single braid that ran along the top of my head and collected in the bun. Her own attempts at making me look presentable for the evening's festivities. She'd believed the braid would bring me luck; so, to appease her, I sat without complaint as she yanked and pulled to finish it. If it made her feel better about me leaving, I was happy to oblige.

During the long days of labour all year round, it made sense to have a shorter style of hair. But as I watched the guards ride ahead, I knew their style was for show. There was no reason for the elegant style. Then again, it's not like we were in war. The guards were nothing more than puppets for the king.

The evening breeze blew across the wagon, bringing the night's slight chill with it. I pulled my hands into my long sleeves, concealing them from the crisp bite. If I'd known the journey would have lasted into the night, I would've brought a jacket. I added the chill to the ever growing list of complaints I had sorted in my mind.

The shorter of the two guards carried a flag at the top a pole; it made frantic sounds as the night wind blew at it. The King's emblem had been embroidered onto the material. I traced the same symbol on my knee with my fingernail, the symbol of the Niraen elves. A knot of roots that looped around a tree in a circular motion. The same symbol carved into the guard's shoulder plates and the signs we passed on our way to Olderim. King Dalior's mark.

The wagon bumped over a ditch and I shuddered at the vibration it caused to run up my spine. The bows on the guard's plated backs bounced with momentum, making a high-pitched clacking noise, wood against metal. The bows were unlike any I had seen, vastly different from the flimsy, yew wood bows I used back home. The thick wood was embellished with designs of vines and leaves painted in gold and silver hues. I could only imagine the power the bows held.

The taught strings and the sturdiness of the frame looked unbreakable. I'd kill double the pray with it. *If only.*

I lost myself in thoughts of hunting, my eyes fixed to the guard's bows. It wasn't until I heard a familiar voice that distracted me from my own imagination.

"I've heard the Prince still has no mate, I think it's time I changed that…"

My ears twitched in response to the name used at the end of the wagon closest to the guards. I diverted my attention towards it, not shocked that it was Illera.

"I wonder what he'll be wearing tonight?" Illera fiddled with her deep chestnut braid, twisting it around her finger. "Something *tight*, I hope…"

Alerior chuckled, nudging Illera's shoulder with her own. "You're terrible, truly!"

For as long as I could remember, Alerior and Katill had followed Illera around like doe-eyed puppies, always feeding her with just what she wanted to hear. I knew steering clear of her was the best option. I'd gained her unwanted attention before and became the brunt of her boredom. It didn't end well. I felt almost sorry for whoever it was they gossiped about.

"I can't wait to see his face when he sees what you're wearing later… or what you are *not* wearing." Katill also had a filthy mind, it was her one redeeming quality.

Illera's laugh was shrill, forced. "We'll see. I had to sneak my dress past father. He would drop down dead if he saw what I'd done to it." She motioned with her two fingers, "Snip, snip, snip."

My laugh even surprised me.

The snort burst out of my nose, which I tried to cover up with a cough. It didn't work. I turned away, looking back over the side of the wagon but their conversation had ceased. I didn't have to see to know Illera was looking at me, her gaze burned into the back of my head.

"Something funny?" Her voice was sweet, though I could taste the sickly undertone as she questioned me.

I looked to Illera's violet eyes, full of intrigue. Her sharp brows pinched above her sinister smile.

Here we go.

I shook my head and held her gaze, biting my tongue.

Don't fall for it. Don't fall for it.

"No?" Her cackle pierced my ears. "Well, let me see… you must have been daydreaming about your father, who will no doubt fail *miserably* at the hunt this evening," she drawled.

My canines bit into my bottom lip and my mouth filled with salvia and copper.

"Oh, I know, I know." She jumped in her seat, raising her hand in the air. By this point, the entire cart was listening, watching. "Was it the thought of your mother having to beg yet *again* for food? Yes, that must be it. Because that is hilarious" She threw her head back and roared with laughter. If that was not enough of a kick to the balls, she clenched her fists pretending to rub fake tears from her eyes.

I kept my eyes on her, ignoring the laughter that had erupted around me. I leaned forward to close any space between us, a smile plastered on my face. For a slight moment, her own smile faltered; she knew what was coming.

I knew better than to get personal. But when it came to Illera, I found great pleasure in wiping the smug smile from her face.

"Sorry for the confusion…" I paused, taking a slow breath to allow those listening to quiet. I wanted everyone to hear this. "But I must thank you for your concern. You seem so interested in something that has nothing to do with you. If you *really* want to know what I found so amusing, I'll tell you. I was just daydreaming about your parents and how they

❋ 6 ❧

didn't even bother to see you off this morn… but then again, who can blame them? I too would be more than happy to see the back of you." I leaned forward even more, and brought my voice down to a whisper. "I've heard they've been praying to the Goddess this day would come…seems she has been listening."

Her smile dropped, and her eyes lost their sinister sheen. She opened her mouth to respond, but came up short, shutting her thin lips, her face blotched red with embarrassment. Katill laughed first and was soon followed by Alerior, whose eyes bulged as she fought back against her own giggle. Illera turned and snapped at them, even going so far as to slap Katill's leg who cowered away from her.

"Shut up!" Illera shouted, a vein bulging on her forehead. I still didn't drop my gaze and to my pleasure, she didn't look back, looking everywhere but at me. Illera cut a look to the crowd who watched on, stifling their muffled laughs.

Satisfied she'd not comment back I turned away, fixing my attention on the darkening sky. If Illera was clever, she would keep to herself the rest of the journey.

The sun had set. The golden wash faded, leaving a moody blue haze across the land. I closed my eyes and slowed my breathing. Sleep was a welcome friend.

⌒

I AWOKE TO silence. I blinked through the haze in my mind and looked around, disorientated. At first, I forgot where I was, but I followed the eyes of those who were still awake and watched as we passed through a village. There was something off about this place. Not a single sign of life amongst the leaning shacks and the closed shuttered tavern. The moon hung bright in the sky, and illuminated the deserted streets.

There was a smell that hung in the air around us, but I couldn't place what it was. The cart bumped across the road, and the remains of a building came into view. If it wasn't for the standing doorframe and the ruminates of bricks and wood, I would have passed it without thought. But as it came into view, I could see it was not the only building left in that state. The guards directed the wagon through the destroyed portion of the village, not saying a word or responding to the worried murmurs behind them. I watched in confusion, finally realizing the smell was smoke. Moonlight shone across the blackened building remains. The air was thick with smoke still, yet all signs of fire had dwindled.

I looked to the stars and began tracing the constellations, working out how far Horith was from here. Growing up in such an open, detached village, I had grown used to the stars and the stories they told. Fa had taught me to use them as a tool of navigation, a skill that came in handy during the many evenings I spent hunting when sleep didn't come to me.

I didn't recognize this village, but could tell from the distance of Orion's belt we were miles from home. *What had happened?* Thoughts spiralled in my mind, but the lack of reaction between the guards was enough to subside my worries.

We left the deserted village behind, and I watched it shrink into the distance until the night swallowed it whole.

It didn't take long for us to pass through another village. It was full of life. Many elves lined the streets to watch us pass, some waving, others turning their backs. I saw the glint of jealously in their eyes when we passed. It was not common for elves like us to be called personally by King Dalior. I also noticed the lack of younger faces amongst the crowd. I could only guess those born eighteen moons ago had already left for Olderim.

The whispers in the wagon had stopped, instead swapped for the occasional snore or grunt from the many who slept. I glanced over the faces, taking note of Illera who'd also fallen asleep, her head bent back and tilted up to the sky. There was movement from the opposite side of the wagon. A shadowed elf clambered over the sleeping bodies in my direction. My heart dropped when *he* stepped closer into view. *I hoped he'd not do this.*

"I'm glad to see you're up!" Petrer whispered. He stepped over one elf who'd decided to make space on the floor of the wagon to sleep, then squeezed into a space between the two sleeping elves in front of me. I rubbed the sleep from my eyes and forced a smile. *Illera would be better company.*

Petrer looked like a giant next to the elves beside him. It would be impossible to ignore that he'd been blessed with the body of a God. In comparison, I looked miniature. The only muscle I had was on my arms, thanks to the bow work and labour on Fa's farm.

I drank in his familiar features, his plump lips and obsidian eyes. The top two buttons on his faded shirt were unbuttoned, revealing his defined chest and the tuft of curly black hair nestled between his pecks. I couldn't hold his eye contact. I wouldn't. I caught his wide smile, but quickly looked to my hands and began fiddling with my dirtied nails.

"Not tired?" I asked.

Petrer ran a large hand across his shaved head, "Not really." His yawn suggested otherwise. "I've been waiting for you to wake. I thought this would be the best place to catch you since I've had the hardest time finding you these past two weeks. A sane person would think you've been avoiding me."

You'd be correct. "Fa's been keeping me pretty busy."

"Is that it? When has that ever stopped you for finding the time for me?"

"I didn't think Olderim was this far away from home," I said. Changing the subject was the best option.

I had to stop myself from melting when Petrer chuckled. "If I see another mountain or hill in the next thirty moons, it would *still* be too soon."

I rolled my eyes. "You've never been one for a pretty view."

"What do you mean? I've come to sit opposite you, *of course* I enjoy a pretty view."

I cringed. If he had said that two weeks ago, my response would have been much different.

I looked to my feet, trying to hide the creep of red that had crossed my face. "Have you tried sleeping? I managed to sleep well, even if it was only for a moment," I said.

Petrer and I had grown close over the past winter. We'd found *many* ways to waste those cold dark days: hunting, talking, and spending endless nights with our bodies intertwined. Memories that now only made me cringe with distaste and regret. We were better off as friends; at least that's what I'd repeated to myself over the past two weeks.

"The only thing that has fallen asleep is my arse, it's so numb!" Petrer replied, wiggling in his seat.

"Shouldn't be long now," I replied, pushing the thought of his bare arse from my mind. "I can smell salt in the air."

Petrer's nose twitched and he nodded, "So, do I. I can't believe I didn't notice it before!"

I'd not seen the sea for years, but I still recognized the smell. It brought memories of my last visit to Olderim with Fa many moons ago. I longed to see its aqua hues and bubbling froth, the shadows from schools of fish swimming in the ocean's belly. I took a deep breath, welcoming the unfamiliar scent, and my stomach flipped with anticipation.

"How about I go and see…" Petrer whispered, rubbing his jaw with his thick thumb. "It would only take me a moment and I'd be back before I'm noticed." He nodded at the guards.

It was pointless telling Petrer what to do, he was never one to listen. "Why ask me? You're going to do it regardless of what I say."

Petrer smiled a gorgeous, large grin and leaned back with a wink. "You know me *too* well…"

I wish I didn't.

I was used to seeing the dark shadows snake from his body, engulfing him in their embrace. But no matter how many times I watched it, it still fascinated me.

Sweet apples and burnt wood coated my nose as the smoke concealed Petrer, shadow and skin blended together. It was the only sign of a shift I'd still not gotten used to. It took seconds for the smoke to then vanish, leaving a raven that hovered inches from my face. Its beady black eyes bore into mine, the same eyes I had peered into hundreds of times. Petrers.

The sheen from his black feathers caught glints of moonlight and he kept eye level with me, turning his head side to side. I nodded and Petrer shot up into the night, blending in with the black around him. Even with my heightened sight, I struggled to keep track of his blurring form. The guards didn't stir, not showing any sign that they knew one of us was missing. Although I was sure they'd been listening in the entire time.

Minutes passed before I felt the faint burst of wind beneath Petrer's wings, signalling his return. One moment he was invisible to the night the next he was shooting for the wagon, cutting through the dark.

Silently, he unravelled in a plume of smoke and sat before me like nothing had happened, not a feather or beak in sight.

"Three miles or so north," Petrer whispered.

His words caused a mixture of excitement and anxiety to whirl in the pit of my stomach. I sat on my hands to stop them from shaking. Adrenaline raced through me. "It's even closer than I thought! What did it look like? Did you see the water?"

"It was hard to see much beyond the wall, but yes, I saw it, the ocean I mean. It's pretty hard to miss," Petrer said, resting a hand on my knee, "Something that is also hard to miss is how I've not kissed those..."

He leaned forward, but I turned my head when his mouth came close to mine. His lips brushed against my cheek and I closed my eyes.

In truth, I wanted nothing more than to experience the familiar sensation of Petrer's mouth crashing against my own, but I couldn't.

Before I could come up with a response, we were both interrupted by a call from the end of the wagon. Illera awoke and shouted as she pointed towards two specs of light in the distance.

Her call was loud enough to wake everyone who was asleep. Half of them began scrambling to get a better view. With the newly gained space, I stretched my legs out and groaned in pleasure. I recoiled when my foot bumped against Petrer's foot, although part of me wished I kept it pressed against him.

The guards pulled up to the entrance, stopping just before the threshold.

The outer wall to Olderim was monstrous. An endless stretch of stone dwarfed its surroundings.

Before us was a door, its metal surface etched with detailed depictions of elves riding elks, branding weapons, and wielding magick. Its beauty was inspiring yet intimidating. Two burning torches stood on either side of the entrance, illuminating the metal designs in hues of red and orange. No other signs of life stirred outside the walls, the night swallowing up all but the entrance before us. Everyone was silent, awaiting the next move.

A hollow sound grew from behind the doors and they began to open. Dull light spilled from the crack as they opened wider. Hands rose to blocks eyes, mouths aghast in wonder at the vision presented before us. The wagon was pulled forward into the light, into the city beyond. The last thing I heard as we entered was Petrer's long drawl, "Fuck."

CHAPTER

TWO

"WHAT TOOK YOU so long? Everyone else has arrived already." The guard beyond the gate spoke only to the two who had brought us, not once glancing back at the wagon.

"What do you expect? They're from the furthest village from 'ere," one replied. It was the first time I'd heard his voice since leaving Horith.

"Anything to report?" The gate guard asked.

"Seems like they got to Talnot. It's a ghost town back there."

The gate guard's face twisted. "I'll pass it on to the King." With that she waved us forward, and the wagon began to move once again.

Olderim had changed a lot in the years since my last visit. Although, visually, the details of the streets were hazy in memory, it was the scent of burning coals and the sea that reminded me of a time long ago. The once contained city had since tripled in size. Ancient, deep oak structures blended with newer sandstone buildings, a patchwork of architecture.

Olderim was the primary Elven settlement in Thessolina, a walled fortress bustling with life. Home to the King and what was left of the royal family; the citadel was the most important in the land. It'd been built next to the ocean and used as the main trading port since its creation, naturally becoming the hub of all major trading between Morgatis and Eldnol.

My eyes scanned the streets of Masarion, the outer rim of the city, as the wagon jolted across its cobbled streets. The domed stone roofs of the newer buildings towered above the rickety dark wood shacks sitting crookedly beside them. The older structures I remembered, but the grand stone buildings were new to me.

Fa had told me of Olderim's growth every year he arrived back from trading, but I never imagined such a large change in such a short period of time.

The streets of Masarion bustled with life, the most I had seen since leaving Horith. Smoke seeped from open doors of taverns as elves of all ages disappeared into the red glow of the buildings. Strings of material hung across the narrow streets, tied between shutters from opposite buildings. Slacks, cloaks and other clothing pieces hung from it, swaying in a choreographed dance with the breeze. I thought back to the time I'd visited, when I was only seven moons old. It was a struggle to remember the time, but I saw brief images of embers burning in open hearths and tankards spilling with an amber liquid. I'd loved city life, even begging Fa every year since to bring me back. But he never did. With each moon that passed, my memories of Olderim faded and warped into an incoherent string of images that did not match what I saw before me.

The wagon jolted, knocking me from my seat. I landed on Petrer's lap, thrust forward by the sharp bump. Others too had fallen, some laughing and others shrieking. The guards turned to look back, but said no words of apology.

"Sorry…" I mumbled as I pushed off his lap, although Petrer's smirk suggested he didn't mind at all. I stumbled back to my seat in time to see a haggle of elven women dressed in deep burgundy cloaks entering the loudest tavern we'd past yet. I took a shuddered breath when the door opened, my mouth watering over the scent of ale and steamed meats that poured onto the street.

Petrer pointed, noticing the glowing interior before the door slammed shut. "Shame we can't sneak in there for a quick pint, my mouth is as dry as the Morgatis desert."

I nodded, cutting the conversation short so I wouldn't miss a single detail of the fascinating place. Petrer huffed and leaned back in his seat, clearly bugged from my lack of response. *At least he got the hint.*

∽

WE PASSED THROUGH the maze of interlocking streets, dim alleys and countless archways. Hanging bowls of fire lit the way, casting orange shadows across the path ahead. I rubbed my hands to warm them, every now and then blowing hot breath onto them. I was jealous of the passing fires, they seemed to tease me with their heat and glowing embers of comfort.

The wagon rolled over a bridge of marble and smooth stone. I leaned over the side of the wagon and caught a glimpse of the waterway beneath us. Silver finned fish propelled above the water, moonlight reflected across their scales. I'd never seen water so clear, each grain of sand visible in the depths below. The lakes and rivers in Horith were muddy and dark, nothing like the one beneath us.

Calls from younglings sounded to my left. I turned to their cries to see a small group, each taking turns jumping into the river, their light laughter bouncing across its surface like a skipping pebble.

Even in the belly of night, the city was burning with life. It was contagious; I longed to join them and bathe the day's journey from my skin.

We reached the end of the bridge and I spotted a sign, the word *Thalor* carved into its wood. The middle district of Olderim, a place I hadn't visited before.

Only grand structures of white stone stood, lining the streets of Thalor.

From what I could see, it was like stepping into a different world. If I didn't turn back to see Masarion over the bridge, I may not have believed we'd ever been through it.

I looked up to admire the buildings that towered above. Grey slated dome roofs, each a work of the best craftsmanship and stature sat atop each building. I could only imagine those who lived inside, each rolling in coins and power. These were not made for common folk, that much was clear.

Apart from the candlelight from the many rooms, there was no other sign of life in Thalor. Not a single elf walked by. There was no laughter from taverns, or noises of evening trades. Silence wrapped around the wagon, the echo of rolling wheels and elk's hooves were the only sounds in the city.

Once we passed through the wider streets of Thalor, we arrived at a second bridge. It was twice the size of the first we'd passed, and on either side, stone pillars stood erect like silent guards watching over us as we passed beneath. At the end of the bridge stood towering gates. The moon was visible through silver metal vines, its sharp points glinting in the faint light.

We came to an abrupt stop before the gates, and the two guards dismounted the elks and shuffled to the rear of the wagon. They opened the gate at the back and we began to file out. It was a mess of bodies clambering over each other; I had to hold onto the side to keep my balance as others pushed past me.

Petrer went ahead and I followed, jumping from the wagon with a soundless thud and joining a group of elves, each who stretched and looked around in awe. The worry of leaving Fa and Mam had melted away, leaving only room to absorb everything around me. The gates creaked open and our two guards began to herd us through them. Petrer stepped in close behind me and placed a hand on the curve of my back, guiding me forward. I contemplated pulling away, but was too caught up with what was beyond the gates to think of anything else.

The palace. It was the biggest building I'd ever seen. The moon appeared small in comparison.

Like the buildings in Thalor, the palace was made from alabaster stone, glowing in the limited light from the moon and stars. Endless windows covered the outer walls, each lit from inside by the warmth of fire and light. I strained my eyes in the dark trying to make out every detail possible. A colony of bats danced around the pointed towers of the palace, flying in and out of alcoves in the walls. Deep jade vines had overtaken the outer walls, and bustling gardens of flowers and shrubbery lined the grounds below.

Captured by the beauty of the palace, I didn't realize the walk had stopped until I bumped into someone ahead of me. I looked up in time to see our two guards standing beneath the palace doors waiting to address us.

"Welcome to Vulmar, home of our loyal King," the taller, blonde haired guard announced. "In a matter of hours, you are to attend a feast. You are to bathe and make yourself presentable for an audience with the King. It is an honour to have such a prestigious invite so please do not waste it. We do not have long to prepare as the journey has put us behind schedule."

A hollow bang sounded from the grand oak doors, signalling for the two guards to move to either side of it. I craned my head over the crowd, anxious to get a look inside.

I lifted my hand to cover my eyes from the blinding light spilling from within. Once my eyes had adjusted, I could see the endless corridor that welcomed us, a rose stained carpet lining the floor disappearing into the palace.

"You are to follow in an orderly fashion. We will be guiding you to your assigned sleeping quarters for the remainder of your stay. I trust you will not forget the way as you will *not* be shown again."

In tandem, we followed the guards through the threshold of the palace. I stumbled over the back of someone's feet and gained myself a sharp look of disapproval.

"Watch it!" he hissed.

I raised my arms and whispered an apology. Making more effort to keep distance between the others and myself.

∽

THE RICHES OF King Dalior were everywhere, from the intricate detailed paintings on the walls to the thick rugs that lay beneath our feet. It was clearer now more than ever how our tithes were spent. Silks draped across the stone walls beside us. It would've been impossible to count the number of candles balanced on clawed footed candelabras.

The shaven heads of the elves before me turned in wonder, taking in every grand detail like it would be the first and last time they would see such beauty. We were worlds away from Horith, worlds away from our simple lives.

We moved ahead through an arched doorway, leading to a winding case of stone steps. Our footsteps echoed across the bare stone walls as we climbed the steps, only the occasional window allowing the moonlight to spill in and light the way. I reached a hand out to the wall, my coarse fingers running over the smooth surface to keep me steady throughout the climb. The stairway went on longer than I expected, but unlike the others, my legs moved at a constant pace, showing no sign of ache or strain. I silently thanked the hours of climbing trees and hunting, I wouldn't have the endurance without it. I spotted Illera up ahead, her steps slow and shoulders moving heavily as she struggled to stay in the lead. It didn't surprise me; I knew she'd do anything to make an impression.

We must have reached our destination because the guards pulled into a room off to the side of the stairway and stopped. As I passed under the archway, I noticed a familiar design etched into the curve above me. The King's emblem was everywhere, carved into stone walls, woven into rugs and wall hangings.

The room we entered was open and large, the same width of my entire home back in Horith. I counted five doors on either side of the floor, each marked with the King's emblem, although faint in the worn wood surfaces. The guards looked around, waiting for the entirety of the group to enter, their faces steel-like, not giving away any emotion. I turned back to the stairway and watched the last few join us. They were each panting, heads damp with sweat from the climb.

"This is where you will be staying," the taller of the guard shouted. "Through these doors, you will find your sleeping arrangements..." She motioned her stocky arms to the first four doors closest to them. "Through the door towards the end of the corridor you will find the baths. You may use it and prepare for the evening. The water is filtered from the ocean and warmed in the morning and eve. Be mindful to leave hot water for your fellow elves in your quarters. We *will* return shortly to collect you." Without another word, they both swept through the crowd, and headed back for the stairs.

"Is that it?" Illera moaned, eyes rolling as she turned for the group. I watched her with burning distaste, unsure of how I was to survive being in such close proximity to her during our time here. However long that would be. The invitation hadn't specified.

"Not the sleeping arrangements you expected, Illera?" Petrer couldn't hide his sarcasm.

Smirking, she gestured to the closest door to her left, ignoring Petrer's remark. "This room," Illera pushed it open, "is mine." It was final, her words not allowing for anyone to argue. Not that anyone would. Alerior and Katill followed behind her and slammed the heavy door closed.

"Anyone else want to volunteer to stay with them?" Petrer asked, pulling me to his side.

The group exploded in countless refusals, enough of an indication that no one wanted to join her. I couldn't blame them.

Petrer yanked my arm and led me through the door opposite the one we had watched Illera disappear into.

"If we're quick, we can pick a bed with a view," Petrer said.

I drew back, unsure how to break the news that I would *not* be sharing a bed with him.

∽

THE ROOM WAS cramped. The thin width left only enough room for a handful of bunk beds to line the walls. Petrer picked our bunk, throwing himself on one at the end of the room next to an open, glassless window. The view was of the endless ocean, a blue expanse that blended in seamlessly with the night sky. Small vessels bobbed on the gentle currents below, wry lights dotted across the coastal line. A breeze blew through the window, surrounding me in fresh bursts of salt that tickled my face and neck.

It was tempting to reach for it, to answer its call. I knew it wanted me to. I looked behind me, noticing that Petrer's attention was diverted. For only a moment, I lifted the lid to the cage within me. Only a small amount of magick was needed, I didn't want to control the air, only feel its familiar embrace. A relaxing sensation washed over me and I took comfort in its familiarity and grasped a hold of it.

"First come, first serve." Petrer chimed to those who entered the room, breaking my lapse in control. I fisted my hand, pushing the lid back on the metaphoric cage and stuffing the sliver of magick into its hold. Keeping it buried within me was the easiest way for me to control my urges.

I turned from the window to see Petrer who'd taken the bottom, leaving me with the cramped bunk on top. There was not much room between the bunk and the low ceiling, yet it was nicer than the lump of material I was used to sleeping on.

"Since I'm not used to *being* the bottom, I thought I'd pick it for once." I didn't miss Petrer's wink. *Gross.*

"Too far?" he asked.

The face I pulled was enough of an answer. I turned my stare away from him and studied the sage coloured sheets that covered the straw mattress and the single pillow that lay at the head of the bed.

"I could get used to this…" Petrer mumbled through a yawn.

"Me too," I replied.

I pulled myself up onto my bunk, but stopped when Petrer grabbed at my foot.

"Join me down here, just for a moment," he pleaded, his eyes wide and blinking.

"That's not a good idea Petrer." My voice was cold, final.

I pulled my leg from Petrer's reach and rolled onto my bed, the mattress lumpy beneath me.

"Suit yourself," he grumbled.

It didn't take long for the room to fill. I counted eight elves who claimed the remaining beds. I recognized most of them from home: Demitria, who had joined me most nights out when I went hunting, and Gwendolyn, the daughter of Fa's childhood friend. Gwendolyn smiled my way as she unpacked her bag, placing her set of chalks and parchment on her bed. I liked her, so I smiled back.

I laid down, losing myself in the sounds of the waves crashing against the rocks at the bottom of the palace beyond the window. I was used to being by myself, not sharing a room with so many others. It had even taken me weeks to get used to having Petrer beside me. How I would sleep later was beyond me. But to my surprise, the quiet chatter only aided me, and I drowned in the waiting pits of sleep.

ThRee

"WHY DIDN'T YOU wake me?" I hissed, prodding Petrer in his side. The room was already half empty thanks to the guards who'd propped open the doors to the room, ushering everyone out.

"Oh, so now you want me to talk to you?" he whispered whist moving for the door. "And plus, you looked too peaceful to disturb."

As Petrer passed me, he smelled of fresh lemon and salt. He'd changed into a new set of clothes, tight fitting in shades of dull greens and browns. I scanned around at the elves who'd begun to leave the room, all fully dressed in stunning sets of furs and other beautiful materials. Each ready for the feast. Whereas I still sat in my bunk, gaining displeased looks from the guard who stood at the door.

"I don't care if you thought I was dead Petrer, you should've woke me!"

He shrugged in response and I moaned, jumping from the bunk and reaching for my bag. I'd only a few moments to change my dirtied clothes into suitable evening wear before I was left behind.

I pulled the set Mam had packed that morning from the sack, stripping the sticky clothes from my body and throwing them to the floor in a heap. A simple white tunic and leather trousers had been packed for me, the best Mam could buy on such short notice and little coin. As soon as I pulled them out, I could smell the familiar scent of home. It tugged at my heart.

My eyes burned as I lifted the tunic over my head, the stench from beneath my armpits enough to offend anyone. I needed a bath, to wash the grub and dried sweat from my body.

I hopped, keeping balance whilst I shoved my boots on. They were scuffed and muddied but would have to do. Petrer turned and smiled from the doorway, raising his brows silently to hurry me up.

"I'll meet you out there, stall for me!" I pleaded.

Petrer closed the door behind him leaving me alone in the room. Quickly, I turned for the window. I wasted no time before releasing the lid on my cage and calling for my magick. It seeped into my consciousness and I lifted my hands to the window. In a rush, I pulled the moist wind from beyond the window into the room. I twisted my fingers slowly, the air listening and changing course from my body to my face. The welcomed stream of air washed the remnants of the days travel from my skin, dissolving the stench beneath my armpits and cleansing my hair of the oils that coated it. My loose tunic billowed in the wind as it ran over every inch of my skin, completing the job I called it forth for.

Satisfied, I pushed my magick back into its hold, not leaving a single bit left. It was a risk, one I had to take. Mam would be horrified if she found out I had gone down unwashed and smelling like shit. I had to represent my family, even if I broke their rules to do it.

The door burst opened to Petrer's face popping around the threshold. "Come on, they're not waiting for yo..." He tilted his head, squinting his eyes as he looked me up and down. "How did you..." The last call from one of the guards sounded outside the room, distracting him from his train of thought.

"Hurry!"

⌒

THE WALK TO the main hall passed in a blur. We'd caught up with the rest of the group by the time they were half way down the stairway, filing in behind them with ease as if we had been there all along.

Naturally, I began mapping out the palace, mentally sorting details in my mind. Using the same technique I would in a forest during a hunt, I picked out visuals around me and replayed them back in my mind. By remembering small details, the stained-glass mirrors and faded maroon rugs, I knew I could find my way back to the sleeping quarters.

I whispered the directions to myself. Carvings on the arch, sixty-nine steps down, narrow corridor, vases of ruby and blue, fifth door to the left, rose covered walls.

No one spoke during the walk. The only sound was of cloaks brushing against the marble floor and the clatter of jewellery.

I smelled the destination before I saw it, and from the flaring noses of the group I knew I was not alone. The scent of rich meats, steamed vegetables, and fresh bread filled every inch of the corridor ahead. Beneath grand doors, a sea of elves stood waiting. They spoke amongst one another, some turning to look at us, others ignoring our existence.

I scanned the many faces, each different from the next. It was hard to tell which elves were Niraen, Morthi or Alorian. The Niraen wood elves like myself bled red, and the points of our ears were usually rounder at the tip. Unlike the Alorian high elves who bled gold and ears were sharper at the point, or the Morthi whose blood ran black and had two points on each ear; there were no other visible differences between the three races.

The two guards who had guided us sauntered over to the line of others who stood on either side of the door, watching over the crowd.

It was the most life I'd seen in the palace since arriving. I'd started to believe we were the only ones here. But it was certain, as chatter burst around me, that the King had sent his mysterious invite to more than I could've imagined.

Petrer remained behind me. He dipped his face to my ear, his breath warm against my skin, and spoke, "And here I was thinking we were the special ones."

I laughed, a short quiet bark. "All I can think about is the food. I swear my stomach is about to start eating itself if I don't get any meat in it." On cue my stomach growled.

We stood around waiting for what felt like a decade until there was a sound behind the door and the entire crowd silenced in response. Petrer's hand clasped mine and squeezed like he had so many times before, but I didn't respond. He dropped my hand quickly, but I tried to act as if it hadn't happened. Ignoring it was easier for me.

Footsteps echoed across the black-veined marble floor as we walked into the room, fighting against the crowd of elves who pushed in from either side of us.

It was a long room, the towering walls on either side finishing into arched panels that cut across the ceiling above. Everything dripped in wealth. The marble floor reflected the many dancing flames from the hundreds of candles within the room. I followed the crowd ahead, admiring the gold leaf paintings and deep maroon materials embroidered with the King's emblem.

In the middle of the room were four, long oak tables. On top of their dark oak surface lay a deep red cloth that ran down the length and flowed off onto the floor. I was pushed to a table and stood behind an empty seat. Aware of the sudden lack of Petrer's presence, I turned to look for him, but he was lost in the sea of heads. The room was a mass of moving bodies as the crowds of elves found seats somewhere amongst the other three tables.

I gripped the carved wooden antlers on the back of my seat, my hands clammy with anticipation. I caught Petrer's face; he was at a table two over from me. I was thankful for the space, but being left around strangers was not something I enjoyed.

The guards flooded the room and moved from the sides of the hall. They started to stomp their feet, first a slow beat that soon built up into a frantic crescendo. My heart matched their tempo. Then silenced reigned, they stopped, and the doors to the room slammed closed. All heads turned towards them to see a tall figure draped in silver move from its shadows and walk directly for the throne at the head of the room.

King Dalior.

He walked past the tables, his face burning with a smile. His cloak swept against the floor, a gentle lush song as he stepped up the raised dais where a throne of wood and thorns sat.

I half expected him to sit down, but he didn't, instead he turned and faced us all.

He was the definition of elegance and strength. His onyx hair fell down his back like a waterfall, stopping at his waistline. Like a statue, carved out of the richest stone, King Dalior scanned the room with a shining smile. His ears pointed through wisps of hair, standing out further than most. But it was his eyes that drew me in. Two orbs of icy grey nestled in his long, sharp face.

A circlet of jewels sat on his crown, cutting across his forehead. They glinted, winking at the crowd in welcome, the largest ruby almost seemed too heavy to wear. Yet he showed no sign of discomfort as he opened his arms wide and spoke.

"Do not stand for me, my children… please, sit." His deep voice boomed across the room.

The screech of chairs brought me back to focus. I copied those beside me and sat down, my eyes not leaving King Dalior for a single moment.

Once the room was seated, King Dalior nodded, his smile still wide.

"My children, welcome to Olderim. I am certain you all have many questions as to why you have been invited here, but I must thank you first for accepting my invitation. It warms my heart to see so many of you here in my home."

He took the three steps down from the dais and began to prowl along the front of the room, his arms clasped behind his back. I strained my neck to keep a gaze on him as he walked, heads blocking my view.

"This is the first celebration I have held in Thessolina for years, and hopefully the first of many more to come. As my son, Prince Hadrian, turned eighteen moons this year; we have decided to hold a feast in celebration. I felt it right to invite all others across our glorious land who also share the same moon as he, to join in with a feast like no other."

The room was held in silent captivity as King Dalior spoke.

A figure cloaked in shadow began moving forward from behind the throne, stepping into a single stream of light beside it. I could hear King Dalior still talking, but everything stilled as the prince came into focus.

Like his father, Hadrian shared the same long black hair, only the prince's hair ended at his broad shoulders. With thick dark brows and a strong face, he smiled at the crowd, bowing his head in greeting.

I noticed his different choice of clothing that held many similarities to the guards that flanked them. Purple and bronze hung off his muscular frame, hugging his arms and shoulders. He moved closer to his father, placing a hand on his shoulder.

I was surprised to see the lack of jewels covering his hand, not like King Dalior whose hand seemed heavy under the weight of many rings and stones.

"… It warms my heart to see so many of you, each with different stories to tell and experiences to share, sitting in one room. I do hope you enjoy your stay here, no matter how short. Please, eat, drink and celebrate with us."

King Dalior's hands clapped together, and instantly the doors lining the room burst open, elves dressed in white rushed forth. They each held numerous plates balanced on their hands and arms. It was like a dance; within moments, all four tables had been filled with steaming food. My stomach growled in response. During the distraction, King Dalior and Prince Hadrian were now seated. I looked their way briefly, but the urge to shovel the gorgeous plates of food into my mouth was almost too much to ignore. The smell was a siren call to my growling stomach.

No one touched the food. Not until King Dalior called from his seat. "Please, eat up before the food goes cold."

Plates knocked against overfilled goblets and the room began to eat. I chewed on chicken legs, the skin crispy beneath my teeth. I piled my plate with soft carrots, mashed potatoes and bread, which didn't last long before I devoured them.

The throne room filled with laughter, and the feast got underway.

∽

AS THE PLATES were being taken away, the elves dressed in white brought out replacements, not leaving the tables empty for a single moment. Plates of meat and bread were swapped with desserts. Sugared buns towered on brass trays and fruit of all kinds spilled over bowls. It smelled divine, yet tasted even better. I bit into my third honey bun, licking my lips and fingers to remove the sugar that laced them. The pressed apple drink was the perfect chaser after such divine desserts.

Every now and then I would look over at King Dalior. He sat and watched with delight at the satisfied crowd, not once joining in the feast himself. Prince Hadrian also watched, although there was something behind his expression that I couldn't put a finger on. I quickly forgot about it when more plates of food were brought out.

I ate and ate, unsure if I would ever stop until it finally caught up to me. My stomach was swollen with food. Bloated and aching, I leaned back in my seat, rubbing the back of my hand across my mouth to discard the flecks of sugar and juice that coated my lips. The elves on the table around me had also started to slow down, huffing with pleasure and giggling at each other's bulging stomachs. For me, being full was a new sensation. One I welcomed.

My attention was directed to a loud noise on the table opposite me. It came from a boy who was slumped, with his head in his arms. The goblet he'd knocked to the floor rolled beneath the table and bumped against my foot, leaving a trail of scarlet liquid across the black marble floor. I kicked out under the table to wake him, horrified at the thought of the King seeing him asleep.

"Oi!" I hissed, aware of the sudden lack of noise in the room. The boy didn't wake so I kicked again, knocking my foot against his shin harder. There was another sound beside me. I turned and my mouth went dry. All around me, elves slept.

I was not the only one left awake as a few others from neighbouring tables began to stand up and step back in worry.

I fumbled to join them, knocking at the one who slept beside me until she fell from her chair face first to the ground. I cringed at the impact.

The doors burst open to an uncountable number of guards who filled the room. I looked to King Dalior who still sat in his throne, his face calm. The guards streamed forward, and began lifting out those who slept from their seats and walked from the room. The white dressed elves also entered the room and began clearing the knocked over goblets and leftover food from the table as if it what was happening was completely normal.

I scanned for Petrer, relieved as I saw he too was still awake and moving out of the way of the girl next to him who was lifted over the guard's shoulder and taken from the room. It was not common to see Petrer worry, but his face was pinched with it. He caught my gaze and mouthed something that I couldn't make out.

"Do not worry…" King Dalior called from the steps, his voice spreading a blanket of calm over the remainder of the room. "You must excuse me, for I have to admit that I have not been honest with you all. Your friends, they will all be taken to their rooms to rest for the evening. They are in safe hands, I can assure you." His draping sleeved arms waved at the last guard, urging them to leave with haste.

"Before the feast, I had the kitchens lace the food with Forbian. Which as you have seen has had the desired affects that I intended. My heart truly aches that I have not been honest with you from the start, but it was imperative that I separated you all from the crowd without causing suspicions amongst your peers."

I wasn't accustomed to herbs and plants, but I knew Forbian well. Fa used it during a winter four moons ago when Mam was sick. She had caught a fever during the winter months and she'd been bed bound for weeks. He'd brought the herb from a passing merchant and used it on Mam that same day. She slept for hours, no coughs or fits. Fa told me it was to help her rest. The drug forced the user into a sleep, for how long depended on the dosage.

"You all must be wondering why you have not been affected by the Forbian." His ivory white teeth glistened behind his thin lips.

Someone called out, and all heads turned towards the speaker. "Because Forbian doesn't work on us..." Illera shoulders were held back as she called forward. Although my body burned with distaste for her, my heart sank as King Dalior moved slowly to where she stood.

"That is right, my child..." Within seconds he stood behind her, both his elegant, long hands rested on her shoulders.

"And what is it that you are..."

There was a pause, before she lifted her grinning face, "Shifters."

CHAPTER

FOUR

I CHOKED ON a ball of spit lodged in my throat. My heart skipped a beat and my entire body chilled. I looked around at the smaller group, Petrer, Illera and Gwendolyn all a part of it. I was stupid not to connect the dots, I should've realized.

I tried to calm my face, mask the worry that filled every inch of me. King Dalior walked back to the dais where Prince Hadrian stood, watching our reactions. I caught his golden eyes for a moment, biting my lip and smiling.

"Why didn't you tell me you could shift?" Petrer didn't look at me when he spoke, keeping his eyes trained on the throne. I could hear the disappointment drip from every word he spoke. *Seems like we both had secrets.*

My magick.

It was the only possible answer. I was not a shifter, but it was possible the Forbian did not affect me because of what I could do.

Panic seized my muscles and the monstrous worry burned through my mind. My magick stirred within its cage, teasing me.

"Huh?" Petrer huffed, but I couldn't find the words to answer him.

King Dalior spoke up, "You may all be wondering why I have taken such drastic measure this evening, to separate you from the rest of your companions..." His voice oozed with authority, "As shifters, you have a natural ability that puts you above most Niraen elves. The ability to change your appearance at will should not be wasted on farms, or the simple lives you have been living. You all deserve more, and that is what I want to offer you…"

Petrer was mumbling under his breath. The atmosphere was thick with excitement, whereas I fought the urge to run back through the doors we had entered through not long ago.

"I want to invite you all to join a special force within our military. A legion of shifters who will help protect the land that we love so dearly. You will be trained amongst our guards and military, utilizing your abilities in a way that will not be wasted. You are each powerful, more so than any other in Thessolina. And it is imperative you join us, especially now. We need you more than ever."

I caught the blur of Illera's braid as it flew over her shoulder. She turned to look behind her long enough for me to catch the smug smile on her face.

"Of course, your families will be sent coin as payment for your service. Riches that will stop their hunger and lessen their woes. By joining, you will be given a rank in Thessolina that will demand respect and loyalty." At the mention of payment my panic seemed to subside. The idea of my family having coin was enough to still the greatest of my worries. It could change their lives.

The doors behind us opened, followed by a shuffle of heavy footsteps. I turned to look along with King Dalior and the rest of the room. I was not prepared for just how quickly the atmosphere changed.

Two guards dragged a hooded figure between them. The strange elf was slumped in the guard's hold. A sudden hint of copper coated the back of my mouth and my face twisted in disgust. My eyes fell on a thin trail of black blood that oozed from behind the body and onto the floor. All my worry erupted in fire and burnt to ash the moment the body was dragged past me.

The crowd parted to let them through. I heard someone gag, but couldn't bring myself to tear my eyes away to see who it was. I only looked to King Dalior who still smiled, whereas Hadrian looked different. His brows were turned down and his full lips were pale. Seeing his clear distaste set my nerves on fire.

The guards stopped before the King and dropped the body like it was nothing more than a sack of shit. I cringed at the loud crack as the hooded figure's knees connected with the floor, its blood blending completely into the black of the marble floor.

Black blood. Morthi.

"This…" King Dalior waved a hand before him, "is proof of the evil that dwells beyond Thessolina's border. I am sure you have all heard whispers and gossip over the past months of villages and towns being attacked. Destroyed. I regret to inform you, they are nothing but truth. The Morthi are flooding our land, destroying villages and murdering innocent lives. Why, we do not know. It was not until this past winter that our military was able to obtain proof that it was in fact the Morthi and not some other hidden beast. Their motives are still unclear, but I am certain this is only the beginning of something much worse."

King Dalior looked to the guards who stood on either side of the body. They both stood alert, as if the Morthi elf between them would jump up and attack at any moment. Yet I knew it wouldn't; the amount of blood that puddled beneath him was enough proof that it wouldn't try anything.

King Dalior's next words dripped from his lips in a deep hum, "Show them."

As commanded, one guard moved swiftly, grabbed the top of the dirtied sack and ripped it off his head in one fluid motion.

The elf beneath it was mutilated beyond recognition. Its eyes swollen shut, meshed with bloodied gashes that covered its purple, bruised skin. Black blood and spit dribbled from its slashed lips, dirtying the already stained tunic that hung from its thin body. The Morthi breathed and slumped to the ground, his palms slapped the floor.

"Blood elf…" King Dalior called across the silent group. "Morthi. The creature was found amongst a village not far from here. It, alongside what we believed to be over a dozen companions, had killed the inhabitants, leaving the buildings levelled and blood running through the streets." As I blinked I saw the destruction, Fa had always complained that my imagination was too strong. I turned away not able to look at the Morthi a moment longer. I rubbed the heel of my palm against my eyes, pressing hard until all I saw were flashes of light. Anything was better than the view before me.

"This, my children, is the threat Thessolina is facing. That is why we need you. The Morthi may have their own abilities, but those weak powers are nothing compared to what you can do. You are unique to our kind, blessed by *our* Goddess."

At the mention of the Goddess we all pressed a thumb to our temple in respect. All except the King. He waved his jewelled hand that prompted the guards to hood the blood elf and remove him from the room. I didn't watch as he was dragged out squirming. I kept my eyes on the ground where he was yanked from, only a puddle of inky blood left in its wake. King Dalior's reflection rippled across its surface, his face a picture of disgust.

"What about Queen Kathine of Eldnol, has she offered aid?" A red-haired elf called from the crowd, her voice high and childlike.

King Dalior shook his head, "No. The Alorian elves have made it clear that they will not intervene. But that is not something I can touch on currently."

"But the peace treaty…"

"Has been destroyed, null and void!" he shouted, his entire demeanour changed before my eyes. For a moment, he seemed like a different person until his anger melted into a smile again, "War is coming, my sweet girl, and it is on the cusp of blooming and staining our seas red. That is unless we stain it black first. It is up to you all now; with you, we have a chance at gaining the upper hand. Will you join? Will *you* fight to protect those you love?"

The room lit up with the cries of agreement. Petrer who pumped his fist into the air and howled, cooing the others to join, knocked me to the side. I too found myself joining with the chant. The cries were infectious and they pulled me along like the current of the strongest river. King Dalior's smile burned and he brought his hands together, pleased with the response.

I wanted to join, to fight. But I also wanted to leave. I was not a shifter, and even if I wanted to stay and join King Dalior's cause, how could I keep up the illusion without revealing my magick? As my mind toyed with the idea, an image of Fa and Mam receiving coin from the King was enough for me to make up my mind. Yet the possibility of my magick being revealed sent daggers into my thoughts. No one could find out.

"Tomorrow, first thing in the morning, you are to return here." King Dalior spoke above the ruckus of the room. "Until then, you are to return to your rooms where you will find the rest of your fellow elves already asleep. Do not tell them of what has happened here, for it will only instil fear and envy into their hearts. When the time is right, although I hope there will not be a need, we will explain to our people what is happening. Until then, ignorance is bliss. It is up to us to protect them." His eyes swept the room, his arms clasped behind his back. "Sleep well, for tomorrow your training begins."

CHAPTER

FIVE

I KEPT MY head down, trying to evade all attempts of eye contact from Petrer during the walk back to our room. Every time I closed my eyes, all I saw was black blood and when I opened them, I saw the reality of my situation. Both horrified me.

I felt sick and exhausted. My legs ached this time around as we climbed the stairs to our rooms. It was just myself, Petrer, Gwendolyn and Illera who trudged back, silently. Numerous worries flooded my mind. What was going to happen to those elves who slept? Would they leave us in the morning? How long would I keep the illusion in place to hide my power? My head throbbed. I was thankful when we reached our floor and dispersed back into our rooms.

Petrer pushed our door open with caution. I walked in first, scanning the many who slept in the bunks around me.

I stripped my clothes, leaving only my pants and a thin under shirt to sleep in. I kicked at the pile of clothes sending it to the corner of the room in a heap. I would sort them tomorrow because all I could think about right now was sleep.

"Are we going to talk about this?" Petrer whispered from his bunk where he was sprawled on top of his sheets.

I refused to turn to him, "There is nothing to talk about." I was lying and he knew it. I reached up for the wood to pull myself onto the bunk but Petrer sat up.

"Zac, what has got into you? There *is* lots to talk about!" he hissed, his grip heavy on my wrist.

"Now is not the right time," I said, pulling my arm from his grasp. My wrist ached from his grip. "Don't *ever* grab me like that again."

Even in the dark I could see Petrer's face soften. My words shocked him, and he looked to his hands and back to my face. His eyes wet and cheeks red. "I'm sorry, I didn't me—"

"Just get some sleep Petrer." I pulled myself into bed, tears pricking at the corners of my eyes. I hated this.

Petrer didn't speak another word. I couldn't see him, but I felt his body roll over beneath me, the bunk shifting under his weight. I told myself it was better this way, better not talking to him and instead aiding the distance that we needed. Or rather, the distance *I* needed. I had buried what he had done to me and ignored it. It was his actions driving a wedge between us. It pained me to act that way, but the wedge could *never* be removed.

∾

I STARED AT the domed ceiling, counting the bricks in hopes it lulled me to sleep. I tried numerous techniques Mam had taught me. I imagined myself as the top of a tree and, in my mind, travelled from the tallest leaf to the very bottom of the roots. She'd told me that once I reached the earth, my mind would still and the darkness of the soil would in turn be the blackness of sleep. It didn't work.

I listened to the faint song of rolling waves crashing against rocks from outside of the open window, and the rustle of sheets inside. I rolled onto my side to get a better view beyond the window, giving up on the idea of sleep. The moon hung in silence above the glass-like surface of the sea, half formed. From here it looked big enough to touch, as if I could reach out the window and run my hand across its imperfect surface. As I contemplated it, a breeze trickled in from the window, dusting across my bare legs.

Time slipped past me, how much I was not sure. Petrer's heavy breathing became constant; he was in the grasps of sleep. Gwendolyn also slept, I could hear her heavy breathing from my bunk although her back faced me.

I looked back to the window, delirious from lack of sleep.

I had to leave.

Now.

Careful not to bash my head against the low ceiling, I sat up. I closed my eyes, it was always clearer picturing the magick within me. I pushed off from the bed, calling for the air to cushion my landing, silencing the heavy thud that should have sounded when my feet touched the ground.

The urge to leave was too loud for me to ignore.

I ran. I ran for the window and jumped until my world was alight with screams of the air.

∽

I WAS FREE. I fell fast towards the rocky ground below, my body filled with adrenaline. The stone walls beside me blurred, the separate stones blending into one. I took pleasure in this moment when all that was around me was air and night. A cold trickle of tears smudged up the side of my face from the downward force. It was all happening so quickly.

I threw open my fists and pushed out every ounce of magick I had into my landing. The air began to harden around me until my body felt like I was swimming in thick mud. I turned my hands, guiding my body to the right position. The cold ground bit at my bare toes the second my feet touched the rough path. I released my hold on the air and it regained its natural form. The chill of night smashed into me in that second, almost knocking me sideways. I threw my arms around me, trying everything to contain the warmth before the night bled it away. I looked down, my bare legs illuminated by the moonlight.

Idiot.

I looked above at the window. It was now nothing more than a dot in the distance. In my rush and stupidity, I'd left without anything but the few clothes I wore.

My wind still spun around me, but I felt its weakened state from my overuse. Pain bubbled, an empty pressure that always followed when I used that much power. I released my magick until the night stilled and the air left me. I squinted back up at the window above. The power I would need to get back was too great for what I had left. I felt it cower inside of me at the thought of using it again.

I looked around me, trying to gain my positioning. I stood on some sort of walkway at the back of the palace. Only a few feet before me was the edge of the walkway that disappeared into the rocky ocean below. I shuffled over to it and peered across the ledge. It was a sheer drop into the ocean, tips of rocks that protruded from the water's surface. There was no way down.

I ran, my feet slapping against the ground as I searched for a door, anything to find my way back inside the walls of the palace. I came to a stop before a sharp cluster of rocks that blocked the path ahead. I could climb, but I had no idea what was on the other side and my feet would suffer.

There was no way back. I was stuck. On either side of the walkway the same cluster of rocks stopped me from passing. *Idiot! Idiot! Idiot!*

Defeated and void of energy, I slumped to the floor and pressed my back against the palace wall behind me. I brought my legs up to my chin, and wrapped my arms around them. I rubbed at my exposed skin, trying anything to fight the numbing cold.

The moon's cold light cut into my bones. I scolded myself for even thinking it would work and the lack of thinking that went into the stupid decision.

I released a deep sob that racked my chest, my vision blurred with tears. I looked between the palace wall, and the twinkle of lights that flickered over the sea and wept.

Occasional bursts of water rained on me as a wave broke over the side of the walkways edge, washing away the tears that stained my skin. I buried my head in my hands and screamed until my throat burned. With the light magick I had left I encased myself in a shield of air, attempting to keep in the minimal heat around me before I froze to death.

$\backsim$

TIME MELTED AWAY. The sky changed, the constellations replaced with pink tinted clouds whilst the sun peaked over the horizon. With the morning light, I saw a glint of metal out the side of my eye. At the far right of the walkway was a door, a simple weathered wood door that had sunk deep into the wall. I hadn't noticed it before. I jumped up and ran for it, my body numb, my mind exhausted.

I reached for the ring handle, rust flaking beneath my hand. I pulled and pushed, using any strength I could muster to force it open. It didn't budge.

Frustrated, I smashed my shoulder into it, trying anything to break it open. It was locked. I stepped back, giving myself enough running room and shook my arm, readying it. Then, I pelted towards it. The side of my body smashed into the door, shoulder first. It swung open. I braced myself for the fall, closing my eyes and releasing a silent scream. But arms wrapped around me, halting my fall.

"Careful, careful!" the voice called. "You are ice cold. I thought I was going crazy when I heard crying, but apparently it is not I who is the crazy one..." Two golden eyes glared with concern beneath the hood of the stranger.

Prince Hadrian.

I stumbled over my reply, unable to conjure a lie fast enough.

The prince reached out a hand, his soft skin brushing across my face. His hand was warm, his breath fresh like he had been chewing mint leaves. He looked even more ethereal so close, his midnight hair fell across both shoulders, his eyes wide with recognition.

"Here." His voice melted my panic, "Take this." With the grace of a performer, he pulled the cloak from his shoulders and wrapped it around me. My body warmed beneath the thick material. I pulled it tight around me, concealing my body. Embarrassment warmed my cheeks.

"I told the guards to leave out the initiations with the new recruits. I guess they do not seem to listen to me very well. How long have you been out here?"

My voice cracked when I replied, "I'm not sure, your highness. I—"

"No need to explain yourself." He reached a hand for me. "I will talk to the guards later. Let me help you get back to bed, it's the least I can do."

Prince Hadrian closed the door and we fell into bleak darkness, all apart from the candle in his hand that I'd not noticed before. His smile glowed red above the flame, "Come."

My hand was small compared to his. I let him pull me along.

We headed forward into the darkness of the room, the light from his candle illuminating the space in a halo of orange light. The brush of the cloak against the floor muffled the slap of my feet, both still numb and sore.

"I suppose it is only fair that I know your name." His deep voice vibrated off the room's barren walls.

"Zacriah, your highness," I replied. In the now dark room, I could only see the candle bobbing ahead, but not him.

"Zacriah…"

"Zacriah Trovirn."

"Well, Zacriah Trovirn, you need to be careful; this may not be the only initiation test the guards put you through during the coming weeks. Personally, I do not see the point in them, but it seems to keep them all entertained."

I didn't know what he was talking about, but I felt the best option was to just go along with it.

"Thank you, your highness."

"I can see why they picked on you," he chuckled. "They normally start with the better-looking initiates." I blushed, pulling the cloak around me tighter, glad he had not turned around to see me. "Regardless, I will speak to them."

We didn't speak the rest of the walk back. It didn't take long for me to recognize the part of the palace he led me through. When I came to the bottom of the stairwell, I was glad that we were almost there.

Not once did Prince Hadrian ask for direction to my room, he just knew. That unnerved me, but I was too exhausted to worry about anything other than sleep.

"I trust I can leave you here to find your way back?" Prince Hadrian said, stopping beyond the stairs into my sleeping quarters.

"I can. Thank you," I replied, short and sweet.

I walked past him, straight for the door to my room.

"Sleep well, Zacriah Trovirn," he called from behind me.

"Thank you." I nodded, but stopped in the threshold, "I should give this back to you." I pulled the cloak from my shoulders and held it out to him.

I watched him walk away, leaving me holding the cloak out. Before he turned down the stairwell, I heard his voice a final time.

"Keep it."

CHAPTER

SIX

I AWOKE TO three loud bangs at the bedroom door. At home, it would be the call of birds or the sweep of a broom against the street outside my window that would wake me. I peeked my eye open enough to see the room awash in morning light. Dust danced in the rays of sun that cut into the room, twisting and turning like falling snow.

My head ached, the dull thud across my forehead reprimanding me for not sleeping when I should've. I stretched my arms above my head and listened to the guards as they called names from beyond the door. Once the names were called the guards explained to them that they would be returning home. It caused a buzz of confusion as those who began to pack looked between Petrer, Gwendolyn and myself. I even heard one elfin boy question the night before, complaining of his missing memories. I didn't respond, and the questions soon ceased.

I pulled the pillow from beneath my head and pressed it to my face, feathers scratching me through the thin cover. I yawned into it, exhaustion too hard to ignore.

I heard a muffled cry and I looked up again to find the cause. Gwendolyn. She released a sob from her side of the room, her eyes rimmed red and her body shaking. She held onto Demitria, planting wet kisses across her face and whispering through her tears. My stomach twisted as I watched them. Demitria and Gwendolyn had been together for as long as I could remember. Since childhood they had been inseparable.

"Why aren't you leaving with me?" Demitria asked, running her hands over Gwendolyn's cheeks to rid of the tears. "Tell me!"

Gwendolyn just shook her head. "I can't, I'm sorry." She buried her head into Demitria's shoulder and sobbed. Demitria tried to question her more, but gave up and planted a kiss on her lips.

Today was going to be a long day.

∾

IT DIDN'T TAKE long for those whose names had been called to leave and the room to fall silent once more. My stomach flipped, anxiety coursing through me. I lay waiting for the guards to return, wondering whether Prince Hadrian would tell anyone about our episode only hours before. I still felt the bulk of the Prince's cloak beside me where I hid it beside my sheets. It was the best option, I didn't want anyone finding it and asking questions. It clearly didn't belong to me; it was too fine to go with anything I owned.

The lack of sleep drained my body. I wasn't a morning person anyway, but today I felt even worse.

I needed some comfort, anything to take my mind off how the rest of the day would play out. It was not a good decision, but then again, I was beginning to get used to my poor choice in actions. I climbed from my bunk, and joined Petrer in his, nestling up to his chest. His warm arm wrapped around me and we lay there, not saying a word. He smelled of open air and cedar wood, a scent that brought back memories of home. We had spent many nights like that, locked together in a silent embrace. I almost expected him to pipe up and grill me about not telling him I was a shifter, but he didn't. He just lay behind me, his breath brushing against my neck whilst he slumbered. I knew how wrong it was, but for just a moment, I allowed myself to push back the memories of *them*.

The door creaked open; the female guard from the previous night poked her head around the frame to look inside before inviting herself in. Another followed in after her, one I'd not seen before. She had to duck when she walked into the room, making sure the metal antlers that stood from the top of her helmet didn't knock against the doorframe. She was young, younger than any of the other guards I'd seen. Although her face was smooth and youthful, her hair was peppered with grey strands. She was tall, beautiful. Her eyes were a bright mahogany. She carried a pile of clothes in her arms, a heap of purple tunics and black slacks very similar to what she herself sported beneath her armour.

"Put these on," she commanded, throwing a set to Gwendolyn and two onto the end of Petrer's bed. "I'll be waiting outside, don't be long."

∽

WE CHANGED IN haste and left with the guards. Just like the previous night, we were headed straight for the throne room.

In the morning light, the throne room seemed like a different room entirely. Streams of light hit the bone chandelier that hung proud in the center of the room, reflecting off the hanging crystals.

In the day, it was easier to make out subtle details that I had missed last night. Vines clung to the walls and spread across the arches of the ceiling. Pedestals covered in flowers each sat in the four corners of the room, a waterfall of colours and aromas. The four tables had been removed, leaving an open space for us to stand while we waited for our instruction. The once blood-stained floor was clean and spotless, not a speck of black blood left upon its surface.

King Dalior was absent. I didn't need to look for him because I could just *feel* his lack of presence. Instead, I watched another elf walk forward and take her place before the throne.

She was dressed in the same purple and gilded armour of the royal guard, a long sword hanging from the bejewelled belt around her thick waist. Her hair was cut short to her scalp, highlighting her wide, strong features. She was pretty and fierce, but there was something off about her stare. Something disconnected. She kept one hand on her armoured hip, the other on the hilt of the sword.

"Initiates, listen up." Her deep voice spilled across the room, stilling all conversation amongst the group. "My name is Alina Faethana, King Dalior's first Commander of the royal legion. But you *will* address me as Commander. King Dalior has tasked me to oversee your training and introduction into the royal legion, which begins today. When your name is called, you are to step forward and shift. Depending on your level of shifting ability you will be separated into one of three ranks. Each rank has been organised by King Dalior himself to ensure you are trained with those with similar abilities and strengths…"

I missed what she said next for panic took over. I felt my heart beat faster and my breath become too heavy to take in. I kept my gaze plastered to the Commander, and I scratched nervously at my hips. My secret would be spilled like the blood of the Morthi who'd kneeled in the same place I stood.

She gestured for a guard at the back of the room and the guard with the antler helmet stepped forward. She walked through the crowd, her metal boots clattering across the stone floor. When she passed me, I saw she carried a scroll in her hand, tied in a purple ribbon. At the bottom of the steps, she kneeled before the Commander. It was clear the guards had a great respect for her.

She didn't move from her bow until the Commander made a sound, prompting her to stand and pass the rolled parchment into her outstretched hand.

Slowly, the Commanders scarred fingers pulled the ribbon and dropped it to the floor for the guard to pick up. The parchment unravelled before her, stopping inches from the ground.

With an extended finger, she clawed the parchment, the sound of nail on paper sent shivers up my arms. She brought her finger to a rest at the top of the parchment and lifted her gaze over the top back at us.

"Let us begin. If I call your name step forward." The Commander scanned the crowd a final time and looked back to the parchment. "Illera Daeris of Horith."

Illera shuffled through the crowd, her head held high. She made her way to the space where the Commander pointed and stood.

"Shift," the Commander said.

I tasted Illera's shift before it began, the same as always. I'd never seen her shift before, but I had heard whispers of the beast she became. The tendrils of smoke moved like angry snakes, pulsing from her body. They wrapped around her and twisted into a note of darkness that blurred her body. The darkness buzzed and burst outwards until it dissipated into nothingness. What was left in its wake was a pure white lion.

I'd only ever seen them in books for they were native to Morgatis, not Thessolina. She was white from her fur to the large, pointed teeth she showed off when she opened her jaw. Her red eyes stood out against her face in contrast. She looked monstrous, strong. One elfin girl jumped backwards with a shriek when Illera prowled too close. She was showing off.

"Rank Mamlin…" the Commander called, her eyes not wavering from the beast. She pointed towards the furthest guard who stood closest to the left wall, signalling for Illera to wait there. As if to say she understood, Illera roared. The guard, who waited, was painted in worry.

Illera padded slowly in his direction, her beastly face kept low. She closed in on him and picked up her pace. I saw him flinch and his lips part in a silent gasp the moment she pounced. We all watched in shock, but mid jump, she shifted back into her elfin form and landed with a giggle. *Bitch*.

The Commander called out the next name, her voice pulling our attention back her way.

"Merlara Abenim of Thatchm."

Another girl walked forward, one I'd noticed the previous night. Her honey coloured hair had been scraped back into a ponytail, accentuating her hooked nose. She walked forward with confidence, but her hands shook violently at her side. She wasn't fooling anyone.

"Shift."

Merlara's opal smoke burst from her chest and she morphed into her secondary form. I first saw the black feathers. A speck of white sat at the base of her elongated neck, like a diamond hanging from a necklace. I had never seen a swan like it, not as beautiful nor powerful in size. I was used to seeing them back home, guarding the waters of the lake in the middle of the village, but nothing like Merlara's form. Petrer sucked in a breath beside me, mirroring my own admiration.

"Rank Falmia," the Commander cooed, her eyes wide, a hint of a smile cracking her serious face. Merlara melted into smoke. She reached out her wide wings and raised beak to the arched ceiling as skin replaced feathers.

Names were called forth, shifts were displayed and the elves were separated into their ranks. I watched, stunned as some shifted into snakes, a ferret, and many different species of birds. One girl shifted into a field mouse and was the first sent to Rank Clarak. It was clear that the less impressive shifters were sent to Rank Clarak.

The larger beasts were put into Rank Mamlin, and the winged shifters were sent to Rank Falmia.

With each shift, my worry grew. The crowd around me thinned, it was inevitable I would be called soon. My palms were clammy and drips of sweat broke away from my hairline to drip down my neck. I had to focus on calming the storm within my mind whilst keeping my magick buried within me. My panic only spurred my magick to life.

When my name was finally called, my body froze.

"Zacriah Trovirn of Horith."

The Commander looked up from the list when she didn't hear me step forward and called my name again. Petrer hissed something beside me and pushed me forward. There was no denying the Commander didn't see me.

"Step forward…" she muttered, beckoning with her hands for me to hurry up.

My mind told me to step forward, but my body was not responding.

"Well this is a first, looks like we have someone suffering with some nerves."

I tried to ignore the hint of sarcasm in her voice and took a step forward, then another until I stood before her. She peered down at me, the whites of her eyes dull and yellowed. She looked me up and down, her tongue clicking against her teeth.

"What are you waiting for?"

"I… cannot shift," I stuttered, holding her burning gaze.

"Speak up, boy."

"I cannot shift, Commander."

My response surprised her at first. But, her face twisted and three loud barks exploded from her mouth. Her laugh urged the rest of those watching behind me to join in "Of course, you can shift!"

I looked away from her gaze to my feet and just stood there. I stopped fiddling with my nails and tensed my arms to keep them by my side. I could feel the judgement of those watching behind me burn into the back of my head.

"I *won't* tell you again, shift and stop wasting my time," she shouted, all signs of laughter gone.

I dug my nails into my leg, anything to stop my shaking hands. The Commander stepped down from the dais and I felt her hot breath, her face inches from mine. I looked up, her face covered in faded marks and scars, a constellation of battle wounds.

"Do it," she seethed.

"I can't," I said.

She held my gaze a few moments longer then looked away, taking the longest inhale through her nose. "Fadine, come."

Fadine stepped forward, "Take over, I will be back."

The Commander thrust the parchment into Fadine's hands and turned to leave the room. When she reached the door, she turned to me. "You, follow me."

I ran to her; my deep-seated anxiety had taken full control over my body. I caught Petrer's gaze as I walked passed him, his eyes wide.

We left the throne room through a side door.

My footsteps echoed as I hurried through a grey stoned hallway ahead, matching the frantic pounding in my head and chest. The Commander didn't turn to check if I followed, only moved forward. I kept my eyes trained to the back of her neck and I noticed a dark symbol that sat underneath the neckline of her garment, a sigil unknown that I didn't recognize. I could only see the top of it peaking from above her collar, unable to make out the shape or design. It was uncommon for elves to mark their bodies with ink and piercings. To see the King's first in commander with such a mark shocked me. It was not a common practice; even my Mam lost her mind when I turned up with two piercings in my right ear two moons ago.

The walk was endless, the hallways and stairs blurred into one. She'd not uttered a single word to me since we left. I wanted to ask where we were headed, but I didn't need to.

This part of the palace dripped in wealth, more than I had seen in any other part. Cases of jewels and strange stones lined the hallways, and elaborate paintings of King Dalior and his lost wife covered the walls. We were headed for the King.

She stopped before a door at the end of another corridor and knocked with purpose. At first there was no reply, so she knocked again, harder. When a voice piped up from inside the room, my heart almost dropped when I recognized who it belonged to. It was not the King.

"Enter."

She pushed on the oak door, the smells of burning incense greeting us. The room beyond was huge, the ceiling so high it was dark in its own shadows. Bookcases lined the walls, each filled with different sized tomes. The walls were a sandy stone colour, and the floor was covered in faded red rugs. Beside the bookcases there was only a desk and behind it sat Prince Hadrian.

His hair hung limp over his shoulders, but kept from his face by the silver circlet placed around his head. He didn't look up when we entered, only carried on scanning the open tome before him. The candles burned on the edge of the desk, flickering from the breeze that followed into the room from the open door.

"Please close the door, Commander, I have only just gotten over a cold and I really do not want another," he drawled, still refusing to move his attention from the book before him.

She listened and slammed the door with a bang.

The prince released a long breath, "I never understand how some can deform the page of a book." He pulled at the thin ribbon attached to the book and placed it gently across the page. "Bending a book's page should be banned. I am in the right mind to ask father to pass it as law. I prefer to treat a book like a lover, always handling it with gentle, tender hands." He looked up and smiled. Without looking down, he closed the book and pushed it to the side.

"And how can I help you, Commander?" He turned his gaze to her, and stood from the desk. The heavy chair squeaked across the floor as he stood.

"Unfortunately, this elfin boy has decided he wants to ignore a simple command," she replied. "During this morning's separation of the shifters he *refused* to shift for me."

Prince Hadrian didn't say anything, only nodding as the Commander spoke. I caught his gaze as he looked towards me, a glint of interest passing behind his eyes. "Is that so..."

"Yes. And since King Dalior is occupied, he's asked that you are the first to deal with requests whilst he is... busy."

Prince Hadrian walked around the desk to the other side and leaned against it. He crossed his arms over his chest and pouted. "Thank you, Commander, for bringing him to me. You can leave him with me and return back to your task," he said. "Please, do not let him occupy any more of your time."

"Thank you, your highness." It was clear that her thanks pained her from the involuntary twitching of her face. She bowed her head and ushered me forward. Prince Hadrian moved for the door before the Commander could reach it. He opened it wide and gestured with his eyes for her to leave. He watched her walk away, and closed the door when she moved from view. He turned back to face me, his smile still wide.

"It would seem we are unable to stay away from each other, Zacriah." Hadrian's deep laugh filled the limited space between us. "I must admit I am not too sure what Commander Alina is asking of me, but I suppose, for today, you can stay with me until I figure out what we are going to do with you. I have a few errands to run in Masarion this morning you may accompany me on. That will give us time to *properly* get to know each other."

"I would be honoured to spend the day with you," I lied.

"Fabulous." He pulled a cloak from the back of a chair and threw it around him. "I don't suppose I need to give you another one of my cloaks?"

"No, your highness."

"Please, Hadrian will do. I get enough of the title from Alina and the rest of the guards."

A silver pin clasped the folds together, keeping it wrapped around him. He moved to the candles, blowing them out one by one until a single line of smoke lifted from the wick. "I am starved, you must be too. I know the best market stall in Masarion who serves the best steamed buns."

"I don't have any coin on me your highn—Hadrian." The thought of eating with him was not one that excited me.

"Then I suppose I shall be treating you to breakfast."

CHAPTER
SEVEN

MASARION WAS ALIVE with movement. Elves' selling from market stalls, the narrow streets full of package wagons, and carts with goods for trade. The scent of fresh baked bread and dried herbs from the passing vendors made my mouth water as soon as we passed the bridge from Thalor.

Hadrian must have felt the same, for he'd steered us to a man who sold us each a fresh brown loaf that steamed in our hands. The trader was adamant that he wouldn't take Hadrian's payment, but didn't notice when Hadrian slipped two silver coins into the loose pocket of his apron.

The bread was the best I'd ever had. The crust was hard, the perfect crunch. The doughy innards were the perfect balance between moist and cooked. I picked at it as I followed Hadrian from the trader back on route to his destination.

When I had visited Masarion with Fa, we had spent the entirety of the first day haggling with vendors to sell our trinkets and loot with the passers-by. I remembered one Niraen man who wanted the china set Mam had asked us to sell. The man was persistent that the price he offered was final, but I managed to up it by the time he bought them. I chuckled at the memory when I passed a similar man haggling with another to our left. The nostalgic feeling was pleasing. My shoulders were relaxing the deeper we walked into the winding streets, immersing ourselves in the crowds around us, leaving the palace behind.

Children ran up to Hadrian, some even playing games with him, jumping around corners and from behind stalls. Hadrian played along, pulling them up and swinging them around in the air whilst they shrieked with glee. It was clear his people loved him.

We left the children and walked forward only a few steps before Hadrian halted. A group of young girls, each covered in dirt and rags, sat in a shadowed doorway off the side of the main street. I stayed back but stretched my hearing enough to hear what Hadrian said when he greeted them.

"Here..." He broke the bread and passed large chunks into their frail hands. The girls squeaked their thanks and started ripping the bread to shreds and devouring it.

"Where are your parents?" he asked, kneeling on the ground before them.

The oldest of the girls spoke up, "Dead, sir." She didn't look up from the bread when she spoke. Her accent was rough, much different from Hadrian's. It was similar to mine. She was not from Olderim.

"How?" Hadrian asked.

The oldest girl finished her piece and looked up, "The monsters, sir."

"Yeh, the monsters with black blood." One of the smaller girls chimed in, speaking through a full mouth.

"You!" Hadrian shouted at a patrolling guard. "Take these girls to the palace and be sure to have them cleaned and fed."

The guard nodded, his armour golden in the sunlight. Hadrian turned back to the girls. "My friend here is going to take you to the palace where you will be treated like princesses. Do you like the sound of that?" The girls peaked at the mention of princesses. They jumped up, bouncing with excitement.

The guard directed them back onto the path back towards the palace. Hadrian stood and watched with his face pinched. I stepped forward, conscious that I should have given my bread to them also. "Will they really be treated like Princesses?" I asked.

"They have my word." It was all he said. His voice was cold and distant as he watched them walk off with the guard. Once they were out of view, he turned and smiled, beckoning me to follow.

The silent journey gave me a lot of time to think, time that I wished was filled up with other thoughts. I was surprised that the topic of the morning had not been brought up, since that was the only reason the Commander had dumped me with Hadrian. I knew the conversation would rear its ugly head soon. I'd have to tell him, there was no way around this.

Lost in my thoughts, I didn't notice that Hadrian had stopped again, not until I walked straight into his back.

"I'm so—" I started to say, choking on a piece of bread that had lodged in my throat. But he only seemed amused when he turned to steady me.

"Am I that bad company that you feel the need to attack me when my back is turned?" he replied, arms raised in defeat.

"I wasn't watching where I was going…"

Hadrian only laughed, patting my shoulder and gesturing to the dark wood building that was before us.

"Clearly. No harm done. We are here now, let us get inside before you cause some real damage."

With that, he turned, pushed the door to the building open and disappeared into its smoky interior.

∽

THE ANTLER & Wagon, as it was not so perfectly named, was unlike any tavern I'd visited before, and not one I thought a prince would ever be seen in. It was small, cramped and dark. Smoke filled the room from the elves sitting around small tables puffing on pipes that smelled of burned moss and oils. I noticed that the whites of their eyes were tainted red and smoke slipped from their relaxed mouths. Their faces were a painting of pleasure and exhaustion, a look that suggested they no longer sat in the room, but off in a faraway land. I'd seen the smoke before, and knew from the lingering smell what was in their pipes. Weelm. The drug had a relaxing effect on the taker. It dulled the senses until they were non-existent. Those who sat in the corner of the tavern would not hear, see or smell anything, not whilst they continued to puff away on their pipes.

Hadrian pointed at a small ale stained table at the opposite end of the tavern, motioning for me to go and wait there. He didn't follow; instead he headed straight towards the stocky barmaid who'd not stopped watching us since the moment we entered.

I waded through the sea of thick smog that hung in the air, trying not to gag on the strong scent that displeased me. There were no windows; the only source of fresh air was from the closed door we had walked through. Weak flames hung in the corners of the room, filling the room with patches of light. Enough to illuminate the alabaster smoke and dirtied floor I walked over.

I sat down on a rickety stool, trying to focus on not coughing as the smoke invaded my lungs. Hadrian soon returned with the two tankards, slamming them on the table in front of me, froth spilling over the rims.

"Stinking Pig, one of the best ales in Thessolina."

I looked in disgust at the thick brew before me, a new smell weaving in with the Weelm smoke. It didn't look appetizing, but the name did explain the smell.

"Is there not any water I can have instead? I am not a big drinker of ale." I lied for the second time. I loved ale, beer and cider, but I thought it best to have a clear mind.

His eyes widened, his hand rose to rest on his chest as he heaved in a shocked breath. "Water! You cannot possibly have water when I present you with one of the best drinks that has ever been brewed in our lands." The sarcasm that poured from him was becoming unbearable.

I studied the ale again, deciding it best just to drink without thinking too much about it. The metal handle was cold in my hand, but I ignored it and tipped the ale into my mouth.

As the warm brew slipped past my lips, a burst of fruit and sugar coated my tongue, a taste I wasn't expecting. It was delicious, refreshing and the perfect temperature. I looked over the tankard to Hadrian whose face beamed with pleasure. "I told you it is nice!" He chuckled.

I nodded and downed the entire drink, tipping the tankard upside down to allow every drop to enter my mouth. "I suppose I will have to get you another."

Some dribbled from my mouth as I responded, "Please."

Hadrian plucked the empty tankard from my hand and moved back towards the waiting barmaid who stood cleaning the side with a dirtied rag. Much help that seemed to be.

The ale soothed everything, dulling my need for fresh air and coating the worry that had made home in the pit of my stomach.

Hadrian returned with another tankard in hand, placing it down in front of me before sitting at the table.

"Take your time with this one, it shall be your last." His golden eyes were trained to me. "Did they not have anything like this back home?"

"No, nothing like this. We had a local cider, but it seems dull in comparison."

"And where is it you call home?" he asked.

"Horith." I didn't want to give too much information away. "It's a small farming town somewhere south-west of here."

"I have heard of it before, although have never visited. If I am correct, I believe Horith had made a name for itself from the production of the incredible potatoes grown there?"

It was true, Horith's weather created the perfect growing conditions for the crop; the constant wet climate helped them thrive. It was the village's claim to fame amongst neighbouring towns, so it came to no surprise that Hadrian had heard about it.

"Yes, we are the town famous by the potato."

Hadrian laughed. "It could be worse."

"I guess so." I took another sip and looked around the room. Keeping my eyes on everything and anything but Hadrian.

"I think it best that we get a certain conversation over with," he began, placing his tankard on the table and crossing both arms across his broad chest. "About what occurred this morning, and what left Commander Alina so flustered— which I must thank you for—it is a hobby of mine to see her face flush red."

I took yet another swig. A large gulp in hopes that I would choke and not be able to answer. "Would you believe me if I said it was nerves?"

"Possibly, although that is not something my father is going to like to hear. I do not think he would appreciate such a wet excuse. And I do suggest that being honest with me will be the best decision you make."

"I am being honest," I lied, again.

Hadrian cocked his head to the side and raised both brows. "It must be a habit of yours to get yourself into trouble. You know what is funny? I spoke to the guards this morning who each informed me, by oath, that they did not run any initiation rites last night. So, you must understand why I am confused as to why you were outside if no one put you out there."

A nervous laugh bubbled past my lips. I had found myself in a deeper hole then I had been in before.

"So, I ask again. Why is it you did not shift when asked to?"

"I'm not a shifter, that is why." I looked down at a stain on the table.

"As in, you cannot shift because you didn't want to, or you are not able to?"

"I'm unable to," I said.

"That is impossible, Forbian does not affect those who are shifters and you were one of those left standing at the end of the night, correct?" The Prince ran a hand across his chin, scratching his head with his other hand.

"That's correct," I said, my voice louder than I expected it to be. I glanced to the group of elves in the opposite corner of the room, but they showed no sign that they had heard me.

"It's possible that you have yet to connect with your shifter ability, although I've never heard of that to happen. You are telling me you have never shifted, nor showed a single sign that you have the ability?"

The second he finished speaking I knew exactly how to answer, with yet another lie. I almost felt guilty, but then, if it meant hiding the truth I would do it.

"I've never thought about it like that," I said, bringing my voice back to a whisper and locking eyes with him, "I suppose that might explain why."

"I have not heard of that being a case before, but I will be sure to speak to Commander Alina when we return and explain the reasoning."

"Or, you can send me back home. I am not a fighter, never touched a weapon in my life, and I am pretty sure the

Commander wouldn't mind seeing the back of me. Can't you tell her it was all a mistake and I'd not eaten during the feast?"

I was almost shocked at my own words, asking the prince of Thessolina to lie to his own people. But he didn't seem fazed by my request.

"Oh, you definitely ate, Zac, but nice try." He laughed, leaning back in his stool. "You will not be returning home, as you heard we need all the help we can get with the..." he looked around, "threats. And plus, with the calluses on your hands, and the slight crock of your two fingers, it would seem to me you are very well in tune with a bow and arrow."

I peered down at my hands, noticing the same marks that Hadrian had pointed out. Nothing got past him, not even such a small detail.

"Finish your drink. I have somewhere to stop before we head back. I would not want to keep you all day, and I have some duties to complete this afternoon, so training will have to begin tomorrow."

"Training?" I asked, confused.

"You really think you are going to be missing out? I will not have it. You will train with me personally; I have always wanted a project and this seems like the perfect opportunity to begin."

I smiled to appease him, although I wanted nothing more than to throw his drink in frustration at the wall.

My head spun, more from the ale than the over load of information. I downed the last of my second drink as Hadrian finished his first.

I had to grip onto the table when I stood. The ale had caused a slight dizziness to settle over me. Hadrian pulled up a velvet pouch from his person and placed a coin on the table, then turned away and walked for the door. I followed close behind, squinting at the sudden light beyond the door as we left.

THE ELVES IN Olderim were so different from those back home. Even those who lived in the cramped, leaning houses that lined the streets still beamed with happiness. I noticed many differences between those back home and the elves around me. My hair was up in its silver messy bun, the back and sides had been shaved close to my skin. Those around me all had the luxury of long, wavy hair—all different colours and shades, a style that suited city life, not the working life on a farm. Their body shapes were all so different, all blessed with the abundance of food that those back in Horith didn't have. I noticed as one young elf I walked past pointed to my left ear, noticing the two ringed piercings that glinted in the sunlight, another clear indicator of what set us apart. I wonder what they all must have been thinking of me whilst I trailed behind their Prince.

Hadrian lifted the hood of his malachite shade cloak, concealing his hair. It didn't stop the passing crowds to spot him and point.

I kicked at loose stones, sending them skittering over the uneven street. I could still feel the ale. I felt giddy and light. A mixture between a burp and a hiccup escaped past my lips and I threw my hand to my mouth. Hadrian laughed ahead, and I was glad he didn't turn around to see my face burning red with embarrassment.

We passed through a maze of streets and finally stopped beside one of the oldest buildings in that part of Olderim. It was clear that it had no upkeep from the faded paint that was peeling from its dark wooden surface. A sign hung from above the marked doorframe, the image of an anvil painted on the panel that swung in the breeze. To the side of the door, a large window allowed passers-by to see inside at the many objects displayed. I first thought it was my drunken vision that seemed blurry, but I soon noticed on closer inspection the window was covered in a thick layer of dust. I squinted and rubbed a circle rid of dust. I could make out the outlines of swords hanging from walls and shields propped up against the tilted cabinets inside.

"I shall not be long," Hadrian said, giving me a quick smile. The door creaked when he pushed it open, rusted metal hinges screaming in protest. "Wait out here, and please refrain from going out by yourself. These streets are not always kind to the lone traveller."

And with a final nod, he entered the shop.

I peeked inside of the shop's window, expecting to see Hadrian walk by. But he didn't. It was dark inside, not a single light or sign of life.

Giving up on the idea of spying, I leaned against the ledge of the shop and waited, losing myself in the crowds that sauntered past.

Time moved on and with it my curiosity peaked. At one point, I even believed that Hadrian had forgotten about me. That he had taken a secret exit from the building and left me alone. What would a prince possibly want from a rundown weapons shop when he could have access to finest choices back at Vulmar Palace?

Giving into curiosity, and wishing for another way of passing the time, I moved closer to the window and peaked back inside.

The usual, rusted and simple made weapons were similar to those back in Horith. Long swords with broken handles, stained shields and miss-matched armour filled the room, giving the impression that it was more of a burial site for old weapons than a shop selling them.

I caught movement in the corner of my eye and heard the faint scurry of small feet. A rat, deep brown with long white whiskers ran across the floor. I watched it bob and weave around scattered weapons until it disappeared into a small hole in the wall. My breath hitched at the object that hung above where the rat had disappeared. A bow, unlike any I'd seen before.

It was made from deep oak wood. From where I stood, I could see purple vein-like rivets etched into its surface; it left me speechless. Facing me on the handle sat a large green stone, dulled from the dust that lay atop it, but still bright enough to show the importance the bow once had. The bowstring was frayed and ruined, but its body seemed timeless.

"See something you like?" I jumped, surprised to see Hadrian beside me.

"What is this place? And why is it not open for business? There are so many weapons that would sell, and many that wouldn't." I said the last part under my breath.

Hadrian's face creased, his thick dark eyebrows pinching together, one down and the other lifting up.

"The owner is leaving town for a while. He had to close up shop."

I shrugged my shoulders, "Get what you need?"

"I suppose so," he replied whilst walking ahead on the street. "I have a few more errands to run back at the palace."

"Being the prince and all, don't you have people to do these things for you?" I asked.

He laughed. "Why get someone to do a job you can always do better yourself? And it's a good excuse to get out of the palace for a while."

"I don't mean to pry."

"Valid questions deserve valid answers," Hadrian replied, walking off without another word. I followed him, but not until I risked one more look back at the bow. But the dirtied windows only illuminated my own reflection. My face alight with want.

CHAPTER
EIGHT

THE MIDDAY SUN became unbearable. My skin prickled with discomfort under the thick clothing as the warmth of the day shone down on me. The heavy material was stiff and impractical for such warm weather. During similar days in Horith, it was rare for clothing to be worn, or at least so much. I wanted nothing more than to rip the tight top from my body and allow the breeze to tickle across my bare chest.

Hadrian had stopped briefly at the end of the bridge and turned to the river we'd just passed over. He walked down the carved steps that'd been cut into the stone wall beside the bridge, following down to a platform that extended out into the water. It was crystal clear in the daylight, its pale blue surface allowing the rays of light to cut through it. It was like looking through a rippling window, one that was clean and not at all like that of the empty shop we'd left.

Hadrian reached the edge of the platform, knelt before the water and reached his hands into it. He cupped silvery liquid and lifted it over his face until it trickled down his cheeks. It was a good face, strong and sharp. Perfectly even on both sides. As the rivulets of water ran down, clinging to Hadrian's lashes, it was clear just how handsome he was.

I didn't need an invite to join him, the lure of the fresh water was enough for me to run down to his side and mirror his actions. The cobbled floor was rough against my knees as I bent towards the water and splashed it onto my arms and the back of my neck.

I released a sigh of pleasure.

"Fancy a swim?" Hadrian asked. The urge to throw myself into the river was hard to ignore, my body craved its slippery embrace.

"I wish…" I replied, the sun warming my wet face.

"Well, I do not see anything stopping us!"

"Can't swim, never learned," I answered.

Hadrian stopped and turned to me. "You cannot swim?" There was something about his tone that suggested he didn't believe me. That and his one raised brow.

"That's what I said, wasn't it?" I snipped, my embarrassment getting the best of me. "But I love water. The ocean is my favourite part of the Olderim, I just admire it from afar."

"Well, if training goes well. I will teach you."

"Thank you, but truly you don't have to. It's a skill I don't need back home. And I'm sure you're busy with other duties." I pushed on my knees to stand.

Hadrian looked up at me through his long lashes, biting at his bottom lip. "I would not offer if I did not have the time, Zac." He rubbed another splash of water on his arms then stood up.

"Of course," I bowed, turning back to the stone steps that lead to the main street.

"Hold on just a moment," Hadrian called. I could hear the slap of his boots as he chased up the steps after me. "Is that a yes or a no?"

"It's a maybe," I replied. "And my name is Zacriah." Only Petrer called me Zac, but I didn't want to say that aloud.

"Maybe is just a polite way of saying not a chance."

"For a Prince, you are pretty clever," I said, the ale gave me the confidence to be abrupt and honest.

"For a farm boy, you are a pretty good liar."

I didn't respond. We both knew what he was getting at and it didn't need to be mentioned again.

⌒

IT DIDN'T TAKE long for us to reach the palace. The streets of Thalor were still empty, which aided us in reaching the final bridge and passing to the palace gates quickly. Even in broad daylight they were still as impressive and grand as they seemed during the black of night. Two guards opened the gate for Hadrian, who thanked them. Hadrian began to talk with a familiar looking guard. Fadine. I stayed back and watched from a slight distance as he took her hand in his to shake. "Fadine, I must admit that I did not expect to see you on gate duty."

"It was this or cleaning the stables, and frankly, I'd spew pretty much everywhere if I did the latter," Fadine replied, her long, black hair tied into a bun on the top of her head. The flecks of grey even more evident in the sunlight.

She was dressed in the same uniform I wore. Purple and brown leathers, except for the rose gold scaled armour and metal that encased her strong legs and arms.

Whilst they spoke, I took a better glance at her helmet, admiring it from afar. Twisting metal designs extended from the helm giving her an air of importance, a dramatic difference from the shorter horns of the guard that stood next to her.

"I heard I'm not the only one who has pissed off Commander Alina." She gestured to where I stood, her dark eyes glaring at me then back to Hadrian. "You know, I would say the entire guard has heard about it. They all seem impressed. Not that it takes much to impress this bunch of idiots."

Hadrian laughed.

"What did you do then?" Hadrian asked. "You must have annoyed her to get placed on gate duty."

Fadine brushed a loose strand of hair behind her pointed ear. "What didn't I do? Your little friend has put her in the foulest of moods; you only need to breathe around her to get on her wrong side today."

"Right…" I could tell by his face he didn't believe her. "But what is it *you* did, Fadine? I like to believe I know you well enough to know that you enjoy stepping on Alina's toes, especially when she is the most vulnerable to fall for it."

Fadine's eyes rolled, she shook a long finger at Hadrian and tutted, "Nosey, nosey…" her voice dropping to a whisper, she seemed to be one for dramatics. My type of girl.

"I may, or may not have caused a tad, incy wincy brawl in our quarters at lunch, which may or may not have resulted in Dameaon being sent to Healer Browlin with a bloodied nose."

"I am guessing he deserved it?" Hadrian replied, his face alight, amused by the whole story.

Fadine's hand rested on her adored hip, "Of course he deserved it!"

Hadrian raised both hands. "If you say so."

"I think it's time you and your *little* friend go inside before Commander comes looking. We wouldn't want her seeing a guard talking to the prince, oh the scandal," she giggled.

On cue, the guard who'd stood still to the side of her the entire time, moved to open the gates. I walked forwards as Hadrian gestured again for me to follow.

I didn't need to look to know Fadine's eyes were trained on me whilst I passed, burning two holes into the back of my head. I felt self-conscious under her gaze. So much so that the hairs on the back of my neck stood up.

"Do not mind her. She is very protective over me. I have known her for as long as I can remember," Hadrian said, as if reading my mind.

"Is she always that welcoming?"

"You wait. It is only your first day. You have seen *nothing* yet."

∓

"I EXPECT TO see you bright and early tomorrow," Hadrian said, calling over his shoulder. "We would not want Commander Alina to think I'm giving you *special treatment* instead of putting you through the same training as your fellow peers."

We'd made it beyond the palaces main doors and were walking in the direction of the stairway that led to my sleeping quarters. I followed steps behind, unaware of just how much time had been wasted in the city.

"Where do I meet you?" I asked, skipping a few steps to catch up with his long strides.

"I will find you, don't you worry." He turned and winked.

We passed the familiar details I had studied when I first arrived and knew that we were close to the turn off for the stairs.

"I have very much enjoyed my time with you today," he said, looking over my shoulder. "Rest up, tomorrow will not be as relaxing. I will speak to the Commander and inform her of my decision." With that, he bowed his head and I forced myself to do the same. By the time I looked up he had already begun to walk away.

∓

IF I KNEW Petrer was going to grill me the moment I returned to the room, I wouldn't have come back straight away. I would have wasted hours wondering the palace, exploring my new dwelling. But instead I was stuck in the room with him. The effects of the ale were wearing off and so was my patience with Petrer's string of questions.

"What did he say? I heard you went into the city with him? Is he a dick like they say? Are you a shifter?"

"Petrer, honestly! I am exhausted. All I want to do right now is sleep."

"All right, touchy, you can't blame me for wanting answers. You disappeared this morning after Commander Alina took you away. I was worried, is that such a crime?"

I released a frustrated breath and rolled over to face the wall beside me.

"Oh, come on, Zac…" Petrer called from below, "You have to tell me something, just a little bit of information is all I need to quench my thirst."

I knew Petrer well enough to know he was not going to give up until he got his way, it was the same as always.

"Please…" His voice droned like a child begging their mam for candies.

Anything to just shut him up.

"Yes, I was with the Prince…" I couldn't see Petrer from my bunk, but the silence was enough to tell me he was surprised with my answer. "Alina… Commander Alina was unimpressed with my *lack* of shifter display and thought my best punishment was to be saddled with Hadrian."

"On a first name basis, are we?" Petrer mocked.

"Jealous, are we?" I replied, sharp.

"Not at all." The pause that followed told me that Petrer was, in fact, jealous. "Are you not going to ask how my day was?"

"Not really interested, to be honest. I'd rather sleep." For the first time today, I was telling the truth. At least in sleep, I had a break from the torment of worry my mind put me through.

"Something has really gotten into you, Zac," Petrer said, huffing from his bunk below me. "But tomorrow you best be in a better mood. I'm starting to get the impression I've done something to upset you with the way you are acting."

You have no idea.

CHAPTER
NINE

MY HEAD SNAPPED backwards against the pillow. I gasped in pain and opened my eyes. A force gripped onto my shoulders and shook me again. I bolted upright, coming face to face with the Commander. Through the haze, her features seemed blurry, but it was clear she was seething.

"You seem to have a habit of ignoring my requests!" she spat, jumping down from the side of the bunk, Petrer moaning when her foot connected with his side.

I rubbed my eyes, clearing the sleep, my hands still numb. The sunless, misty view from the window told me all I needed to know. It was too early to be up. Yet awake I was, and looking at a living nightmare.

My heart felt like it was going to explode. I couldn't decide on what was worse; the dream I'd been ripped from or the red face of the Commander before me.

"I'm sorry, Commander," I replied, fighting a yawn. "I'm a heavy sleeper."

Gwendolyn peeked her face above her bunk, her brows pinched in distaste.

"I have waited long enough, get ready and meet me outside immediately."

"But, Commander, I have to meet with P—"

"Immediately!"

She stormed from the room. The door slamming against the wall as she threw it open.

I stuffed my face into the pillow, screaming into the feathers. I was exhausted. My eyes were heavy; all I wanted to do was crawl into a ball and sleep. As if reading my mind, Commander Alina slammed a hand against the door, urging me out of bed.

Changed, I knelt beside Petrer's bed and nudged his back. He rolled over and looked at me through squinting eyes. His face crunched in annoyance at being woken yet again.

"Zac, I love you to bits, but I love my sleep just a little bit more," he murmured, stretching his toned arms above his head.

"I love my sleep too, but the Commander is waiting just outside the door for me."

Petrer rolled his eyes. "I heard."

"Listen, the Prince is going to come looking for me this morning and I'm going to need you to tell him where I have gone."

"And where is it you are going?"

I rocked back, stumped. "I don't actually know. Unless she had screamed it when I was still sleeping. Just tell him that Commander Alina came for me, he will find her."

"Leave it to me, sweet thing."

I ignored his last remark and turned for the door.

I closed it behind me, waiting to hear the click of the door as the latch fell into place. The Commander stood with her back to me. In the candlelight of the corridor, I could see that she wore a nightdress. No armour or fancy uniform in sight. No wonder she was so annoyed. Her boots peeped from under the hemline of her dress, muddied and scuffed. It was clear she had been in a rush to get here.

I stepped forward into her line of sight, "Sorry to keep you waiting Commander." I forced my sweetest and most believable voice as I addressed her.

"Don't do it again, boy," she said, still not facing me but looking off beyond the window at the end of the corridor.

"Can I ask where we are going? I promised the Prince that I would meet him here this morning."

She looked at me. I almost flinched under her stare. "Oh, did you? Well pardon me, but King Dalior has given me *direct* orders to take you this morning so I am afraid the Prince is going to have to wait. King Dalior feels that until you prove yourself as a shifter you are going to be working in the kitchens every morning to earn your keep. Each morning you are to make your *own* way to the kitchens. Alone. I will be in contact with the staff to keep me informed of your timekeeping."

My lack of response must have pleased her. She smiled at me, one that did not fit her face nor reach her eyes. "Anything wrong with that? Any complaints you would like me to pass back onto the King?"

"No not at all, in fact, I would love to help. My only request—which by the way, thank you for asking me if I had any, so *so* nice of you—is that I do hope I can encourage you to change your mind about escorting me each morning…" I paused, allowing my statement to sink in like the tip of a knife before I sunk it in to the hilt. "I've not enjoyed company like this since I was placed on duty at the morgue back in Horith." There goes the hilt.

The Commanders face morphed before my very eyes. I watched her neck blotch with red patches, a single blue vein visibly pulsing on her forehead. I tried not to laugh as she made her attempt to compose herself, fists clenched when she moved for the stairway. My smile didn't falter; I almost wished

Fadine was there to watch. I knew it would be something she would enjoy.

The Commander didn't address me the entire walk, nor did I question her again. I thought it best to leave her.

‿

THE KITCHEN WAS huge, a common theme for most rooms in the palace. The smell was the first thing I noticed, the air thick with steaming meats and boiling oats. My stomach clenched in sudden hunger, my mouth began to water as I watched food being prepared from the doorway. The Commander had pushed me forward inside of the kitchen and left without giving me any instructions. I just stood awkwardly, watching elves dressed in white garments bustle past, each ignoring my presence. I attempted to step forward, but jumped backwards when one elf almost bumped straight into me. I could hear the grumble of insults as she passed me, the many pots she balanced in her arms rattling around.

I took a step back, hoping if I edged towards the door I could leave without anyone noticing. My back slammed into something hard, the door. I reached back with my hand and grasped for the handle. Beneath my touch it felt a lot softer then I would imagine it to be.

"Oi!" someone squeaked behind me. "You'd think you'd keep your wits about you whilst trying to escape this hell hole. If I have to cut carrots, you'll have to as well."

The girl I'd bumped into was familiar, her sharp nose and freckled face was one I was sure I'd seen the morning before. She too was dressed in the whites of the staff; her long ginger hair tucked behind her pointed ears was concealed beneath the tall hat that sat askew on her head.

"I wasn't trying to leave, I was just…"

"Nyah." She extended a freckled hand towards me, "And you don't need to lie to me." She tapped the temples of her head and smiled. "I'm glad to see another familiar face, you can help us."

"Zacriah," I replied, taking her hand. "And what do you mean *another* familiar face?" I asked, looking around the room again and noticing a few other faces that I recognized beneath oversized hats.

"I know who you are," she replied, her grip strong as she squeezed my hand. "Seems like all of us in Rank Clarak have been told to work the kitchens. Most of us don't mind though, the leftovers are worth it."

I pulled my hand from hers and rubbed away the ache from her grip. "Sorry about that. It's not usually what happens when I first meet someone, promise." I felt the need to apologize.

"Forget about it!" Her laugh was odd, but nice. It reminded me of a woodpecker, loud and shrill.

"You know, you are going to get pretty hot in those," she said, her eyes glancing to my outfit, "If you don't fancy smelling like stock and onions for the rest of the day, I suggest you go through those doors and change into something not so… tight." She pointed to a door at the other end of the room. "Don't expect anything too fancy though, the choices are not the most flattering."

I didn't have to be told twice, the heat was already getting to me. I could feel my skin dampening under the heavy, warm air. I walked over to the doors, dodging others as they rushed around the stations, shouting for peeled potatoes or scrambled eggs. Nyah was behind me still, directing me forward.

The room we entered had towering shelving units on either side, each covered in mixture of clothes and pans. Nyah closed the door behind us and looked me up and down before passing me a set of white clothes from the shelf. She was much taller than me, more than a foot in height. She was built incredibly, muscles everywhere. As I took the set from her hands I noticed her bulging forearm. She handed me a pile and turned away, crossing her strong arms.

"I promise I won't peak."

I laughed, already feeling completely at ease by her presence. It was a strange feeling, I could feel like trickle in the back of my mind the moment I touched her. She oozed with positivity.

I peeled the training attire off, placing it on an empty shelf and changed into a loose fitting set that Nyah had passed to me. I toyed with the idea of leaving the tall hat, but decided against it. I didn't want to stand out any more than I already had.

～

ONCE CHANGED, NYAH pulled me back into the kitchen towards a station in a less busy area. Only a few other elves stood around us, the rhythmical thud of knifes against wood matching the smashing clangs of pots and pans. Nyah picked up two knives, the blades weathered and dull. She passed one to me, and kept the other for herself. We began, slowly making our way through the never-ending pile of carrots before us.

"I wasn't joking about the carrot chopping," she said. It was hard to keep up with her speed and technique, it was clear from the way she held the knife and the fluid movement of her wrists that she was well versed with them.

"I can see that," I replied, my hand already stiff.

"You know everyone is talking about what happened with you yesterday," she said. "But I'm already sure you know that."

"I've heard." I'd also noted the number of glances I'd gained myself already in the kitchens alone.

"I wouldn't worry about what they say. People talk, I know that well enough."

"And what are they saying?" I asked, unsure if I wanted to know, but curiosity got the best of me.

"That your shift is weak." I had to commend her honesty. "But it could be worse, right? My shift is a moth and Makrus over there is a worm. Literally, a worm. It can't be much worse than that."

I laughed, and so did she. We leaned forward to hide our giggle from Makrus who turned our way when he heard his name.

I rolled my wrists for the hundredth time to stretch the stiff from them. "I wish the Commander saw the same hilarity in it as you do. I didn't think it was possible for someone to despise another like she does with me," I said.

"I wouldn't take it personally. It would seem she pretty much despises the entirety of rank Clarak since we are the only rank that have been placed on any type of duty," Nyah replied.

"Is it bad that I feel slightly relived her attention has spread to others and not just me?" I picked up another carrot, chopping it into thin chunks and throwing it into a pot of water beside me.

"A little, but I get it. Seems like you truly are her favourite. I noticed she dropped you off personally this morning."

"You saw?"

"Hard not to." She giggled.

Someone across the room shouted at us for talking. I could see, from the corner of my eye, Nyah's shoulders heave from laughter. I had to bite my lip to stop myself from joining.

TIME PASSED AND with it the pile of food before us lessened. I didn't stop my flow of work until the door to the kitchens burst open, catching me off guard and causing my knife to slip. I gasped as deep, red blood dripped onto the side board and I stuffed my finger into my mouth to suck and still the flow of blood. Everyone was silent, even Nyah's eyes were wide as she looked to the door. I turned, following her stare, to see Hadrian. His face a picture of anger, eyes searching. I caught his glare the moment they landed on me, my breath hitching. Heads of those watching followed Hadrian as he strutted across the room, right to me.

"She brought you here?" His question was directed at me. I could feel the warm creep of embarrassment flush over my face.

"Did she?" he shouted, slamming a palm onto the side.

I pulled my bloody finger from my mouth to reply, "I tried to tell her, but Commander Ali—"

"Come!" he interrupted, moving back for the door.

I turned quick to Nyah whose emerald eyes burned with concern.

"Go…" she whispered, passing me a wad of material to wrap my finger in. I took it and thanked her, moving to the door Hadrian exited from.

He didn't look back to check that I followed, not until we had walked up two flights of stairs and reached an empty corridor.

"I knew she would do this, I should have come sooner," Hadrian hissed, his voice riled with frustration. "I went to collect you, but your roommate explained to me what happened. Finding where she brought you was a hassle, one that I could have evaded if I only came for you sooner."

He walked back and forth before me, his breathing harsh.

"She said King Dalior gave her the command," I said, leaning against the wall behind me, catching my breath from the quick walk.

"I know her, Zac, she had a part in this. I spoke to father last night and told him I was to train you. He did not mention anything about you working to earn your keep. I am sure Alina had her say in this since. And I am *not* having it."

I would have told him not to call me Zac again, but it wasn't the time. Between the throbbing of my cut finger and the anger that radiated off Hadrian, my anxiety spiked.

"I honestly don't mind."

"Well I do. Now come. I think it is time I pay her a visit."

CHAPTER

TEN

WE SLIPPED INTO the room. Hadrian didn't tell me where we were going, it seemed like everyone in this blasted palace lacked necessary skills in communication. No one noticed us enter, not the crowd sitting in the elevated stands, not even Commander Alina who stood in the middle of the room.

I first thought she was dancing. Until I saw the double ended staff in her hands. She threw the staff into the air, moving like water, throwing a leg into a wide kick then snatching it back into her hands. Her feline movements were precise, strong. The staff whistled through the air again and she cut, swung, and bashed at invisible enemies. All the while not noticing the two new occupants in the room.

We kept in the shadows of the towering walls, giving me a moment to absorb the details around me. The room consisted of two levels. My eyes were drawn to Illera first; I then caught onto other faces I recognized. The entirety of Rank Mamlin watched in awe as the Commander demonstrated her movements below them.

I turned to still a wobbling shield that threatened to fall. I'd been too transfixed by the Commander to watch where I was going. My heart stopped, worried it would fall and give our presence away. But it didn't, and nor did it catch Alina's attention. I then noticed more shields each pristine and painted in of reds and blues. I could tell they were nothing more than decoration from the lack of marks across their surfaces.

Lining the bottom of the walls, countless wooden weapons sat propped up, just like the one spinning in the Commanders hands.

Hadrian stepped forward and made a coughing sound from his throat. Gasps from the watching initiates spread like a wave. Distracted, Commander Alina dropped the staff in a loud clatter against the floor. She turned towards us, ready to reprimand who ever had interrupted her lesson, but choked on her words when she spotted who it was.

"Prince Hadrian..." She bowed, her eyes not leaving him as she dipped. "I didn't expect a visit from you today."

"I too did not expect to be visiting you today, Commander," he replied, gesturing dramatically around him, "but here I am."

Her eyes flickered over his shoulder towards me where I stood, still in the shadows. I held her intense glare until she dropped it first. Her lips tugged ever so slightly, pulling downwards into a frown.

"I see Zacriah has left his staff duties early, I'm sure King Dalior would not be happy to hear this." She slammed a foot down onto one end of the staff, sending the other end up into the air before she snatched it. The slap of her hand against the wood made me cringe.

"He is to be brought to me for training, not wasting his time staffing. I find it odd that King Dalior did not inform me of his decision last night over supper and why I had to find out this morning instead."

"Yet, it is still King Dalior's wish for him to work to earn his keep. That is until he decides if he is ready to share his shifting ability." Again, she shot her eyes right at me. "Train him your highness, by all means, but Zacriah is to work mornings in the kitchens with the rest of Rank Clarak until he proves himself. If you have an issue, please bring it up with your *father*. As you can see, I am otherwise occupied."

I couldn't see Hadrian's face from my vantage point, but I could hear the slow clicks of his tongue whilst he walked forward and snatched the staff from Commander Alina's hand. Commander Alina's face burned red and that same bulging vein I had seen this morning began to push through her skin.

In truth, I was used to sticking up for myself. But seeing someone—let alone the Prince of Thessolina—getting so angry over my own fate had me on edge. *Why me?*

"Prince Hadrian..." I walked further into the room, paranoid that he was about to use that staff against the Commander. "I feel as though we've taken up too much of Commander's time, I'm happy to return back to the kitchens and carry on working as King Dalior has requested."

"Do you hear that Prince? Your *pet* is rather happy slaving away instead. I'm sure he is used to it were he is from, aren't you, boy?"

I heard a laugh in the stands above. A familiar snigger. I didn't need to see who it came from. Illera.

I wanted to leave the room as soon as the words dripped from her mouth. I was embarrassed with Hadrian's behaviour, I didn't care if he was the prince or not. Dragging me here, before a crowd, allowing the Commander a chance to belittle me. Her comment rubbed me the wrong way. The two days' worth of frustration burst from me as I stormed forward, only to be stopped mid-stride by Hadrian's outstretched hand. I was ready to tell her *exactly* what I thought, but Hadrian spoke before I even had a chance.

"A duel," Hadrian said, his strength holding me in place. "In two weeks' time Zacriah is to duel a guard of your choice, there he will prove his worth. Until then, he will carry on his time in the kitchens, but if he wins he will be relieved of his duties."

I looked at him, my anger turning in his direction. I didn't care about titles, royalty or who he was. I hated that the moment I entered the palace my fate had been ripped from my own hands and placed into the hands of others.

"I will need to check with the Ki—" the Commander began, but was cut off by the high shrill of Hadrian's laughter.

"Of course, a loyal dog always follows the orders of its owner, rarely trusting their own instincts. Regardless of what King Dalior says, I am prince and I demand a duel. It's the least I deserve; call it a late birthday gift. I could do with the entertainment, it may lighten the mood for the palace during these times."

She bowed, slow, pointless and exaggerated. Once she was done she stood up and turned for the initiates who watched in shock from up above.

"What a good idea. Two weeks, I pick the competitor and we can *all* watch as your little pet either shits himself or lies in a puddle of his own blood." She grabbed the staff back from Hadrian's hand.

"And don't worry…" she said with all her attention focused back on me, "I will make sure whoever I pick won't hurt your hands, we wouldn't want your skills in the kitchens to be affected."

I couldn't stop myself, I spoke before I even had a moment to register what I was saying. "It's not my hands you should worry about, but rather what I'm doing to your food when I prepare it."

I felt a warm hand on my shoulder, gently urging me back before I pounced. Hadrian whispered something to me, but I didn't hear, not through the roar that filled my mind.

I kept my gaze pinned to the Commanders. My next words I made sure were loud enough for every single elfin in the room to hear. "I suppose we have some work to do, your highness."

"That we do," he agreed.

Commander Alina said nothing more. Instead, she watched as we left the room, leaving the door wide open. I kept breathing, in through my nose out through my mouth. Hadrian was behind me, his hand placed on my back. With every footstep, the idea of duelling sank into me deeper. By the time we reached our next destination, I was in full panic mode.

CHAPTER
ELEVEN

"KEEP YOUR HANDS up and cover that pretty face of yours, unless you want me to hit it." Hadrian moved like a snake, weaving from my punch with a smile. "And I really do not want to ruin it."

"Don't worry about me," I said, breathless.

My arms ached from holding them up in defence for so long. "If you are so worried about ruining it, why don't you stop deliberately aiming for it!" My legs burned from squatting and dropping repeatedly to avoid Hadrian's advances. Although my attempts at dodging him seemed to always end in Hadrian catching yet another undefended part of my body.

"Keep it protected and you won't have to worry about my attempts," he replied, dropping his fists. "Fetch two of those swords, it's time we move on."

Hadrian was built like a statue. I watched, mouth agape, as he yanked his shirt over his head and dropped it to the floor. The muscles on his back rippled when he rolled his shoulders and flexed his arms, both in perfect proportion to his thick torso. I looked away, quickly busying myself and picking up two wooden swords on the wall beside me.

"I do not think you are ready for weapons." Hadrian spoke from behind me; I could feel the heat from his topless body warming my back. "But we are going to need to work every angle of training in the limited time that we have to get you ready."

I did not turn to him, my face still red. "What makes you think I haven't used one before?"

Hadrian's hand shot from over my shoulder and snatched a sword from my grasp, pressing the butt of it to my spine. "Because you are a bow and arrow type of guy, not a swords master."

"If you say so." My voice dropped. I turned fast, throwing the sword out to the side as if to prove my worth. He was right, though; I had no clue how to use it. In the blink of an eye Hadrian blocked my slash and slammed his sword so hard onto mine that I dropped it on the floor.

"Don't get ahead of yourself." He smirked. "Pick it up and try again."

∽

THE ROOM WAS cramped, with only the light from a few candles that dripped wax down the alcoves on the stone walls. It was enough light to catch Hadrian's movements, but not to illuminate the entire room.

I ran my hand down the wooden sword, feeling the marks and rough design. Hadrian paced in front of me, his sword held out before him. His gilded eyes squinted in my direction.

"Remember, protect your face, keep a wide stance and do not drop eye contact." Hadrian stopped moving and bent his knees, smiling.

"Got it." I took a deep breath through my nose and released.

"Good luck." He winked.

He didn't mean it.

I couldn't keep up with his movements. He bobbed and weaved, his body blurring. I advanced. I spun my sword, bringing it down onto his. The slap of the wood echoed across the room, vibrating up my arm. He swiped his across the floor, and slammed it to my shin. I bit back a cry of pain. Distracted, he took another swing for my head. I dropped, rolling to the side. A sudden burst of wind brushed beside my ear. I threw out a leg, aiming for his. He jumped. I missed.

He must have swung the sword again because my head snapped backwards and my cheek stung from the slap.

"What the fu—" I thrust my sword at him, hitting him for the first time in the crook behind his knee. His howl of pain was music to my ears.

My next two attempts made contact, one in the side of his stomach and the other under his arm. Pain and anger blended together within me and urged me on. I pushed all my strength, although it was beginning to dwindle. My next movement had managed to send his sword tumbling from his hands. Hadrian's face, a painting of surprise.

"Ha!" I shouted. I'd spoken too soon. He growled and moved forward, side stepping my frantic attempt to stop him.

His fists struck me in calculated movements. He moved like a viper, sending sharp punches to my arm. I stumbled backwards, falling over my feet and landing on the ground. He leaped on top of me, pinning me down with his weight and straddling my stomach.

"Never be cocky. You do not win until your competitor is on the ground," Hadrian said, flecks of his spit and sweat on my face. "And right now, *you* are the one on the ground, which makes me the winner."

I tried to wiggle free, but failed. Hadrian was heavy, a lump of pure muscle. "I get it. You can get off me."

Hadrian rolled me over. He yanked at my arms and wrapped his legs around my stomach. I pushed, trying anything to get the upper hand. But my energy was spent.

"Enough!" I pleaded, less with Hadrian and more with my magick as it stirred within me. I pinched my eyes closed and pushed at it. My lack of energy was working against me. I couldn't see Hadrian, but only felt the lack of his weight when he let go of me.

I could feel the stuffy air in the room throbbing around me, begging for me to take a hold of it. It screamed at me, it wanted me. Every ounce of strength I had left, I threw it down against my magick, finally stopping its rush.

"Cheap shot." Hadrian wheezed beside me, still clutching his crotch. "Looks like we are both on the floor. Neither of us wins." I must have kicked him as he rolled on his back, grasping his groin.

"If training is going to be like this for the next two weeks, I think I would prefer working in the kitchens and forfeit the duel."

"If training is going to *end* like this," Hadrian moaned, "I think I will have to insist on training with you as often as possible."

I pushed off the floor, my legs screaming as I attempted to stand. I stumbled to the wall on the far side of the room and sank my hands into the fresh spring that dripped from a hole in the bricks. Its cold touch was refreshing against my aching fingers. My face chilled once I rubbed the water across my warm cheeks.

My ears twitched as Hadrian stood from the floor behind me and picked up both the fallen swords. "I am impressed, Zac, truly." He joined me next to the spring. "I'm not going to lie, I first thought you were a lost cause. But by the end of this session I could see the want to fight back in your eyes. You just need... persuading."

"Persuading!" I laughed, turning towards him. "You call that persuading?" I gripped onto the wall, fighting back the urge to strike him. It was easy to forget he was the prince. I would wipe that smug smile from his face one way or another. "And my name is Zacriah. Call me by it."

"Ease up!" He raised his hands in defeat. "I shouldn't have been so hard on you. It has been a while since I trained with anyone and must admit I got a little carried away. But if it is any consolation, you did best me... sort of." His eyes flickered to his crotch which his hand covered as he spoke.

"Well next time, ease up," I said.

"What is that..." Hadrian moved closer to me, inspecting my arm. "You bruise easy, I'm sorry."

I looked down to see what he saw. My arms were already covered in purple and black spots. I pulled my arm from his clammy grasp. "I forgive you. I bruise easily; Mam always said I was like a petal."

"Like a petal. I like that. In fact, if I can't call you Zac, I believe petal is just as good of a choice."

"Tell me you're kidding."

"Never, Petal."

"Is training over?" I asked, taking my eyes away from the small curls on his chest and ignoring his teasing. He stood right before me, both his hands on the wall on either side of me.

"We can stop now."

"Great." I slipped under his arms, and headed for the door, unsure where I was to go. But the latent hunger that rumbled in my stomach told me I needed food.

"But before you rush off I have something for you."

∽

I FOLLOWED HIM for the third time that day. All hope of escaping for food had disintegrated into nothing as we moved through the dark corridor ahead. Hadrian had forgotten to put his shirt back on, although it didn't cross my mind to remind him. At the end of the corridor, we reached another room.

He turned for me before opening the door to it.

"My father believes, and rightly so, that allowing our soldiers to each pick a weapon of their choice gives our army an advantage. Alongside the bow and arrow and sword that is given to all who join, it is also custom for each solider to pick out a weapon that is of their personal choice." He pulled open the doors. "Welcome to the armoury."

I was stunned into silence. I passed glinting objects that hung from the walls, weapons of all different sizes and designs. The room was full of shelving, each covered in dusty swords and scabbard to match. We moved through a small space between two units, a row that seemed to never end. Hadrian headed straight for a cabinet up against the wall ahead. It was made from some type of burgundy wood I didn't recognize. Its surface was glossy, reflecting the minimal light around it making it seem wet. I peered over his shoulder and watched him pull open the top drawer. Within the drawer short iron swords, daggers and unfamiliar armaments each laid on a purple silk cushion. The weapons were different from those that lined the walls and covered the shelves we had passed. Obsidian daggers with handles crafted from bone, intricate iron throwing stars and swords covered with razor shape teeth. They each lay in their own space within the drawer, amongst the mounds of silk.

"Looks like a lot have already been picked by your fellow shifters," Hadrian gestured to the pile, "but there are still some good choices left."

"They're beautiful." I had never seen anything like it. Each had been crafted with detail and beauty. I ran my hand over them, careful not to cut myself on their sharp edges.

My eyes landed on a lump of metal chain that had been pushed to the back corner of the drawer. "What is that?"

"Nothing of importance," Hadrian lifted the bone dagger, "What about this? The dagger is small enough to be concealed on your person but large enough to penetrate and leave a lasting impression on any enemy."

I tugged the tangle of metal, ignoring Hadrian and the dagger he held out to me. As I lifted it from the drawer, the tangles of metal unravelled, the metal links chiming together when they fell. "They look like…"

"Claws," he answered for me.

I tilted my head, looking over every possible detail. Metal spikes protruded from the tips of what must have been finger caps. I tapped my palm over the tips to see how sharp they were. A prickle of adrenaline spread beneath where they touched me. "I want them."

"Really?" His eyebrows pinched in confusion, "Out of all of this, you want these?"

My look alone shut him up. He raised his arms, dropping the dagger carelessly back into the drawer. "They are yours. Here, let me help you try them on. They may not fit, you haven't the biggest hands."

To Hadrian's displeasure and my delight, they slipped on easily, each one of my fingers filling the capped space inside the claws. The chains hugged my hands as Hadrian clipped the clasp around my wrists. They did not fall off, slip or move. I lifted both hands before me. The curves of metal reflected in the candlelight as I spun them, flexing my fingers and allowing the claws to move back and forth.

"Copy what I do," Hadrian instructed. He held his hand out, fingers splayed and quickly flicked them into a fist.

I copied, clenching my fingers into a fist. A small pop-like sound followed. I lifted my hands again, this time looking closely at the tips of my fingers. The points had retracted.

"Are you sure you want them? I am not confident on how well they work in battle," Hadrian said.

I could not pull my gaze from them. "Sounds like I'll be the first to find out. You told me *I* could choose, so I have. I want these."

I mimicked the movement again, flexing my fingers outwards until the pop sounded. The points were back, sharp and elegant as before. I ran my new hands over the cabinets' surface, running my claws across the once perfect wood. I pulled my hand back and noticed the four marks that I had left and the rolls of peeled wood that sat in their wake.

"What did the cabinet ever do to you?" Hadrian asked, blowing the flecks of peeled wood and brushing his hand across them. My stomach answered for me, rumbling in hunger.

"Let's get back, Petal. I think someone needs feeding," he said, pushing the drawer closed.

"You're really going to call me that?" I asked, but he only laughed in response.

I kept my hands behind my back and we made our way back to the throne room where the scent of steak and boiled potatoes greeted us. Hadrian dropped me off at the door, instructing me to remove my claws, although I attempted to protest his command.

"Trust me, if word gets back to the Commander about which weapon you picked they could use that against you in the duel. Keep it a surprise for the day."

I unclasped the first buckle with my teeth and Hadrian helped pull it off my hand. The second was easier to remove without the constraints of metal. "I shall drop them off to your room myself. Go and eat."

"Thank you." Hadrian nodded. I watched him walk off but before he turned a corner I shouted for him. "Hadrian, sorry about your jewels, it was a dirty move."

He didn't turn to me, but his laugh did reach me. "I like dirty."

His comment stayed with me and I walked into the throne room with a red face. Petrer waved from across the room, and I headed towards him.

I was thankful for the mindless chatter about his training as we ate. I asked question after question, it was my way of steering conversation away from me. It wasn't until we left the throne room to return to our room that I realized it was the first time I had forgotten about my woes with Petrer. My mind was too busy racing about another.

∽

WHEN WE RETURNED to our room I headed straight for the baths. I was excited about the idea of washing, it would be the first time since arriving. *The first without my magick.* I lowered myself into the warm embrace of the water, my entire body relaxing.

Losing track of time, I replayed the day's events until I noticed the lack of light from the window and the sudden chill of the water. Wrapping a stiff towel around my body, I padded to the room, leaving wet footprints behind me. Everyone was already asleep when I entered.

As I lifted myself up I saw my claws placed on my pillow. Hadrian had been here. I lifted them up, ready to move them into my sack for safe keeping, when I noticed a single red Rose petal placed beneath them.

I smiled.

CHAPTER

TWEL VE

NYAH HADN'T STOPPED talking from the moment we left Masarion on our errand run. Despite the straw bags that were draped off both her arms and the pace she walked, she was unfazed. Where I was exhausted. Her freckled face was raised to the sky while she nattered about some boy she had met the previous night.

"He is seriously good looking. And his voice, honestly, his voice. It's rich like cocoa, sweet as honey. I practically melted into a puddle right before him when we spoke."

"I'm guessing he didn't mind that you spilled food across his back?" I asked, attempting to wipe the sweat from my chin with my shoulder as I too carried two full straw bags.

"Well, it depends on how you define 'we spoke.'"

"Right…"

"He kind of gasped and shouted, but that was because the soup was pretty hot," she replied.

"You've got to be joking." I chuckled, struggling to keep up. "Did you even have a conversation, or did he just shout at you?"

"Not really. By the time I coughed up an apology he was halfway out of the room."

My chuckle had turned into a fit of laughter, so much so that I had to stop and drop the bags to the floor. "Honestly Nyah, you do make me laugh."

"Well laugh all you want, if you saw him you'd have melted on the spot."

"Oh, I'm sure I would've."

We'd been sent to the market with a large list of goods to collect for breakfast. The head chef's handwriting was rushed and hard to read, we only hoped we'd retrieved everything. The last thing I needed was for word to get back to the Commander that I was not following instructions *again*.

It was still early morning, and apart from the shouts of the market it was relatively peaceful in the city. That was until Nyah perked up again and listed off questions about my training with Hadrian.

"You're limping, which suggests your training with the Prince was intense," Nyah said, picking up one of my bags as I stopped to catch my breath. She was as strong as an ox, carrying over double the bags I did and showing not a single sign of struggle.

I shrugged, "Sure, it wasn't that bad. I'm certain Hadrian—Prince Hadrian—forgets that I have no experience in hand to hand combat."

Nyah looked over her shoulder, one eyebrow raised. "Word is he likes you. You know he hasn't spent this much time with someone for years... at least that is what is being said."

I huffed, "It's been three days since we arrived. I'm certain he doesn't like me any more than I like him. And why is it that this entire palace thrives off gossip? Sounds like everyone knows more about what's going on than I do!"

"Lying again," she teased.

"What makes you think you are so good at reading me?"

"I have my ways." She peaked over her shoulder and flashed a grin. "Speed up. You're so slow!"

I decided to direct the conversation onto another course. Talking about Hadrian became boring, fast.

"Well, hopefully you pick your weapon today," I said, speeding up to keep up with her.

"I hope so. I'm holding out hope that the dagger is still there, sounds like something I would work well with."

"If your skill at cutting carrots is anything to go by, I'm sure you will be the best knife wielder in Thessolina," I replied.

We dropped our voices as four of the King's guards passed by on elks. I'd seen the same guards pass by already since we'd left the palace; they must have been doing a routine check of the grounds. We kept our heads down and walked past. I was sure I heard my name from one of them, but I didn't look up to check.

I looked up to the sky, the light disappearing behind a large dark cloud. I held hope for rain, it'd been days since it last did and it would help wash away the muggy atmosphere that clung around the city.

"About the shifting, or lack of shifting. Has Hadrian helped you with that?"

I bit my tongue before responding.

"Between me and you, no. He hasn't even mentioned it for a couple of days. I guess I am just a late bloomer." The lie was sour in my mouth.

"Don't worry, I am sure *it* will happen soon enough." Her reply was cold.

She picked up her pace again and I struggled to keep up.

∽

THE GREAT HALL was filled with the loud laughs and conversations of the many elves that sat at the long oak tables, all who were waiting to be served. I looked out over the room at the sea of purple and black, guards sat next to the shifters, chatting and banging tankards together. I caught a glance at

Petrer who looked content sitting amongst a group of guards and two unfamiliar shifter girls who flanked him on either side. His wide smile lit up the room, a beacon of familiarity in a sea of uncertainty.

Nyah was nowhere to be seen, I'd lost her once we entered the kitchens when we arrived back from the city. It was a rush of unpacking bags and preparing to serve the great hall.

∽

I STOOD AMONGST the many other workers, each who balanced trays and jugs in their arms. We waited around the edge of the room; for what I was still unsure, but I kept my head forward and waited for instruction.

There was movement from the dais that stilled all conversation in the room. I couldn't see from where I stood, a large pillar blocked my view, but the deep voice that sounded was unforgettable.

"Good morning to you all…" King Dalior said, his voice filling every inch of the throne room, his words dripping in lush tones. "I must first thank you all for your hard work during training. I have heard many things from Commander Alina who has expressed such pleasure in your efforts over the past few days." The crowd looked at each other, faces alight with pride. Somehow, I felt his words were not for me, not at all.

"My dear, *dear* children…" he paused, taking in a breath, "I am afraid my visit is not a positive one this morning, for I bring news of an attack. I regret to inform you that there has been yet another, this time at the peaceful farming town of Vlaroi. When news reached me this morning I had learned of the level of destruction of Vlaroi. It has been a brutal and unprovoked attack."

The temperature in the room dropped. I listened, my heart beating. King Dalior's voice had dropped and as he spoke I could hear the sadness that laced his words.

I knew of Vlaroi. It was a town Fa had visited before. Close to the forest of Vlamour, the deep woodland cutting across the entire country like a belt. Many did not pass through it, or even venture close. It was believed beasts and creatures lived amongst the dense woodland of Vlamour. Creatures that sucked at the bones of younglings and restless spirits that melted the mind with a touch. The stories were enough to keep anyone from its depths.

"Unfortunately, that is all I can share with you at this moment, but although this tragic event has caused us such worry, I want this opportunity to remind you of your importance to Thessolina against this threat. You must not let this news deter you, only encourage you to train harder and prepare you to face it."

King Dalior stood amongst the elves that sat at the four long tables, his ruby cloak spread behind like a pool of blood.

"Please, enjoy your feast this morn and gather your energy for another day's training. Train harder, faster. We must be ready for their next attack. The Morthi behind these attacks will not get away with it again."

He bowed his head and turned back to the throne, disappearing through a doorway behind it.

It took a few moments for the room to shake themselves from the shock of the news. I missed the clap, our signal to place the food on the tables, and only began to move when I noticed those next to me step forward. I moved through the room, my mind focused on nothing but Vlaroi. Once I placed the platter of food onto the closest table to me, I headed straight for the kitchen, numb.

I picked my pace up and by the time I reached the kitchens, I ran straight through and out another door. Once beyond, I landed on my knees and vomited across the ground, my stomach cramping as I retched.

I slumped to the wall beside the door, not a single speck of energy left to even turn towards it when it opened.

"Here," Nyah's voice whispered beside me. She handed me a piece of brown bread and a tankard of water. "Eat this." She side-stepped the puddle of sick and moved to sit down beside me, squatting her long legs.

"Thanks." My throat was sore and my stomach empty. "I don't know what happened, one minute I was fine and the next…" I gestured to the sick before me.

"Don't worry about it, it happens to the best of us. I tried to catch you in the hall, but you looked as if you had seen a ghost. You had no colour at all."

"Did I?" It was hard to piece together what happened once King Dalior had left.

Nyah reached out and placed her hand on mine. She was cold to the touch; her fingers gripped a hold of my arm. It was her face that worried me, it was pinched, and she looked like she was in pain.

"Nyah, are you well?" I asked, but she ignored. "Nyah?"

"I'm concentrating…" she said, her eyes closed and her lips stretched until they were white with tension.

"On what?"

A sudden wave of warmth seemed to encase my entire body and my emotions began to change. The panic melted away within me, gone in seconds. Although I had no idea how it kept happening, I could feel its origins. I looked towards the throbbing feeling, it came directly from Nyah's hand.

They glowed, tendrils of red wrapping around me. I would've screamed, but I felt calm. A detached feeling between my mind and body. I watched in awe as the tentacles ebbed and flowed around my hands and arms. Filling me with their light.

She dropped my hand, panting. It was the first time I had seen her out of breath. She leaned her head against the wall, a single drop of sweat rolling down her forehead onto her cheek. I looked to my hand again, expecting to see the red glow, but it had gone. Not a single trace left.

"I feel... different," I said. I could feel the flurry of panic in the back of my mind, but it was buried by a new sense of calm.

"I thought I'd help you out. I must admit it was a slight gamble. I don't normally have such success on the first try." She spoke through heavy breaths.

"Magick," I said, turning my hand before me. "How?"

"Empath, and not a very good one. I haven't had that much practice, so I can only do the bare minimal like alter an emotion and read an aura. Sense a lie." She gave me a side-eye look. "And when you left the hall you were a walking flame of worry."

"You're part Alorian? Part high elf?"

Such magick came from the blood of a high elf; it was not something Niraen elves could do. It was the one main difference between us. The Alorian power came from their blood.

"My Mum was high elf. I haven't seen her since I was born though, she left and never returned." Nyah didn't look at me as she spoke. "Papa said I gained the ability from her, but I never learned how to use it. There was no one back home who had a clue what it was. The other Alorian elves in the village had different abilities, not one was an Empath though. I'm self-taught."

"I know an Empath." I said, "Well, I knew one, I think. I'm not sure if he is here anymore."

Nyah perked up, "Really?"

"I'm not. I ... can't remember his name but my Fa and I stayed with him here many moons ago. I remember him and

Fa talking about it when they thought I was asleep." The memories were coming back to me the more I spoke of it, still in black and white but there none the less.

Nyah jumped up, "Do you think we could find him? I mean, it'd be amazing to learn."

"We could try. I don't... remember where he lives or anything. But he must be easy to find, right? We just ask for the local Empath," I replied, patting her arm.

Nyah giggled. "I suppose!"

The door opened to the head chef who looked between me, Nyah and the puddle of sick. His face awash with disapproval.

"I thought I heard some shouting out 'ere. What do you think you two are playing at?" His eyes were blood shot. "Get your sorry arses back in 'ere before I drag you in myself."

Nyah looked at me with wide eyes, biting her lip to stop a laugh. After the subtle look, she nodded at the head chef, walking silently back to the kitchen. I followed quickly after her, certain Commander Alina was going to hear about it.

CHAPTER

ThIRTEEN

IT WAS HADRIAN'S idea to train outside, swapping the cramped dark room for the open air and uneven lush ground. The cool sea mist blew across my damp neck giving instant relief. We were in a courtyard of sorts, in the middle of the palace grounds. Many guards and staff walked past us, some even hesitating to stop the training when they noticed who was fighting. Hadrian had to call out countless times to tell them he was fine and not under attack.

It still didn't stop their wary glances.

I was beginning to take pleasure in sparring with Hadrian. It'd been a few days since our first session and I could already feel my body and mind evolving. I'd begun studying him, watching and learning every slight movement he made. It was working, for each day I picked up my pace and even Hadrian noticed my improvement.

"Aim here," he said, gesturing to a soft spot to the side of his torso between his ribs and hip. "If you strike hard enough, it will give you a few extra seconds to get in another attack before your opponent has a chance to regain composer to retaliate."

I nodded, readying myself to try.

We'd swapped the wooden swords for fists, a decision I was thankful for. I'd woken up with friction blisters on my palms that Nyah had to help me pop in the kitchens before training.

I swung, hard and fast, following his guidance. My fist passed through the air, missing its mark. Hadrian side stepped out the way, grabbed my arm and twisted it behind my back.

"AHH!"

"Nice try," he whispered into my ear before thrusting me forward.

I stumbled, but didn't waste time in regaining my balance. "You can't tell me what move to try, then use it against me."

Hadrian was about to respond when I surprised him with my next move.

He'd fallen for my diversion.

While he was distracted, I kicked my leg out, turning my body back to face him.

He tried to cross his arms to block his stomach, but was too slow.

My foot connected hard, sending him backwards.

I kept up my momentum and swung my left hand, palm open, up at his neck. The slap caused a passing guard to shout.

I stepped back and stopped my next move as Hadrian gestured with his hands to please the guard. He was covering his stomach with one hand and the other to his neck.

Not quick enough for me to miss the mark I made. *Shit.*

"King Dalior is going to have me *killed* when he sees that bruise. And I bet it's Commander Alina who'll volunteer to do it!" I said.

With a light finger, I reached for his neck and brushed over the dark mark.

"I have had worse, believe me," Hadrian replied, flinching under my touch. "There is no denying your improvement. You never know, you might even have a chance at this rate."

"I suppose." I also didn't want him to up his gear in training and attack harder because I knew he had the ability to do it. I saw it behind his eyes every time we trained, he was still holding back.

"Does it hurt?"

"If it didn't, I would not be as impressed." He chuckled. "There was a reason for me bringing you out here today." He grabbed a water pouch from the ground, tipping the contents of it into his mouth. "I may have brought something for you, call it a gift of congratulations for your improvement."

I caught the water pouch Hadrian threw to me. "What do you mean a gift?"

Hadrian moved towards a deep green sack that'd been propped against the wall of the palace. I hadn't noticed it, for its shade blended in with the thick vines that covered the wall. He bent down and pulled at the two ends of tasselled rope. I watched in awe as Hadrian pulled a bow and set of arrows from within. It was familiar. The sun caught the large green stone that sat in the middle of its frame. Deep purple designs etched into the frame, still as mesmerizing as before.

"Recognize it?" Hadrian asked, walking over to me and passed it into my hands.

"The shop, it was in the shop you took me to!" I replied, almost reluctant to take it.

"I saw you goggling over it, thought it would be a nice present."

I looked up at him, shocked. "Are you serious?"

"Of course, it's all yours." Hadrian smiled, his golden eyes flashing between my hands and my face.

"Thank you so much, it's incredible." I was surprised at how light it was. I ran my calloused hands across the frame, taking in the beauty of its curves and design.

"She is beautiful, isn't she? You are going to need a couple of these too…" Hadrian passed over the arrows. I held the bow between my legs and took them, careful not to touch their heads.

Compared to the bow, the arrows were mundane, simple. They were made from plain wood and iron, not much different from those I was used to. The only difference was the collection of coloured feathers that sprung from the end, a combination of rich blues and mossy greens.

I was desperate to use it. In my own bag, I'd snuck an apple from the kitchens. The idea hit me full force.

"Here, throw this in that direction," I said as I passed the apple and pointed to the open expanse of the sky above. It was the best place for target practice and away from any windows of the palace. At worst, the arrow would land in the sea, but I trusted my skill better than to miss.

I lifted the bow, feeling its balance in my hands. Satisfied with its weight and proportions, I lifted an arrow and notched it in the string.

It was simple, using a bow, as easy as breathing.

Focus on the target, breath in, out, let go.

My hands buzzed with excitement and I gripped tighter, holding it firm before me. I pulled the bowstring back to my ear, relaxing to the chime that sounded as I did so.

My next move was dangerous. I should have resisted, but it was second nature when I used a bow to have my magick aid me. I allowed a sliver to fill my mind, enough that I could listen carefully to the calls of the air around me. I waited and closed my eyes to focus on my magick.

"Now!" I shouted, throwing my eyes open.

Red blurred in the corner of my vision from the apple Hadrian had thrown. My breathing slowed until the moment I saw it flying through the sky before me.

I released.

The thwack of the arrow was a song to my ears. It sliced through the air, beautiful and graceful. I watched it spin, the air holding it within its grasp, urging it to speed towards the moving target. It gained on the apple that now curved from its apex into its descent, just where I expected it to.

You're mine.

Just as the arrow was about reach the apple, the air screamed in warning. I didn't have time to pull the air back with my magick as the arrow shot into the black mass that flew in front of its path.

Hadrian's muffled gasp was smothered by the shrieks of the wind. We both watched the birds' body fall to the ground.

I pulled back at my magick, shoving it into the cage and severing the connection to the air.

It was a raven.

Then it wasn't.

Black smoke spread wide, bleeding into the blue sky.

It all happened so fast. I screamed as the body of the shifter smashed into the ground.

I ran.

I threw the bow to the ground somewhere between where I previously stood and where I now knelt on the ground looking over Petrer's bloodied torso. The grass beneath him was already stained red from the blood that oozed from his chest. His body was colourless, lifeless. I checked for a pulse, my blood covered fingers pressing against Petrer's neck.

Time slowed as I waited for a sign, but it was there, a weak flutter.

Hadrian was shouting from above me, yet I couldn't make out what he was saying. My eyes were trained to the arrow that protruded from Petrer's shoulder, the wood buried deep into his skin.

Hadrian pushed me to the side and kneeled before Petrer.

Petrer.

His body looked strange. Arms and legs lay in unnatural angles. Like a broken wooden puppet.

"I didn't see him, I didn't see him," I repeated, choking on tears.

I followed the river of blood that ran from him and pooled into a puddle at my side. I stared at it, stunned into stillness.

There was a blur of bodies around us, but I didn't look at them to see who they were. One of them swept Petrer into her arms, and began running towards the doors of the palace, leaving me. Hadrian followed her, shouting commands, but not once turning back for me. I was left alone, frozen to the spot, unable to lift my eyes from the blood.

I slapped my wet hand against my forehead. Over and over, I pounded it until the pain clashed with my inner panic. I cried and screamed. I could've stopped the arrow. I knew I could. It was my fault.

Petrer's animalistic scream repeated over in my mind, the loud crunch of his body hitting the ground and the blood. So much blood.

A hand pressed down on my shoulder, startling me. I looked away from my hands, squinting my eyes from the suns glare bouncing off the guard's armour.

Fadine's stern face looked at me through the cuts in her helmet. "Hadrian would have come back to get you, but he has his hands full, so he sent me instead."

I couldn't look at her.

"Is he… dead?"

She didn't answer.

CHAPTER

FOURTEEN

WHEN WE ENTERED the room, it was Hadrian who I first noticed. He was standing in the far corner, his face a mask of concern as he looked over the older elfin woman and Petrer. I followed his gaze to her and watched as she shuffled around the cot where Petrer lay. Her long, grey hair was a nest of knots and ribbons. She was hunched over Petrer, whispering to herself in a song-like tune, as she burned incense around his head.

I knew she wasn't Niraen. Her skin glowed from the golden blood that ran beneath her thin skin. Her ears were sharper and stood out more from her head than mine or Hadrian's.

She was Alorian, a high elf.

The arrow had been removed from Petrer's shoulder before I'd arrived. Instead, white cloth wrapped around him, a bloom of red spreading over where the arrow had hit. I sagged in relief, a momentary release of guilt.

Fadine closed the door behind me just as the Alorian elf's song built up. It got louder, more child-like until it stopped, blue light spilled from her fingers and snaked into Petrer's limp body.

Everything in the cramped room glowed from her light. Hadrian's face was awash with it. Even Petrer seemed to glow from the inside out, burning like a blue flame.

The healer was not like the one back home who was known for her concoctions of herbs. No, she was different.

I watched from the doorway, whilst the healer ran her hands across Petrer's skin and spread her pulsing light across him. It went on for a while, not a word being said. The only sound came from my heavy breathing and the shuffle of the old elf's feet. Right before my eyes Petrer's body seemed to fill with the colour of life and his chest began to rise and fall.

She stopped and turned for Hadrian, the blue light still lingering within Petrer's chest.

"He needs to rest. His body will heal, but his mind needs time." The old elf said, "I ask that you call for me once he wakes so I can assess him and proceed with the healing."

"Thank you, Healer Browlin." Hadrian bowed.

"May the Goddess guide him."

I pressed my thumb to my temple, mirroring Hadrian. She smiled, a wide gum-filled grin and left the room through a small door concealed beside a large cabinet.

I stayed pressed to the door whilst Hadrian stepped forward. Guilt had frozen my mind and body.

I'd done this.

"I did this…" I croaked.

"Don't blame yourself," Hadrian said, moving from beside the cot to me. "There was no way of stopping it. It was completely out of your control. I am more concerned to why he was there in the first place. I have already sent a guard to find out why he was not with the rest of Rank Falmia."

"He won't be in trouble, will he?" I asked, my voice trembling.

I felt the burn of tears in the corners of my eyes, my cheeks sticky from those that'd already spilled.

"I thought I recognized him. He is your friend?" Hadrian placed a hand on my cheek, warm and comforting. I wanted to melt into it, to open the flood gates within me. But I bit my lip and held myself together.

"His name is Petrer. We are both from Horith."

The pinch of Hadrian's brows didn't go amiss. He took his hand from my face and turned to Petrer. "He is going to survive. Browlin has been our healer since before I was born. Her powers are immense."

I was glad for the change in subject. Talking about mine and Petrer's past would only open other wounds that I wanted to keep closed. "She's Alorian. I haven't seen her power before."

"Yes, and we are lucky to have her. She has saved many lives, aided in many births and guided souls during the passing. Petrer is in fine hands."

I walked around the cot to stand by Petrer's side. His face was relaxed in the deepest of sleep, peaceful. His skin still had a faint glow from Healer Browlin's magick, it lingered within his veins ever so slightly. If I'd not seen it happen I would pass it off as a trick of light.

"The training will resume tomorrow, you are dismissed for the rest of the day," Hadrian said, he still stood behind me.

"Thank you..." I pulled my eyes from Petrer, "for helping him."

"Your thanks are appreciated, but misplaced. I only did what was right," Hadrian replied, looking down as he fiddled with the seam of his shirt.

"Can I stay with him?" I asked. "It's the least I can do, to be here when he wakes up."

"If that would make you happy, then yes."

Hadrian's smile wavered, his eyes looking everywhere but at me. "Promise me you will get some sleep? Do not stay here all night."

"I promise." I lied.

As soon as the door closed behind Hadrian, I released the leash around my tears and they fell in desperate sobs. Petrer didn't wake when I climbed into the cot with him. I lay as close as I could, resting my head on his arm.

Hours must have passed whilst I watched the rise and fall of his chest. I longed for him to wake, but he didn't.

"I'm sorry, Petrer," I whispered, "for hurting you."

The tears trickled from my eyes and ran down his arm. I looked at his peaceful face, a face I'd kissed more times than I could count. A face I'd studied in the dark of night, a face that once belonged to me. All until that night when I saw him, the night when he decided he was no longer mine.

After what he had done to me, I never thought forgiving him would be possible. But as I lay there, watching him, it was the first time in a long time I felt ready to let it all go. To open the wounds a final time and fill them with forgiveness.

"You know, I had no idea how to handle it after I saw you and *him*. For days after, I wanted to tell you, to hurt you for hurting me. I wanted to scream so you knew I'd caught you." A laugh burst past my lips, "It's funny. I never thought you would lie with another whilst with me. Not you. But when I saw you in the same place you took me…" I paused, flashes of Petrer and the boy together in the forest filled my mind. "I trusted you. And I've blamed you for weeks. I wanted you to feel the pain I felt, but not like this."

As I spoke I could feel the weight lifting from my shoulders. "Seeing you like this, knowing I'm the cause of this kills me. I never want this to happen again." I took a shuddering breath in and finally said the words that I never believed I'd say. "I forgive you. Just like I hope you can forgive me for what I've done to you."

I leaned across him and placed a single kiss on his head. I held it there, until my tears smudged beneath my mouth.

I forgive you.

The hairs on my arms stood on end. There was a noise, an unfamiliar sound. I stilled, straining my ears to try and place its origins but nothing. *It must be a trick of my mind.* The only sounds I could hear were the shallow breaths from Petrer beside me and the hush of the wind tapping against the palace walls.

Certain it was nothing sinister, I gave into sleep, resting against the gentle rhythm of Petrer's heart.

⌒

THE DOOR RATTLED, yanking me from my light sleep. A chill ran across my mind and I gazed to Petrer who still lay there, unaware.

I heard the noise again. I jolted up, my graze pinned to the door as it creaked open.

"Hello?" I called, but no one answered.

A body of ivory floated in, the ruffles at the bottom of its silk cloak dusting across the floor. Healer Browlin.

"There is something strange about you," Browlin sang, walking on silent feet.

Rich coming from you.

"I'm sorry, I must've fallen asleep," I said, rushing from the cot in a hasty leap to leave. "I best get going."

"Since you are here, stay and help me with his ointments." She turned towards the set of shelves covered in bottles of all shapes and sizes. "Come."

Browlin shuffled her sagging arms through drawers filled with glass vials, each containing liquids or powders that were barely visible through the dusted bottles and faded labels. She picked out a vial, tinted with a deep jade. She lifted it to the subtle light from the single window in the room and purred, "Perfect."

She uncorked the vial, the pop echoing across the room. A warm, sickly scent seeped out into the air. I covered my nose with my one hand and moved to her, her long fingers beckoning me closer.

"Place this vial before his nose and allow his body to absorb the healing properties."

"What's in this?" I asked, reeling away from the bottle thrust at me.

She laughed, long squeaking cackles like that of a youngling's cry. "Nothing to worry about."

I held the vial away from me and walked over to the cot. Petrer was blissfully unaware amongst the ruffled sheets when I held the stinking concoction beneath his nose. The jade smoke snaked its way inside his nostrils, illuminating the many veins in his face before fading once again.

"Beautiful, isn't it?" I felt Browlin behind me, inches from where I stood. I'd not heard her move, yet there she was, like a phantom behind me.

"You seem shocked at this magick, although, I know it is not the first time you have seen it."

"I really should leave," I said, placing the vial back in her hands.

The moment my fingers brushed hers she struck out, her grip iron as her silver hands pulled on mine. Ribbons of light began seeping from her skin, wrapping around me in knots. I watched, stunned as they moved across my skin, inspecting me. The snakes of light lifted and drove into me. I tried to pull away, but it was impossible. She was laughing, giggling as her magick fingers clawed through me. I felt as they spread their chill within me.

"My boy, my boy."

My magick stirred the moment hers brushed up against the cage within me, teasing for a release. I felt its need to join Browlin's magick, the urgency building.

I could feel her presence reach into me more, the ribbons of light curling around my bones, moving through muscle, dancing amongst my blood. I realized my anxiety was not a product of my mind, but from *my* magick that screamed to cleanse my body of Browlin's touch.

"Please, don't," I pleaded, aware of Browlin's attempts to release my magick. "Please!"

A new feeling turned within me and I grasped it. The moment my consciousness made connection with it I felt my magick force Browlin out of my body.

Her blood shot eyes looked *into* mine. She dropped my arms, pulling herself from me in a rush. Stumbling backwards, her feet moved awkwardly to keep her upright. Her face was twisted in shock, hands trembling, her power trailing back inside her.

I wasted no time and ran for the door. It slammed against the wall beyond, but I didn't care. I sped down the corridor, not stopping even when she called after me.

"Dragori…"

The word was no more than a whisper.

I felt sick.

I moved as fast as my feet could take me down the spiral staircase. I ran across a courtyard, the same one I'd trained with Hadrian earlier, no signs of any blood left. I ran back into the palace, not stopping until I recognized my surroundings. I ran and ran, but still felt her presence, in me, her cold whispers filling every inch of my body. The same that had plagued Petrer's…

I stopped, landing on my knees, bile crawling up my throat.

Petrer. I'd left him with her. I crawled to the wall, bringing my knees to my chest and pressing my back against the hanging rug behind me. I wished for the shadows to swallow me whole, I wished for them to take me home.

I closed my eyes and steadied my breathing. She'd felt my power, felt the one part of me I had tried everything to conceal.

My secret was out.

CHAPTER

FIFTEEN

MY HANDS SHRIVELLED from the soapy water in the kitchens by the time news of Hadrian's departure reached me. I questioned the guard who'd broken the news for more details, but she resisted, giving no more information about his whereabouts, or when he'd return.

Frustrated, I slammed my wet hands on table. I needed to train, the thought of missing out on a day's worth of sparring panicked me. The duel was just over a week away, and I wasn't even close to being ready.

"Hit it any harder and you'll be working extra hours to replace it," Nyah joked. For an empath, she really didn't know when to keep her mouth shut.

"I can't miss a day of training. What am I to do? Wonder around the palace all day? I have no rank, and without Hadrian, I have no duties. And Goddess help me, I'm not staying in the kitchens all day!"

"You can train with us," Nyah suggested, "if that makes you feel better. Rank Clarak is not as picky with who can join, as I'm sure you can tell."

"You're sure they'll let me?"

"Honestly, calm yourself. It'll be fine, our trainer is *nothing* like the Commander. I'm sure she will be happy for you to join us."

I smiled at her, my hands submerged back into the basin of water while I carried on scrubbing burned lumps from the pile of pots. "Thanks. As long as I'm not expected to shift."

"Don't worry about that, we won't make you do anything too *impossible*," she replied.

There was something about the way she said "impossible" that had me squinting at her. She only smiled and carried on drying the pans.

"Thank you," I replied through a yawn, unsure of how audible my response was.

"You look like you haven't gotten any sleep." Nyah stopped drying the large pan and placed it on the side. "The bags under your eyes are so... dark and that's the hundredth time I've seen you yawn. What kept you up last night? Maybe that would explain where Prince Hadrian is."

I didn't need to see her face to know what she was hinting at. "It's not like that with Hadrian. It's Petrer, I'm worried about him. I couldn't get any sleep because of it." It wasn't an entire lie, just a twist on the truth. I couldn't mention Browlin.

"Well, after training with us today, you will have no problem sleeping tonight."

"Oh, can't wait."

Nyah knocked my shoulder and laughed. "You think the Prince is sarcastic? You should hear yourself."

∽

I KNEW RANK Clarak was the smallest out of the three ranks, but I didn't realize just how small until I entered the sparring room with Nyah. Besides Nyah and their trainer, there were only six others. She'd led me to a small compact room in the basement level of the palace with no source of natural light. I thought back to the room that Commander

Alina used to train rank Mamlin in, realizing just how worse off Clarak was.

Flames from nearly burned out candles lit the room in patches of ominous orange and red glows. The trainer in charge, who Nyah had introduced as Sulan, was the nicest one I'd met so far. His handshake was firm yet welcoming, and he wasted no time in pulling me into the room and introducing me to the others.

"It looks like we have another sparring partner today," he said, "Zacriah is to train with us, which I must say I am happy about. I have been hoping for a break from Nyah..." He pretended to rub his arm.

He turned to me. "Good luck with her, even Nyah could give the Commander a run for her coin."

Nyah nodded, winking to him. "If you say so."

It didn't take long before we each were given wooden staffs and separated into pairs. Sulan instructed us that one was to defend and the other to attack.

"I'll take defence and you try attack first," Nyah said, throwing the staff at me. I caught it just before it fell to the floor.

Nyah shifted her stance, spreading her legs to gain better balance. Out of the kitchen attire, it was clear just how well built Nyah was. Her black training gear was tight fitting, hugging the curves of her muscles. I could tell before we even started how it was going to end.

With me on the floor. In pain.

I passed my staff between my hands, familiarizing myself with its weight, a trick Hadrian had taught me.

"Forget everything Princey has taught you." Nyah jumped from foot to foot. "Let's dance."

I threw myself and every inch of strength I had into my first move.

I swung the staff one way to throw her off guard before sweeping it under my arm and sending a jab into her stomach. It was a wasted move for she shuffled her feet sideways before bringing down her staff in one big movement.

They smashed together, the impact vibrated up my arm.

Nyah followed with a move that I'd not seen before. One moment our staffs were pressed together and in the next, she had spun hers around and pushed mine out of the way.

With lightning strike movements, she tapped the left side of my chest then the right. As I tried to guess her next move she changed again and thrust the butt of the staff into my ribs.

I jumped back, ignoring the new pain and brought my staff up.

"I thought I was attacking and you were defending," I said breathlessly.

"Oops, got carried away."

I could understand what Sulan had meant about Nyah giving the Commander a run for her coin. She was a natural fighter.

I attempted to attack until Sulan instructed everyone to swap positions. If that was what she was like defending, Goddess help me when it came to her attacking technique.

"I'll go easier on you this time," she added, stretching her arms.

"I'll believe *that* when I see it."

Nyah shot forward, her staff no more than an extension of her own body. She showed no sign of tiring whereas I was ready to collapse on the floor within the first round of her attacks.

I fought through the stabbing agony.

Again, and again, she brought down the end of her staff, smashing it into my ankles, arms, stomach and hands.

My muscles screamed as I whirled my staff around, trying to follow her movements and stop her advances.

At one point, I had to dip low and spin for her to miss. I turned back to face her, but was blinded when the opposite end of her staff smacked into the bottom of my chin.

My head jerked backwards and light burst behind my eyes. I dropped my staff and threw up my hands to cover my face.

I ran my tongue along my lip and winced when I tasted copper. I didn't dare open my mouth in worry for it to spill onto the floor.

"Are you hurt?" Nyah lifted my face. Her expression soured when she noticed the swelling. My entire face was hot and stiff.

I tried to speak, but my words were lost between swollen lips and bloodied teeth.

"Let me take you to the Healer. I hear she is well skil—"

I shook my head viciously. I tried to say no, but could not get the words out.

"There is so much blood, Zacriah, you need to go."

I tilted my head back and gargled, "No!"

"Fine, I get your point! At least let me help clean you up." Nyah called over her shoulder to Sulan who I'm sure had already noticed, "Gotta take Zacriah out."

"What have you done?" Sulan called back, a hint of humour in his voice.

"Urmmm…"

"Just make sure he doesn't spill blood on my floor."

Nyah raised a hand to him, "Leave it to me."

Everyone watched Sulan open the door to let us leave, no more questions asked.

Nyah led me to a room down the corridor. I held my hand to my mouth, still tilted back to stop the flow of blood. The thought of swallowing it made me feel sick, so I just let it build up in my mouth.

The room she guided me to was no bigger than a glorified storage closet, empty apart from two benches on either side of the space and the single stone basin in the middle. Ripples of water reflected onto the ceiling and walls of the room, lit from the glowing basin. Nyah sat me down, pulled a piece of cream cloth from her pocket and submerged it into the water before ringing it out, droplets falling back into the pool like the chimes of a bell. First, she passed me a chalice and told me to spit out the blood. Satisfied that my mouth was empty, she placed the damp cloth to my lip and held it there.

"This should help with the swelling. Sulan showed us the room on our first day, it seems the water has some mild healing properties. Enough that you may not need to see a healer, all depending on how deep the cut in your mouth actually is." I took the cloth from her, holding it to my lip.

I could tell she was sorry, it was written all over her face. "I got a bit carried away in there. You did well, considering. I've just had a lot more practice then you and—"

"You don't need to apologize, or explain yourself," I said, the swelling in my jaw relaxing just as Nyah had suggested it would. "But I think I deserve to know why you are so good. Especially since you nearly knocked my teeth out."

Nyah lifted her legs so that they were crossed on top of the bench. "Growing up with competitive siblings has its perks. Dad felt it was important we all trained in hand to hand combat; he said it would even the playing field when my brothers and I fought."

"And did it?"

"Oh yes, I bested them each time. That was before my brothers enrolled in the guard and left home. They're twins, you see, did everything together, so when Dill mentioned he wanted to join the guard, Bellan also chose to leave with him."

"Are they here, your brothers?" I asked, confused to why she had not mentioned them before.

She shook her head, her red locks falling over her face. "No, I thought they might be, but with the attacks I suppose they have been stationed somewhere else. It would've been nice to see them, it's been almost five moons since they left."

"Have you asked about them?"

"I have tried, but it seems no one is willing to give me any answers." A shadow passed behind her eyes, the topic was a hard one for her. "But what about you, any siblings back home?"

"No, just me. I couldn't imagine having siblings, seems like a lot of work."

Nyah chuckled, and nodded. "Oh, it is! But it is also one of the most incredible things."

I ran my tongue behind my lower lip, across the puckered cut that had already began to shrink in size. "It's gone down, seems Sulan was right about the water."

Nyah lifted a hand to my chin and pulled down my lip to inspect it. "You sure you're going to be all right? I don't want the Prince chasing me down for hurting you."

I pinched my face at the mention of Hadrian. "Very funny."

"I am, aren't I!" She took the cloth from my face and moved for the basin. She hesitated over the water, "Can you hear th—"

There was the sound of pounding feet beyond the room. Nyah looked back to me then moved for the door to check. We both jumped as Sulan burst through before Nyah had a chance to open, his face pale.

"We have all been summoned by King Dalior, there has been another attack."

CHAPTER

SIXTEEN

HADRIAN PACED THE bottom of the dais, his face thunderous, fists clenched at his sides. King Dalior stood before him, addressing the room. We'd slipped in just before he had started to speak.

"During the early hours this morning, word reached Olderim of *another* attack." My body chilled and flashes of fire and blood passed across my mind. "Currently, the village of Nasamel is being held captive by a group of Morthi. As a result, it is imperative we send a group to scout the area and look for survivors. I understand your training has been limited, and what I ask of you is dangerous and sudden, but this is the time to utilize your abilities as shifters. I ask you to step forward and receive respect for your bravery."

My heart screamed at me to join. I wanted to help, to fight, but going would only prove I was not a shifter.

Feet shuffled around me as elves stepped forward, arms raised. King Dalior kept his eye trained to those who volunteered and guided them to join a crowd of guards who stood at the front of the room.

I recognized some from Rank Clarak who also did not step forward.

"I don't know what to do," I whispered to Nyah, but when I turned to her, she wasn't beside me. I looked around the bustling room until I spotted the crest of her red hair bobbing towards two guards near King Dalior. She was going to join.

King Dalior's eyes burned with pride. He watched more than half of the shifters join with the guards, not once looking to those who didn't step forward.

"I thank you." He bowed, closing his eyes. "It is in your hands to help our people on this day. I ask you to save those you can reach. And kill every single Morthi who is found," he spat. His entire being shifted as he spoke, anger drove his words. The crowd roared.

King Dalior looked over the room a final time and turned to Hadrian who still paced behind him. "I leave you in the trusted hands of my son, Prince Hadrian, who will be leading this expedition."

Hadrian stopped his pacing and looked to his father and bowed. I half expected King Dalior to stay, but he picked up his cloak and moved from the room without another word nor glance our way.

I couldn't take my eyes of Hadrian. He lifted his stare to the room and spoke, his voice deep and pained. "Nasamel is half a day's ride from here, which means we must leave immediately to arrive before nightfall. Those who have so *bravely* stepped forward will be briefed during the journey to save time and ensure we leave as quickly as possible. And to those who are staying behind… remember you will all face battle eventually, one way or another. I hope you learn from your peer's bravery and may it inspire you for when you have no choice but to help."

His words, although spoken to the entire crowd, felt like they were directed at me.

I slipped into the crowd moving for the door. I noticed Nyah ahead and I picked up my pace, dodging elves every step I took. By the time I reached her I grasped for her shoulder and she turned, ready to strike.

"It's only me," I said, flinching from her raised hand.

"Why did you not step forward?" she asked, pulling me from the crowd into a nook at the side of the room before the doors. Her expression was shadowed with annoyance, yet stilled when she glanced at something over my shoulder.

"I was thinking the same thing," Hadrian interrupted.

Nyah bowed, lowering her gaze to the floor with flushed cheeks that matched her red hair.

"You are coming, Zacriah, and that is an order," he added, his voice laced with authority. "You will ride with me, understand?"

I could've argued, but figured it was useless. Hadrian didn't seem in the mood to take no for an answer.

I looked to Nyah who smirked, pleased with Hadrian's command.

"I am sorry for the interruption," Hadrian said, grasping Nyah's hand, "it was awfully rude of me."

Nyah bowed again, her hair tipping over her face. "No bother."

Everything seemed so rushed. People still streamed from the room beside us and Hadrian's attention kept flickering to them.

"I need to go, Petal. I expect you will go and get yourself ready and meet me outside in the courtyard. I do not want to have to find you."

With that, he left. I followed the back of his head as he blended into the crowd and disappeared. I turned back to Nyah whose face seemed ready to burst.

"What?"

"Did he just call you Petal?" She choked on a laugh.

"Oh, shut up!" I replied, pulling her back to the door, ignoring her muffled chuckle.

THE COURTYARD BEYOND the palace was a blur of pounding hooves and shouts. I watched from the side lines as Hadrian separated the crowd into three main groups, each led by one guard. The cavalry would start with Fadine, who sat ready atop an elk, her helmet matching the horns she gripped onto. I saw Illera up at the front, a large sword strapped to her side. Next, a group of Falmia stood waiting. Hadrian commanded the shifters to use their ability and stay above them in the skies during the travel. My heart felt heavy looking at them, knowing if Petrer was well enough he would be amongst them, ready to prove himself and his loyalty.

Not to my surprise, Nyah was placed at the back of the group. The weakest last. If only Hadrian had seen Nyah's skill, she would be right up at the front beside Fadine.

There was a cry from the front of the group. I looked at it and watched as the group began to move in two lines through the courtyard, over the bridge that led to Thalor.

"Jump on the back." Hadrian towered beside me, seated on his elk. It too was covered in silver scaled armour, just like its rider. I squinted and looked up to him; the sun sent tears to prickle at the corners of my eyes.

"Don't I get my own?" I asked, already knowing the answer.

"What, have you got a problem with sitting with me? Elmirr here is more than capable of carrying two so jump on." He rubbed his arm down the elk's neck until her head shook in pleasure.

I placed a foot on the stirrup, holding onto Hadrian's outstretched hand and pulling myself up. He yanked me up faster than I anticipated.

I melted into the cushioned seat and looked up to see my surroundings, but Hadrian's helmet blocked the view in front.

With a click of his tongue, Hadrian urged Elmirr forward and we began to follow the cavalry ahead.

We sat in silence together whilst we passed through the streets of Thalor then over the bridge to Masarion. Elves stood, gawking when the cavalry passed, moving for the outer gate of the city. Some bystanders threw handfuls of colourful flowers on the ground beneath the elk's hooves, bowing and whispering under their breath words of protection. Hadrian waved his hand to the crowd to please them, his armour shining brilliantly.

Before we reached the final gate, I felt a droplet of water land on my check. Rain clouds billowed above in the sky, covering the sun with their menacing embrace. Those who watched from the streets began running for shelter, leaving the flowers muddied and crushed beneath their feet.

"Let's hope it holds up for most of the journey. I would not want the morale of the group to be dampened before we reach Nasamel."

I looked up to the sky and wished for it to rain as it wouldn't affect my already dampened mood.

"I should apologize for my unexplained absence this morning. Father had me busy when word of the attack hit," he said, nodding to the gatekeepers for them to open the gates.

"I understand, no need to apologize."

The moment the gates to the city closed behind the cavalry, bursts of obsidian smoke spread across the group and birds of all types shot into the sky. The shifters flew in and out of the dark clouds, cutting through the light drizzle of rain.

Brown flecked eagles danced with pure white doves. I noticed the swan shifter from the first night, her wingspan the largest out of all the shifters amongst her. She opened her beak and let out a sound that boomed across the sky, louder than thunder.

"I made sure Fadine only allowed them to shift outside of the city walls. I could only imagine the reaction if the city folk witnessed it."

"I understand. It took me a while to get used to seeing it," I replied.

"And when was that?" he asked, his eyes trained on the road ahead.

"It's a long story."

Hadrian laughed, "Well, luckily we have a long journey ahead."

I rolled my eyes and pulled the fragments of images through the haze in my mind.

"It was during one of the worst winters I've ever experienced back home. Snow piled up so high it covered the windows and blocked the doors. It was near impossible to leave the house and if we did, we'd never navigate the streets. The cold had seeped into everything, our bricks, clothes, even the fireplace and just when we needed food the most, the Goddess seemed to answer our wishes. One of our villagers was a shifter. His form was a bear, the mightiest one I'd ever seen. It brought, to every house affected, bags filled with stale breads and ale that he'd held between his jaws. Once the snow fall settled he even helped clear the streets into paths. I'd heard about shifters before, but that was the first time I saw one."

"I can only imagine what that must have been like. I wish I could say the first shifter I saw was a bear, instead mine was something more terrifying. I had a nanny as a child who could shift into a spider. Now that was terrifying," Hadrian said. I could feel him laugh as my arms were wrapped around his stomach.

We talked about shifters for a while, yet he still didn't ask about me. I was so caught up in the conversation that by the time I turned around and looked behind us, Olderim was nowhere to be seen and the rain had ceased.

"I want to ask you something," I said, releasing my grip around his waist.

"Ask away," he replied.

"The attacks? Why now? There hasn't been a war between the continents since the treaty and the end of the druids."

His shoulders shrugged. "That is a question that I do not have an answer for. We have only captured two Morthi, both who came with their tongues gouged out. So, you can understand how that makes our methods of obtaining information almost impossible."

"The first time we heard of an attack was almost four months ago, it was the first and only one of its kind until a week prior to the feast. Since then they seem to be happening more often. Too often."

"I'm still confused. The Morthi are allies, they helped defeat the druids. Why turn against us and break the treaty?"

"I know. Father sent a representative for an audience with their King. To justify their actions and remind them of the clauses in the treaty, but it did not go as planned..."

"Surely the Alorian elves will respond to the attacks? Has there been no word from their shores, will they aid us?"

Hadrian removed his helmet, shaking his head to loosen the strands of hair stuck to his neck from sweat. "We have heard nothing from them. I should not be telling you any of this, but they ceased trading with us after the first Morthi attacks. They either want nothing to do with the conflict or, like father believes, they are in on it too."

"But I don't understand why. What is their reasoning behind the attacks?" I questioned.

"If I could tell you, I would. And if I find them in Nasamel, I *will* be getting answers."

I didn't speak any further on the subject, nor about anything else. Hadrian stared ahead and I kept my eyes trained on the path. The landscape was a view of endless fields and hills. In the gloom of the day, everything seemed colourless and odd, only adding to the intense atmosphere.

Hours passed by and I fought against sleep. Elmirr's elegant movements lulled me into a deep relaxation. I leaned my head against Hadrian's back, and allowed myself only a short moment to close my eyes. I was surprised when I opened my eyes to see that the sky was no longer light, but that dusk had arrived.

A shifter squawked from the skies above, diverting my attention to the plume of grey smoke in the distance.

Nasamel. We'd arrived.

"Did you know you snore?" Hadrian said.

"Can't say I do." I yawned, my eyes trained to the smoke ahead. "We made it."

"What is left of it…"

A sudden flurry began to fall in the air around us, dusting across Hadrian's back and hair. I reached a hand trying to catch one, but it crumbled the moment it landed on my palm, turning into nothing more than dust.

My stomach sank at the realization of what it was. Ash.

The flurry grew heavier when we gained on Nasamel. A sudden stench overwhelmed me, a mix of burned wood and something else that I didn't want to dwell on.

Someone was retching off to the side of their elk ahead and others coughed. I copied Hadrian by pulling a piece of my cloak and covering my nose and mouth.

We stopped at the bottom of the hill below, far enough from Nasamel that no one would see us, but close enough to take in the horror of what was left.

My body was stiff when I climbed from the back of Elmirr, joining the rest of the group who stood around waiting for the next command.

Hadrian jumped down onto the ash covered ground and whistled three times.

In response, I looked up to see a white dove flying towards us, its body standing out against the grey sky.

The shifter sank a dagger of sadness into my chest and twisted it with each word he said.

"Destroyed, everything is destroyed."

CHAPTER
SEVENTEEN

AS SOON AS the words fell from the shifters lips, the entire cavalry exploded in angry shouts. Hadrian called out once to still the noise, but no one heard him. Not until he shouted again, his voice fuelled with the same anger, that he battled to silence.

"ENOUGH!"

It was hard not to flinch from his command as he stared everyone down, eyes bulging wide. "Let the boy speak."

With that, he turned to the stone-faced shifter, allowing him to carry on.

"It's completely empty, I couldn't see anything left from the skies," the elfin said. Aside from his grief-stricken face, he was a handsome boy. He looked young, a crop of blond hair, and two large piercing blue eyes.

"Has Nasamel's surroundings been scouted? The forest *and* hillside?" Hadrian's brow creased.

The sandy haired elf shook his head. "I've personally checked the woodlands, but saw nothing. It looks like the Morthi have fled."

"You see the smoke… the blush of it suggests they are still here. The fires have only just stopped." Hadrian pointed at the village atop the hill. "Be vigilant; I don't believe they have gone anywhere. We are to go in waves. I want those from Rank Falmia to take the skies, circle the surrounding areas and signal the moment you see any sign of life. The rest of us will each go in from different directions to cover more ground. I will enter from behind, through the woods. Zacriah, you are to follow me." A rush of relief stilled my worried mind. I knew Hadrian was the safest person to stay with. "I want the rest of you to separate into two groups, one taking the left and the other from the right side which is just north of here. If the Morthi are still here, they will show themselves when it is to their benefit. Just be certain you beat them to it. I know King Dalior has commanded we kill them, but I need them alive…" Hadrian's words dripped with hatred.

Hadrian clapped his hands together, guards and shifters alike nodded and called in agreement. All but me.

"Now, go. Any survivors are to be brought back here. You and you will stay back and wait, just in case." The two guards Hadrian pointed to bowed and stepped back, preparing themselves to wait with the elks.

"Go."

With Hadrian's final word, everyone moved off. Shifters changed around us, until animals filled the space. Birds shot into the sky and a white lion, Illera, pounced off into the distance. Hadrian moved to the left, the opposite direction than the others and began trudging towards the shadows of trees in the distance.

I followed, wasting no time to catch up. If the Morthi were still wandering around, there was no way I was going to be caught alone.

With every step closer to Nasamel's border, my anxiety brushed its fingers against my magick. To distract myself, I unclipped my clawed gloves from my belt and put them on my hands. I flicked the claws out of their clasps. Hadrian had his long sword out, held before him poised and ready. Grey clouds hung above us and as I glanced up. I took comfort in seeing the shapes of birds scanning the skies. They would keep us alert.

It was only when we reached the boundaries to the forest that I understood just how monstrous it was. A wall of dense oak trees shadowed the surrounding area before us. It was ominous, staring into its pitch-black underbelly. Gnarled roots reached from the ground like desperate hands. I had to be careful not to trip over them.

I strained my eyes, but all I saw was darkness. I listened, using all my senses available to search for life, but heard nothing. Not a sound.

Hadrian paced beside me, looking between the forest and the village. When I looked to Nasamel, I could see the movements of guards and shifters prowling over the remains. I almost expected to hear the shout that they had found a survivor. But it didn't come.

"Would you stop that? It's putting me on edge," I said, but Hadrian ignored me and kept up his pacing.

"Something does not seem right about this; do you see the smoke over there?" He pointed to the village, "It is recent, and it has not been long since the fire was lit."

"I'm not sure what you mean?" I followed his gesture, glancing in the direction.

"From when news reached us this morning, the smoke should have burned out by now, but it has not."

"Where would they be, though? The shifters would have spotted them."

"The Morthi are masters of the darkness. Their very magick comes from it. I am almost certain they are watching us right now." Shivers crawled across the back of my neck. I looked back into the forest, an unsettling feeling falling over me.

Hadrian voice dropped to a whisper, "I can feel their retched breath lingering in the air."

A cry sounded from the village, making me gasp in shock.

Hadrian was running, leaving me rooted to the spot. He vaulted over broken brick walls to reach the village. My clawed hand moved for my bow as I turned, an overwhelming feeling of being watched prickled down my neck.

I started running when the next shout sounded from the village.

∽

THE SURVIVOR WAS a mass of deep, oozing wounds and burned skin.

I was unable to tell if they were male or female until the swollen stomach gave me the answer I needed. She shook, sprawled on the ground within a circle of guards. Her bloodied palm left red prints across her exposed belly as she grasped at it. She was trying to speak, her cracked lips trembling, yet not an audible sound coming out of them.

Hadrian dropped to his knees before her, scanning her body with his piercing eyes.

"Can you hear me?" His voice trembled. His normally strong, commanding voice was weak, terrified.

She didn't respond. Her wide eyes only staring to the sky, her bloodied, cracked lips trembling and her hands rubbing her belly. Hadrian ripped at the clasp of his cloak and covered her exposed body.

"You," he shouted, pointing at the guard that had found her, "take her directly back to Olderim, do not stop until you reach its walls." The guard moved forward, scooped the woman into his arms. He carried her through the crowd that had doubled in size since I had arrived, each looking in horror at the survivor. As she was carried past me I noticed a single tear escape and trail down her dirtied cheek. She was smiling.

"What the FUCK are you all doing standing around watching?" Hadrian screamed at the group, the whites of his eyes red. "Find more, NOW!"

No one stopped Hadrian when he stormed off. They only stepped out of his way before resuming their searches. I followed him, pulled by the tether of sympathy that tugged at my heart. Hadrian picked up his pace as he moved back towards the forest. I expected him to stop before it, but he didn't.

My heart jumped when he entered its border, disappearing into its waiting darkness. I was still a few steps behind him, but the second he vanished I picked up my pace.

With each foot fall I thought back to the survivor. She was with child, I knew it the moment I laid eyes on her stomach. The bubble of ignorance I'd lived in had burst the moment I have arrived in Olderim, popped by the lurking evil that dwelled around us.

Branches scratched at me as I ran through the dark underbelly of the forest's trees.

A glint of silver armour flashed ahead.

Hadrian.

I was gaining on him. Rays of light that had seeped through the thick foliage above caused beams to illuminate Hadrian as he ran past beneath them.

Hadrian stopped at a clearing ahead. I slowed down, stopping a few paces behind him. He kept his back to me, but I knew he was aware of my presence.

His fist slammed into the tree closest to him, repeatedly. He was shouting, hitting it without stopping. I moved for him and grabbed onto his arm before he could strike again, his knuckles dripped with blood.

"Calm down." There was a smell that surrounded him, a burning scent.

"Please, leave me, Zacriah." I waited for him to turn, to look at me but he kept his eyes trained on the tree.

"I can't and I won't. You said the Morthi could be here, so I cannot leave the prince alone if that is the case." He looked over his shoulder, his eyes wet.

I let go of him and took a few steps back. Hadrian's bottom lip trembled and his lashes clumped together.

"The youngling she is carrying…" Hadrian choked on his words. He looked up, trying to catch the tears before they fell.

"I know…" I didn't know what to say. The thought made me sick.

Hadrian buried his face in his hands. "How could they do this? Monsters. I want their heads on pikes; I want to wash the very ground with *their* blood. Why would they kill and destroy innocent people like this? What have they done to deserve this treatment?" I knew Hadrian wasn't looking for an answer from me.

Hadrian sagged, his entire body caving when his knees connected with the ground. I moved for him, the urge to hold him too strong to ignore.

My ears picked up a sound beyond the treeline.

I caught the blur of movement and watched in dismay at the arrow head that spun with vigour and power. It flew straight for Hadrian.

My body went cold.

The cage broke apart.

My power ran free.

CHAPTER
EIGHTEEN

TENDRILS OF MAGICK filled every inch of my body and in a split second, I was connected to the world around me. I felt the air of the forest and grasped it, picking up its gentle breeze until I was a cyclone of power.

I reached out a hand and willed the air to latch onto the arrow. I pushed until I changed its course. It passed to the left of Hadrian's face by inches.

I was a spectator, watching the world rip open. I spun my arms, controlling the torrent of air that held the arrow and moved it to arch behind us. With a great push, I controlled the arrow and sent it back towards the cloaked being who'd released it.

A gift for you, I thought.

The spinning arrow whispered to me, soothing my wild control whilst it swam into the tree line. I felt the thud of the arrow, it's hollow vibration as it embedded into a tree.

It'd missed.

More arrows came our way. I threw both hands up before me, a wall of solid air stopping their path. They snapped and fell to the floor.

Everything moved so fast.

Hadrian was already up, running for the attacker. His strong footfall pounding on the ground while he flew into its welcoming darkness. I chased after him, flexing my hands to allow my claws to extend beside me. The winds followed me like a lost puppy. I saw out of the corner of my eyes leaves and dirt burst from the forest floor where my magick dwelled.

I softened my footfall, cushioning my magick beneath my feet. It propelled me faster ahead. I reached Hadrian in seconds. But I ran right past him.

The trees shook, their leaves pulled from the branches against their will. The Morthi were nowhere to be seen, masters of shadow.

I pushed both hands forward, sending my magick ahead of me. The wind screamed against the trees and I reached forward, trying to find them.

There. Only one.

In my mind's eye, I saw the shadow move from tree to tree.

Hadrian's deafening roar merged with the screams of my magick, blending together in a symphony of rage and power.

I was aware Hadrian could see me, but I didn't care. I wanted to kill.

There was a sudden burst of heat behind me and I spun around to greet it. Flames, coursed up trees and under every footfall of Hadrian's as he ran towards me. Fire spilled from his hands like lava, coating everything behind him.

Distracted, I didn't notice the next arrow until Hadrian's fire engulfed it. I threw myself to the ground as it burst into ashes beside my face. I stumbled up, hearing the song of an arrow again.

"Up ahead!" I screamed.

Hadrian roared. I sent my wind forward again, searching for the attackers location, and found three of them. Three shadows.

"Watch out!"

The shadows moved like assassins of the night, disappearing then reappearing in different locations. Impossible.

I threw my hand to the side, my wind knocking the next volley of arrows off course. I couldn't keep up with the shadows.

Hadrian was beside me. He sliced his hand, sending an explosion of green flames at the two arrows I'd missed.

I pulled the bow from my back and started running as I nocked an arrow. I reached out with my power to locate the Morthi again. In my mind's eye, I felt the three of them. Latching my magick onto them, I held the arrow and...

My face connected with the ground first. There was a loud snap somewhere below me and a sharp pain ran across my side.

My magick cut off in that moment. I could feel nothing, but the pain in my stomach. I reached a hand to it, my palm came back wet. Hadrian knelt beside me, his face was flushed red, sweat dripped from his head.

"You are hurt!" he said.

"Don't let them get away!" I pushed at his arms, willing him to move on. Flames no longer poured from his hands, not a single burn or mark laced his body.

"They are gone, it is over!" Hadrian gasped, "You are bleeding. Let me see."

I tried to sit up, but my side cramped. I looked to my stomach to see a broken piece of wood jammed into my side.

"It is only a scratch." I winced when Hadrian pressed his hands against it.

"Bite on this." He pressed something into my mouth. "This is going to hurt, but we must get it out."

I didn't have a chance to decline before Hadrian dug his fingers into my side.

I screamed.

Every muscle in my body tensed when I felt Hadrian pull out the splinter. It was over quickly, an instant relief when the pressure was removed.

Hadrian pulled a vial from a small pouch strapped to his belt and poured the contents onto the gash. My entire stomach went numb the moment the liquid touched it.

"Browlin passed this onto me before we left, she said I would need it. She was right."

The cut had knitted together by the time the first shifter ran through the tree line. My heart sank. Hadrian placed a finger to his lip and turned to those who followed into the clearing. Before he moved his gaze to them completely, I pulled on his shirt. "Please don't tell anyone what I did," I whispered.

He shook his head, "Oh, I won't. We both have secrets to keep."

Hadrian yanked my shirt back into place, his warm hands brushing against my stomach. A shout distracted me, and I turned out to see Fadine. She moved like a dancer, jumping over huge roots and dodging trees until she reached us.

"What happened?" she shouted, not stopping until she scanned the forest around us.

"We were ambushed. Zacriah saved my life. Without him, I would have an arrow in my head." Hadrian stood, addressing Fadine and the crowd. I cowered under their glances.

"Marcues and Jon, I want you to go ahead and see if you can catch a trial on them before those bastards disappear," Fadine commanded to the two guards closest to her. "Nyah and Caro, head back to the elks and prepare for the journey back."

At the mention of Nyah's name I spotted her in the group. Her eyes burned into me from across the crowd. She mouthed something to me, but I couldn't make it out from where I was.

She gave me a quick smile and disappeared back in the direction they had come from.

"The rest of you. Station yourselves around Prince Hadrian. I want you each to keep your eyes and ears on the horizon. If they tried to kill him once, they will do it again."

Hadrian was pulled from me, the guards surrounding him. I stayed rooted to the spot as I watched them leave. Fadine whispered something to Illera who at first shook her head. But Fadine's voice rose, pissed at Illera's refusal. Illera looked my way and I heard her sigh as she walked to me.

"Get up, hero," she said, extending a hand to me.

I reached for it and she yanked me up.

"Thank you," I said, aware of just how difficult this was for her.

She didn't respond, nor utter another word when she walked off towards the group.

⁓

THERE WAS NO sign Hadrian's fire had ever graced the forest. The trees were unmarked and the ground still fresh. I hung back, Illera walking ahead, confused at the lack of evidence.

The broken arrow that had been pulled from my side had been discarded to the ground. I looked around for the rest, noticing them scattered all around me.

I was relieved when I saw that my bow was still in one piece. I picked it up from where I'd dropped it, brushing off the dirt. I placed it back in the holder on my back until the click sounded. I collected the fallen arrows and left. The ominous feeling of being watched no longer hung in the forest. I knew the Morthi had left.

It didn't take me long to walk back through the forest. And as I did so, I studied the ground, noticing the imprints from mine and Hadrian's feet. I used that to navigate back to the village. There was a dull throb in my stomach. I rubbed at the healed cut but knew the pain was from my exhausted magick. I'd never used that much power, nor lost control. It scared me, how fast I'd lost myself. I called for it within me, yet it lay still and weak.

When I saw the light peak through at the end of the forest ahead, I picked up my pace to a jog. I caught something in the corner of my eye. I stopped just before the clearing and turned my attention to the object that stuck out from a tree.

The arrow.

I moved for it. I'd never seen a Morthi arrow before and I was surprised to see how similar it was to the arrows strapped to my back. The only difference was the muted grey feathers, perfect to ensure the arrows accuracy. I ran my finger down the shaft, feeling remnants of my power that still clung to the wood. My finger dipped into the red blood lacing the shaft. A piece of skin jammed beneath the arrow and the blood that coated it.

The *red* blood.

My heart sank and my mind whirled. I'd seen enough of the Morthi blood to know it was black. I'd dreamt of the rivers of obsidian blood oozing across marbled floors since seeing the Morthi elf on my first night in Olderim. I knew well enough that what I was seeing went against everything I'd believed.

The ambushers were not Morthi.

I had the urge to shout it, but there was no one around. I had to think quickly. I ripped a piece of material from my shirt, and yanked the arrow from the tree. I pinched the skin, fighting the urge to gag whilst I pulled it from the arrow. As soon as it was free I wrapped it in the material and stuffed it into my fist.

I needed proof, needed something to show Hadrian that it was not the Morthi that had shot the arrow.

Only Niraen elves bleed red.

CHAPTER

NINETEEN

THE NIGHT HAD come to lay its heavy blanket across Thessolina. The cavalry rode south back to Olderim and what had been endless fields and hills was swallowed by the night.

Up ahead, decorative lanterns hung from iron polls held by the guards, illuminating the cavalry and the pathway around them. I lost myself in the dancing reds of the hanging fire thinking about Hadrian. It was all my mind could focus on, that and the bloodied material in my pocket.

I'd looked behind me more times than I cared to count, checking for gleaming eyes in the distance or signs that we were being followed. But now that I knew the truth behind the attackers, I couldn't help but think they could be around all us, hiding in plain view amongst the group.

The sound of the shifters wings relaxed my worry. I kept my claws out though, and my hand on the hilt of my sword just in case. My magick was still exhausted, even hours after the incident in the forest. I kept reaching for it, hoping to feel its urgent movements. But it remained still.

Hadrian stayed up ahead, surrounded by a moving circle of guards who kept him within their formation. I'd been given a spare elk to ride when we left.

Hadrian was to be kept guarded and separated. I didn't try to join him, nor did he request my presence. He just kept ahead, his face trained to the darkness before him, not once turning back to look at me.

I was drained. The rhythmic pound of the elk's hooves soothed me, but every time I closed my eyes, I felt the heavy weight of the cloth in my pocket. The skin's presence warmed against my leg and I was certain the blood had seeped through the material and onto my skin.

I lost myself in the memories, fighting to stay awake the rest of the way back.

$\backsim$

IT WAS EARLY morning when we finally gained on Olderim. Fadine commanded a shifter to fly ahead and warn the palace to prepare for our arrival, it was the swan shifter who was chosen for the task.

There was not much talk between the cavalry whilst we pulled up to the outer walls of the city. No one had slept the entire journey back, but I could see from their faces that they were as exhausted as I was.

The streets of Olderim were empty. It seemed like the last part of the journey dragged the most. The shadow of the palace in the distance a haunting reminder of my urgency to speak with Hadrian.

When we arrived, countless guards rushed from the palace the moment we passed over the bridge to Vulmar. The courtyard beyond the door filled up fast and before I could jump down from my elk, Hadrian was guided from his and taken inside. I wanted to shout for him, to tell him to stop. Seeing him disappear into the palace caused the latent panic to build once more within me.

I slipped from my elk's back. My legs were numb from the journey; they almost gave way under me as I connected with the ground for the first time in hours.

I turned back to face my elk and ran a hand down its wiry fur. It huffed in pleasure, a cloud of mist bursting from his nose, its wide grey eyes looked straight into mine. "Thanks for bringing me back." I pressed my forehead to his, thanking him.

An elf dressed in white walked over and grasped the reins from my hands. I didn't have a chance to thank her before she pulled my elk away.

In the same direction they walked, I noticed Fadine. She cut through the crowd towards me. From her pinched face, I knew something was amiss. Her lips were pulled firm into a frown and two large, dark shadows hung beneath her eyes.

"The king requests your presence," she whispered under her breath, closing the gap between us and passing a small parchment roll to me. "This was given to me as soon we arrived back."

"Do you know why?" I unrolled it, reading over the simple message for my presence. It gave no reason, and had clearly been rushed. The handwriting was almost not legible.

"I do not, nor do I wish to know his business, but you are to follow me immediately. I am sure King Dalior does not want to be kept waiting." She grasped my forearm, her grip strong enough to leave a bruise. "Come."

She dragged me along. Many watched, their muffled whispers trailing behind us as we passed.

"You're hurting me!" I winced. "I'm not going to run off…"

"Sorry," she replied, dropping my arm. "My mind's all over the place."

I kept up as her pace quickened.

"How did you stop them?" she asked.

"I can't remember. It's all a blur." I lied. "Did Hadrian not say?"

"No, he didn't."

We walked through the throne room till we reached a door beyond the dais. Two guards stood on either side, both who nodded to Fadine once she showed them the King's note. Whilst we passed, I kept my eyes to the floor.

They were not the last guards we had to get past. At every door, Fadine flashed the note before we could move ahead. I'd not been so far into the palace's winding corridors, but was certain the extra security was a result of the events at Nasamel.

When reached the final door it was a barren of guards.

"Strange, the Commander is not here," Fadine said, "It's your lucky day. Take off your sword and bow and give me those strange gloves you wear. It wouldn't be suitable to take them in with you."

I nodded and pulled the bow and arrows from their holder on my back. I unbuckled the belt from around my waist and passed the short sword that hung from it to her. It took me longer to unclasp the clawed gloves, but they soon came free and I dropped them into her waiting hands.

"I'll have them dropped off into your room," she said, knocking twice against the metal surface of the door. It was the first of its kind I'd seen. An elaborate choice, fitting for the King.

Fadine didn't wait for an answer, instead pushed the door open and urged me inside the room beyond.

King Dalior didn't look at me when I entered. He lay across a maroon seat, lifting small fruits from the platter that lay next to him before dropping them into his waiting mouth. Purple juices spilled from his lips, running down his chin before he wiped their trails with the back of his jewelled hand. He seemed relaxed, not what I expected.

The room clouded with drifting smoke from burning incenses. I breathed in, taking in the scents of jasmine and pine that clung in the air, clearing my airways of the memory of burning flesh and wood that seemed to cling to me from Nasamel.

The room was dark, the only light source spilled from the open window at the back of the room. The sky was a deep grey.

I turned back to the door expecting to see Fadine, but she was not there. She must have been waiting for me outside. I took three steps into the room before the King and stood waiting for him to look up.

"Grape?" It was the first thing King Dalior said to me. He held a rounded piece of fruit pinched between his forefinger and thumb towards me. "Try it."

I hesitated, there was something different about him. Not wanting to offend him, I shuffled forward and plucked the fruit he called *grape* from his grasp.

"Thank you, King Dalior." I bowed and took careful steps back.

He didn't drop his gaze from me. I slipped the grape between my teeth, my mouth salivating. I bit down onto it and the grape popped in my mouth, its juices gracing my tongue and quenching my thirst.

"Beautiful, do you agree?" King Dalior said, his voice childlike. He swept a handful from the platter and dropped them one after the other into his mouth.

"I first tried it when a vine was sent as a gift from across the seas. For years we tried to grow them, but failed." He rolled a grape in front of his face, staring longingly at it. "It was simple in the end, replicating an environment that obtained moisture from the ground, much like the temperature of Eldnol. Now I'm able to grow them in abundance. Fascinating, isn't it?"

"Yes, my King." I opted to keep my replies short, anything to get the meeting between us over with.

"Now…" He shifted in the seat. "When I heard of your heroics in Nasamel, I had to personally thank you myself. You saved my son from certain death, an act that will not be forgotten."

Something passed behind his eyes when he spoke.

"I did what I could," I reined in my voice, trying to still my nerves. I was a prisoner to his gaze.

He stood up and moved to his desk. I could smell the sweet fumes emanating from him as he walked past, his shoulder brushing against my own. It took a lot of effort not to shake.

"But, Hadrian did not tell me how you succeeded in saving him from the Morthi's attack. Do you care to enlighten me?" His tone of voice had changed so fast that it caught me off guard. I could feel him standing behind me, but I didn't dare turn around.

"I cannot remember, everything happened so quickly," I said, pushing my hands into my pockets to stop them from shaking. My hand brushed against the clump of cloth and I pulled it from my pocket.

"King Dalior, I found something I need to show you." I unwrapped the material and teased the part of the skin from it. Lifting it between my forefinger and thumb, I held it up for him to see. King Dalior walked slowly around to face me.

His face melted. He snatched the skin from my hand and turned away from me.

"What is this?" He examined the skin with intent, lifting it into a stream of light from the window. The skin had dried at the sides, but the blood was still there, still red.

"I… shot an arrow at whoever was in the woods. I thought I'd missed them, but I think I must have caught whoever it was because I found the skin on the arrow whilst I left the forest where it happened. I think that whoever tried to kill Hadrian was Niraen, not Morthi."

King Dalior didn't say anything for a moment. He stood, hunched over the skin and then fisted it. When he turned back to face me there was a wide smile on his face.

"Thank you for bringing this to me, I appreciate your honesty, but you must understand that if this information gets passed around it would send our people into a frenzy. I would appreciate if you kept this to yourself until I feel the time is right."

"Of course, King Dalior, I understand." *I didn't.* Something was wrong.

He placed his jewelled hand on my shoulder and squeezed. Hard. "I knew you would. And as a way of showing my thanks, you will no longer be needed in the kitchens. A small gesture to show my appreciation for you saving my *precious* son's life." With each word, his grip seemed to tighten on my shoulder.

"Thank you." I tried everything I could to not flinch under his grasp.

"You may retire, I am sure you are going to need the rest after the day you have had..."

He finally released his hold on me and moved back to his seat. Keeping my eyes trained to the floor, I took calculated steps moving backwards to the door to leave. I didn't look up until I opened the door. When I did, King Dalior was looking at me, but his expression changed the moment I caught his eyes.

"Remember what you have promised me, my child," he said, stuffing a grape into his mouth.

"I won't forget, my King."

King Dalior smiled, but it never reached his eyes.

I slipped from the door and closed it behind me. Fadine was waiting, leaning against the wall. I didn't say anything to her as we walked back through the corridors and anti-chambers until we reached the throne room.

"I can trust you will find your way back from here," she said and I nodded.

When she left, I stuck my closed fist into my pocket and dropped the blood-stained material back into it. King Dalior hadn't noticed that I had kept it.

Something was amiss, the entire meeting felt off. King Dalior was different. His lack of worry over my news unnerved me. Between King Dalior's placid face and the way he disregarded the proof made me think that he already knew.

His eyes screamed so.

CHAPTER

TWENTY

I FELT GROGGY after the few hours of sleep I managed.
And standing beneath the front of the palace with countless
bodies pressed in on me from either side didn't help my
irritable mood. During breakfast, we'd been informed that the
King was to give an opening speech to the city and all its
occupants, including the guards and shifters. No one seemed
to know why we'd been called, but once we exited the palace
it was clear the entire city of Olderim buzzed with
anticipation.

I'd still not heard nor seen Hadrian since we arrived and
with every passing hour my worry grew. I had spent the hour
before breakfast looking for him, but he was nowhere to be
seen.

The sun had burned through all remnants of clouds that
had hung in the sky from the previous day, leaving a pure,
blue open expanse. There was no shade, nothing to give us
rest from the burning rays of the sun.

Drips of sweat ran down my neck until they disappeared
into the neckline of my new guard uniform. I stood out more
than ever beside my initiates. They'd been placed on my bunk
by the time I woke that morning with a note from King Dalior
with one simple word attached

Remember.

I'd asked Gwendolyn if she saw who brought it in, she was the only one awake early, but she had not. It unnerved me to think someone had been so close to me whilst I slept, when I was so vulnerable.

Like the training clothes, the uniform was loose fitting. Matching purple slacks and top, each made from a cotton material that allowed more room for me to move. I had spent a while working out how to fit the leather shoulder garments over my head and how to tie them up. Gwendolyn helped me while she asked about the trip to Nasamel and congratulated me on saving Hadrian. News really did travel fast.

"It's what I had to do," I replied.

I'd even asked about Petrer; he was still absent when I arrived back to our room. Yet there had been no news regarding his recovery.

Nyah stood next to me waiting for the King. "What is taking him so long?" she asked. "I'd love to get inside as quick as I can before I start burning. At this rate, by the time King Dalior shows up, I'll be covered in blisters."

"I hope he comes out soon…" I replied.

My mind was all over the place. For King Dalior to call for so many people to gather in one place meant it was important. And there was only one thing I could imagine him telling everyone.

I pushed up on my tiptoes to get a better look around. For as far as I could see, elves took up every available space in the surrounding streets. I saw some climbing up on the bridge connecting Thalor to Vulmar to get a better look, some even sitting on the roofs of the buildings closest to the palace, waving flags with the King's emblem.

I trained my focus back to the balcony. A large banner hung from the wall beneath it, swaying in the breeze. I blocked the sun with my hand, making it easier to see the vines that wrapped around the pillars of the walls and the crystal glass doors between them.

I watched and waited until a shadow passed behind the glass doors and they opened.

Sheer curtains blew out like reaching hands and the crowd roared like one beast as King Dalior stepped out onto the balcony.

He wore pure silver from his shirt to the long cloak that dragged behind him. It was difficult to make out the features of his face from where I stood, but I could already tell he seemed like a different man than the one during my private audience with him.

I was thrust from either side, narrowly dodging fists that pumped into the air. I thought the shouts would never end. But they did when King Dalior raised a hand and everyone silenced.

"My children…" He paused and looked around. "I must first thank you all for coming to visit me this morning, especially when my request was such short notice. What I have to share with you all is something that before this day I thought I would never have to say. As you are all aware I sent a legion of our best soldiers to attend Nasamel after the most recent attack. During the expedition your prince, my son, was ambushed and an attempt on his life was made."

A collective gasp came from the crowd and my blood ran cold with anticipation. He was going to tell them.

"Luckily Prince Hadrian is safe. Protected by his loyal guards, they were able to prevent the attack and kill the assailants."

I turned to Nyah who was already looking at me, her face twisted in disbelief. "Did he just lie?"

"I…" I croaked, looking back to the balcony.

"My children, I cannot keep this from you any longer. You have all heard rumours and seen an unexplained number of elves who have joined our city in the past months. Thessolina is under threat. Not since the druids poisoned our world with their dark powers has a threat been this serious. This time the Morthi have crossed boundaries and are now our greatest enemy. The Peace Treaty, signed between the Morthi, Alorian and Niraen elves is no longer in play. From this day forward, I, King Dalior of Thessolina, declare that we no longer live by the rules set by our enemies and we fight for what is right! I will not stand and watch another innocent Niraen life destroyed by the Morthi. It ends today," King Dalior shouted and lifted up a parchment for the crowd to see.

With every lie King Dalior spoke, his voice grew louder until he was almost screaming. He held the Peace Treaty in his hands and out for the crowd to see. The parchment was crisp white and even from the distance I was at, I could make out scribbles of black ink. In one moment King Dalior was screaming and in the next he yanked hard on the parchment till it ripped in two. The entire crowd fell into a silence as the parchment fluttered to the floor.

"Today, I call for *all* those able to fight to consider joining our military to protect our beloved land. Help us prevent any more bloodshed. Enough Niraen blood has spilled as a result of these hateful creatures, it is time to wash it away with the blood of our enemies."

Everyone around me began to stomp their feet on the ground.

"Do not be afraid, for I will do everything in my being to protect you all. I will not allow another Morthi to take an innocent life, not while I reign."

My breath hitched as King Dalior looked at me. I reached for Nyah's hand and squeezed. She yanked her hand straight out of my grasp while she too stomped her feet.

He smiled. My body ran cold and the hairs on the back of my neck stood to attention. There was movement behind him, enough of a distraction for me to tear my gaze from the King.

Hadrian stepped into view.

He was nothing more than a symbol of war. The boy who sparked the end of the treaty.

King Dalior grasped Hadrian's hand and raised his arm up, turning the crowd beneath them into a frenzy.

"Now, come forward, fight for *your* kingdom."

I didn't hear what he said next. The crowd moved in a surge forward, pulling me along in the tidal wave of succession. I reached out again for Nyah, who walked towards the palace. She turned sharp to face me with a scowl. "What the hell are you playing at?"

"Follow me," I shouted over those who cut between us, breaking our connection apart.

"But that's the wrong way!" Nyah shouted cross the bustling noise. I ignored her and pulled more, navigating her through the oncoming sea of elves.

It took a while to fight our way across the bridge to Thalor. One we stepped onto its streets I moved for the closest alleyway.

"What the *Goddess* is going on!" Nyah pulled her arm from my hand, her voice stern.

"Do you trust me?" I asked.

"You are starting to freak me out, Zacriah! Do you know how crazy you're acting?"

"Do you trust me?!" I repeated.

"Of course, I do but—"

"I need you to go and get Hadrian and bring him to me."

Nyah cackled. "Now you really have gone mad."

"Nyah!" I begged. "You said you trust me, so please. You have to get him for me."

Nyah looked over my face. "I'm so confused, Zacriah. How do you expect me speak to him let alone get near him! And for what? Even if I did, do you think he will listen to me?"

"The King is lying, Nyah. Even you said so."

"I know, but there are worse things than lying about who saved the prince. Like the fact he has declared war and the end of the treaty. We need to go and show our support."

I shook my head. "You don't get it! I'm not talking about that. He lied about the Morthi! They were not the ones who tried to kill Hadrian. I can prove it."

I pulled the bloodied clump of material out of my pocket and showed her. Even in the shadows of the alleyway I could still see her face change.

"Can't you do your empath thing and see if I'm telling the truth?" I asked before she could respond.

She looked up at me, all sign of irritation melted from her face. "If what you're suggesting is true, this is treasonous. You think telling the prince is going to be a good idea?"

"Shift!" I said, the idea hitting me fast. "Shift, no one will notice something so small – no offence. And when you find him, tell him to meet me back at Antler & Wagon in Masarion."

"Did you not just hear what I said!" she replied.

"Yes, but Hadrian will understand. Please."

"I swear, Zacriah. If I get caught and thrown into jail over your crazy theory, I swear I'm going to knock you out." Her words were not at all laced with her usual humour.

"I'm sure you would. Please, hurry."

"I will. You better make sure there is a drink waiting for me. In fact, make it two. I have a feeling I'm going to need it."

"I shall…" I replied as she shifted.

She melted into the shadows of the alleyway within seconds. Nyah may have been a moth in her shifter form, but she was the biggest, most graceful moth I'd ever seen. She landed on my finger, her small legs tickling my skin.

"Good luck," I whispered.

Her wings began to move until they were a single blur. In seconds, she was off my finger and flying through the alleyway.

I ran for the tavern, catching odd glances from those I passed. I focused on my destination and fought the storm that battered within my mind.

CHAPTER
TWENTY-ONE

I ITCHED WITH nerves while I sat waiting for Nyah to arrive with Hadrian. I kept my eyes on the door, hoping it would open, but it didn't. I wasn't sure how much time passed while I was waiting for them, the lack of natural light held me in an endless limbo.

I scratched at my legs and pulled at loose strands of string on my slacks. I contemplated leaving and heading back for the palace, but I was in too deep. This could not wait a moment longer.

Like my first visit, a group of dazed occupants smoked from pipes across the room, each in their own worlds. The whites of their eyes were stained red and their mouths hung open. By the time the barmaid poured four ales, one for myself, one for Hadrian and two for Nyah, I realized I had no coin to pay. I could feel her one good eye on me, burning a hole into the back of my head. I'd promised my friends would pay when they arrived and that seemed to be good enough for her.

I jumped when the door burst open, a cloaked figure rushing in. Hadrian. Nyah entered next, checking behind her a final time before closing the door. As soon as the outside was shut out, Hadrian pulled the hood down, revealing his face. I almost wanted him to conceal it again. He was angry. Very angry. His face screamed with distaste, so much so that I hesitated to call him over.

I didn't need to. He spotted me and strolled straight over.

"Nyah found you without problems?" I asked. He didn't respond, he only picked the tankard up from the table and downed the entire thing. The sound of it being slammed against the table made me cringe and he pulled a stool to sit.

I turned my attention to Nyah. "What took so long?"

"Well, let me see, first I had to find his room. Then by the time I found it, I had to wait for the guards to leave. Then the princey decided to attack me, he lunged for me before I could even explain why I was there." One of her auburn brows was raised, that explained the obvious tension between them. "As soon as I said your name he stopped..."

I looked back to Hadrian who just stared at me. His golden eyes glowing above the single lit candle in the middle of the table. "I have apologized more times than I care to remember," he added.

"We also had to shake off his baby sitters so I'm not sure how long we will have till they track him down. These mine?" She pointed to the spare tankards and I nodded.

I looked between them. Nyah more occupied with her drink and Hadrian not taking his eyes off of me.

"I must apologize, Petal, for not calling on you sooner, but like Nyah told you, Father has stationed guards with me at all times. He has gone overboard with protection after the Morthi attack."

I shot Nyah a look as she choked on her tankard. She hadn't missed what he called me.

"I haven't told him anything..." Nyah whispered over the rim of her tankard. I wished she had. I didn't know where to start.

"I am impressed, I must say. Sending moth girl to fetch me was a pretty risky move."

"If he calls me that one more time," Nyah hissed, placing her tankard on the table.

Hadrian turned to her. "What?"

"If you think being prince will stop me from hi—"

"Nyah! Hadrian, enough!" I shouted, slapping my palm on the table. "Nyah, go and pay for our ales and get another round in. Hadrian, if your guards are out looking for you now, it won't be long until they get here."

Nyah pushed her stool back, and turned for the bar. "Hold on, you were meant to get these. Not me."

"Please, Nyah."

I pulled the cloth from my pocket and placed it on the table before Hadrian. "I found it as I was leaving Nasamel's forest. The arrow I stopped was embedded into a tree and caught under its head was skin."

"That doesn't look like skin…" Hadrian said, picking the cloth up to study it.

"That's not skin, the skin was wrapped inside of it. I gave it to King Dalior when we arrived back, but I was able to keep this."

"You saw the King? Why?" Nyah questioned. She walked back to the table carrying four more tankards. Hadrian didn't seem surprised. He would have been told, I just didn't know how much of our conversation would have been revealed to him.

"He called for me when we returned, to thank me for saving you."

Nyah slammed her tankard on the table, her face alight with excitement. "Why didn't you tell me? That's incredible!" Her enthusiasm made me cringe.

"It wasn't what I expected it to be like." I shook my head. "But that's not the point. He saw the skin of the attacker and still lied."

Hadrian said nothing, but kept his gaze shifting between the cloth and me. His polished nails grazed against it.

"I told him about what happened when we were attacked." Hadrian flickered his gaze to me. He knew what I meant. "He was adamant that it was the Morthi, but I know that's not true. Look…" I turned the cloth over so the stain of red blood was visible.

Hadrian's expression changed the moment his eyes caught the stain. He leaned forward to examine it closer.

I wasn't sure if he was playing dumb or had still not connected the dots. From his pinched brows and wrinkled forehead, I went for the latter. "Hadrian, it came from the attackers, the blood is red… the elves that tried to kill you was not Morthi. I think that whoever tried to kill you was one of us. Niraen."

"I'm sorry, but I don't understand. Why would father say any different if you showed him this?" He dropped the cloth to the table, disgusted.

"I did, and he even kept the skin. He has the proof and told me he would investigate it. King Dalior knows everything, he knew that whoever shot that arrow was not Morthi I'm sure of it."

"I know your confused, Zacriah, and so am I. But father is not someone who lies, at least not someone I thought even had the capacity to," Hadrian replied.

"Well clearly you and your *daddy* are not as well acquainted as *you* thought," Nyah said, clicking her knuckles.

There was a shout outside.

I snapped my head to the door and Nyah jumped up. "I'll go and see what's going on out there."

"Good idea. Let us know the second you see the guards."

Nyah only nodded back to me and made for the door.

"Finally," Hadrian huffed, not even waiting for the door to close. He reached his hand over the table and grasped mine. I stopped for a second, my mind telling me to pull it back but my heart refusing to follow the command. "I am truly sorry I have not spoken to you sooner. It has been a crazy day with the speech and everything."

"I understand." His hands were warm.

"So, you think my father is lying?"

I nodded. "I don't know what's going on, but I am sure those who tried to kill you were not Morthi. It is the only thing I can think of that explains this." I gestured to the cloth.

Hadrian released me and placed his head in his hands. My next question came out of me before I had a chance to stop it.

"What are you? I mean… the fire in the forest. It was amazing, but how?" I could hear how awkward my question sounded. Hadrian looked up from his hands, a confused look on his face.

"The question is what are *you*?" he replied.

"That's not fair, I asked first!"

"Life isn't fair. Elemental? Mage?" Hadrian asked.

I dropped my gaze, embarrassed. "I don't know."

"What do you mean you do not know? How could you not know! I could tell by the way your magick moved that you have used it before. You know it well."

"I meant what I said. I'm not an Elemental, both my parents are Niraen which also eliminates Mage. They know about my magick but they won't talk to me about it."

This was not the answer Hadrian was expecting. He let out a breath, a long drawl of concern. "Interesting…"

"What about you, surly the Prince of Thessolina should not have the magick you have? I've never heard of a member of our royal family ever causing unnatural fire. Does your father know?"

"No, my mother promised me to keep it between us." he said. A shadow passed over his face at the mention of his mother.

"But I thought the queen was Niraen also, I had no idea she was Alorian." I was certain of it.

"She was Niraen. If you are thinking that the two options I mentioned were the only explanation of power, you would be wrong. I'm neither an Elemental nor Mage. I'm Dr—"

The door burst open, bright light and fresh air spilling around Nyah's silhouette. Something was wrong. She ran to the table, her arms gesturing for us to stand. "If your baby sitters come in the shape of four monstrous guards each decked out with swords the length of my arm, then they are right around the corner heading this way."

We didn't need to be told twice. I swiped the cloth from the table and stuffed it back into my pocket. Hadrian called for Nyah to follow and he pulled on my hand. I maneuvered around chairs and tables while he led us towards a shadowed door at the back of the tavern. The barmaid screamed after us, her voice raging with anger. Tables were knocked over in our haste. Once we reached the door, Hadrian kicked it open. His boot smashed into its weak wood frame and sent it crashing into the stone wall of the alley.

The narrow pathway that greeted us was lined with rotting food and sacks of steaming waste. I lifted my empty hand to cover my nose and mouth, but it didn't help shield me from the rancid smell.

Hadrian still held a firm grip on my hand. He stepped over piles of rubbish, avoiding mysterious looking puddles as we ran down the alleyway. Nyah's muffled complaints trailed behind, swearing under her breath.

"I need to get back to the Palace," Hadrian said.

The alleyway came to an end. We stopped before the crossroad, Hadrian peering around the corner, checking each side before turning back to me.

"I would like to carry on our conversation later. I shall send someone to collect you for dinner."

"How romantic." Nyah chuckled, coming to a stop behind us. "Since we are all friends, am I invited?"

"Not this time." His reply was short, he still looked at me intensely as he spoke. "We still have a lot to discuss. Try and keep your head down."

"I will."

"Time to split up," Hadrian said, dropping my hand. "Nyah, it has been a … well, interesting." He nodded to her and she smiled.

"Petal…" He reached for my aching hand and pulled it to his mouth. His warm lips against the back of my hand sent a blush to race up the back of my neck. "Remember, keeping secrets is something I have perfected."

He lifted the heavy cloak hood and covered his head, shadowing his face. A glint of metal flashed at his side beneath his cloak as he straightened it. A dagger.

I didn't look away from Hadrian until he turned a corner and disappeared from view.

Nyah placed a hand on my shoulder. "We should get back, I still want to sign up to join the military even if it is only for the gold bands that are rumoured to being given out."

"Go without me," I replied, "Until this is figured out, I'm not joining."

CHAPTER

TWENTY-TWO

MY ARMS BURNED and my lungs screamed for more air. Shallow cuts laced most of my exposed skin, a result of Nyah's advances. It was her choice to fight with metal rather than wood during training, a decision I wasn't comfortable with.

I lifted a hand and swiped a trail of sweat from beneath my hairline, smudging blood amongst my sticky forehead. The salt from my sweat stung my open wounds, like needles driving into my skin.

Despite the bruises and cuts, I was thankful that my mind was only occupied on my next move and how to balance the sword. I didn't bring up the mornings events and neither did Nyah. The only time it was mentioned was when she found me in the throne room, a gold band wrapped around her forearm.

I was getting used to the way she moved. I'd focused hard on memorizing her steps just like I would do with the constellations during hunting season, marking each one. It had worked at first, but as soon as my energy dwindled I began to fall behind.

Sparks burst beneath my sword when I slammed into the gold band on her wrist. She stumbled backwards, yelping. It only took her a second to regain her composure before she ran at me, sword drawn above. She brought it down on mine knocking it from my grasp.

I was empty handed.

I extended my claws, exchanging one weapon for another. It was the first time she would see me using them.

A loud clap sounded as I stopped her next volley with my open palms. I closed my metal hands into fists around the tip of her sword and yanked it down to the floor.

Once. Twice. On the third time, it came free from her hands.

"Ha!" I shouted, throwing it behind me into the shadows of the room.

Nyah cocked her head to the side and smiled. "Careful now, don't get ahead of yourself." She sprang forward like a cat, her movements animalistic and rushed.

She unsheathed a dagger, but my ears didn't pick the movement up. It sang through the air, and she sliced it at my chest. I dodged to the left, but it caught my shoulder. *Shit.*

"Meet Clarisa…" Nyah sang, bouncing from one foot to the other, her dagger held before her. "I was glad to see she was still there when I finally picked my weapon. Thanks for the suggestion, she is pretty…useful."

"You seriously named your dagger?" I asked, not taking my eyes off her face. I wouldn't give her a moment to move without me seeing.

"Yup, just like the great warriors in my books, I named it."

She jumped forward and kicked at my shins. I gave way to the attack and fell against my will to my knees.

When I looked up, Clarisa was pressed against my throat.

"I win," Nyah said, her emerald eyes pleased.

I laughed. "Are you sure?" I looked away from her for a moment, enough for her to follow my gaze. "Don't get ahead of yourself, Nyah."

My claws were pressed into her inner thigh, inches from ripping one of her main veins open.

∽

"HERE…" NYAH PASSED a vial of water she'd collected from the well in the room down the corridor. "I know there's no point suggesting for you to see Healer Browlin."

I popped the cork, and tipped the glowing blue water onto my arms and neck. My wounds began to fade, skin knitting together in a flush of fresh pink. "Great session today. I could get used to besting you," I said.

Nyah laughed, "Well don't get used to it, you have a long way to go till you can beat me without relying on luck."

"You know. I've never believed in luck. Only skill."

"Sure!" Nyah rolled her eyes with a smirk. "Skill. Don't get to cocksure, it won't do your ego much good the next time you're sprawled on the floor with a dagger to your throat."

I threw the empty vile at her, but she caught it with speed.

"Watch it…" She snorted, wiggling her freckled nose. "We should think about getting back. You look like shit. I suggest washing before your little meal with Princey tonight."

I had forgotten about the dinner as well as everything else during our sparring. "It's odd, but I'm actually looking forward to it." It wasn't just the possibility for answers that excited me.

"I know you are. You're burning with excitement right now, it's all around you." Nyah patted my shoulder and passed me.

I blushed, and I could tell Nyah didn't miss it. "Is that some creepy empath thing?"

"Yes. Although you don't need to have my power to see you're excited. It's written all over your face," Nyah replied,

"Whatever happens tonight, I expect a full debrief in the kitchens in the morning."

"I won't be in the kitchens tomorrow. King Dalior has relieved me of the work."

"Well, aren't you a lucky one."

⌣

THE HEAT OF the water stung my skin the moment I lowered myself into its embrace. I lay there, allowing the heat to relax my muscles and wash away the day's worry and dirt. Someone had filled the stone bath with a thick white foam that floated on the top of the water. I picked up a handful and sniffed at its buttery scent. I placed the handful of white bubbles on my head and wore it as a crown, feeling more childlike than I had in a long time.

I dipped under the water until it covered my head and washed the suds from my silver hair. Holding my breath for as long as I could, taking pleasure in the muffled silence beneath the water. I pushed back from the surface of the water and rubbed my eyes dry. A chill wrapped around my shoulders. I looked around. Someone was here.

"Hello?" I called, reaching for my claws that I'd placed beside the bath. Whoever it was didn't respond. I squinted toward the sound of breathing through the haze of steam. A shadow hung at the back of the room.

"You creep!" I shouted, struggling to find my claws.

I didn't know if it was an illusion caused by the steam or the adrenaline that filled my mind, but I was sure the shapes edges were rippling.

The breathing sounded harsh and soon built into a low growl.

My heart stilled. I looked around for my claws, but could only see my clothes. They were no longer on top of them. My magick stirred for the first time since Nasamel.

The shadow began to move through the room, straight toward me. Without thinking, I threw my hands up. Wind shot forwards, cutting a path in the steam. I pushed as much power as I could muster and reached the shadow. I waited for it to scream, but the moment my magick connected it burst apart. The shadow was gone.

I jumped from the bath, the room vacant of steam, thanks to my magic. Even the aqua water in the bath splashed up the stone sides and onto the floor.

Where I'd first seen the shadow, my claws were in a heap on the floor. Something had been there. I grabbed the towel and wrapped it around my middle. With my clothes in one hand, I walked to where my claws were, expecting the shadow to return.

But it never did.

◠

"YOU LOOK LIKE you've seen a ghost." Petrer said when I threw the door open to the room. I almost dropped my towel when I saw him.

Forgetting everything, I ran to Petrer and threw my arms around him. "You're back!" My eyes scanned him, looking for any twitch of pain or bandages. Any sign of what he had been through. What I had put him through. But there was nothing, not a single blemish. "You look better…"

He didn't hug me back.

"I'm so sorry! I had no idea you were even near us when I was shooting, and you know I'd never intentionally do that to you."

"Do I?" he asked.

I pulled away from the awkward embrace and looked at his dark eyes. They seemed different.

"Are you angry with me?"

"It's funny." He shrugged. "Normally when someone is worried they make more of an effort to check up on someone or at least call for them. But you, nothing."

"I'm sorry, really I am. It's been so crazy around here and—"

"You think it's been like this only for the past couple of days, Zac? You have treated me like shit for weeks. One minute we are all over each other and in the next you are trying to kill me. I don't know what is going on in that little head of yours, but you are delusional to think that the way you've treated me has gone unnoticed."

I couldn't believe what was coming out of his mouth. I watched, mouth wide, as Petrer turned to face his bunk and gathered the pile of clothes that sat on his sheets. I stood, shivering in the doorway, dazed and confused. Anger burning in my throat.

"And why do you think I've been so distant, Petrer? Are you telling me you still haven't worked it out?" I slammed the door shut and moved for my bed, waiting for his response.

"Because you are a selfish prick who only thinks about what he wants and when he wants it. Maybe it's the Prince. Word is you both have been very close over the past few days. Has he been a distraction for you? Does he warm your bed like I warmed yours?"

His words were like daggers to my heart. I turned to him. "The question is, does the prince warm my bed like that boy did in *ours*?"

Petrer turned to me and smiled. "So, my secret is out?"

I went to reply but a slow tutting sound came from the doorway behind me.

"Now, now, now," Hadrian growled through bared teeth.

CHAPTER
TWENTY-THREE

THE TENSION BETWEEN them was so thick, not even my claws could've sliced through it.

I looked between Hadrian and Petrer, both men not speaking, just staring at one another. At first Petrer didn't bow, but when he finally dipped his head I was sure his lip twitched into a snarl.

"Leave," Hadrian commanded.

Petrer didn't need to be told twice. He strode through the room, past Hadrian and me with a face set into a scowl. He slammed the door to the room, making me jump. With his departure, the tension began to melt.

"What a prick!" Hadrian whispered. The word didn't sound right from his mouth.

Hadrian turned from the door and glanced my way. He must have only realized my lack of clothes because he looked me up and down and coughed. "Get changed, before you freeze to death. I'll meet you in the hall."

Hadrian didn't make a move for the door.

"Are you going to go?" I said, prompting him to leave.

Hadrian rubbed the back of his neck and smiled. "Yes. Sorry. I'm slightly distracted." When he got to the door he turned back around again, his cheeks red. "I will just be out here…"

"Thank you…" I replied.

Hadrian opened his mouth to say something else, but must have decided otherwise and left.

I changed in haste, my cheeks warm when I thought of Hadrian's expression when he looked at me. I pulled on a spare set of clothes, a mismatch of training and formal wear. With the passing seconds, I expected the phantom to show itself again, and I didn't want to be alone a moment longer.

⌒

THE WALK WAS silent, not a single word said between us. I caught Hadrian's wondering glance every now and then, but still he didn't say a word.

I recognized this part of the palace, the same corridors, candelabras and gilded mirrors I passed with the Commander on my first day. We were headed for Hadrian's quarters. It wasn't that I was expecting something different. But with each step in the direction of his room, my anticipation built.

It was evident that the palace was filling up. Everywhere we passed Niraen elves stood crowding the numerous hallways, each wearing the gold bands on their arms. When Hadrian passed they bowed and raised their golden wrists at him, a sign that they had joined for him.

Hadrian looked ahead the entire time, paying no mind to those we passed. I smiled at them for him, nodding thanks to those who so desperately wanted to be seen. I could see the disappointment reflected in their eyes when their prince ignored them.

We reached the end of another corridor, one of them reached out for him. Hadrian didn't see the elf move, not until her hand was clasped on his wrist. It all happened so fast. Hadrian turned and yanked his arm from the elfin's grasp, shouting in surprise. She recoiled.

Everyone was watching and Hadrian knew it. He looked up, rubbing his wrist as if her touch had hurt him, and hurried forward. His reaction brought out whispers amongst the crowd. We continued to walk, only stopping when we reached the door to his room.

"What happened back there?" I asked, reaching for his shoulder.

"She scared me, that's all. I suppose I am still on edge after what happened in Nasamel."

I could understand. I opted to drop the conversation before I stepped too far.

"You look nice." His hushed compliment sent warm tendrils to squeeze at my stomach. He pushed the door open and I attempted to hide my smile when I passed him.

"Thank you." I blushed.

It was the first time I'd been back in his room since that morning. The pink light of the sunset reflected on the spines of the books that took up every spare inch of the room. It filtered in from the windows above his desk, giving the room a different mood to when I first visited it.

A subtle musty scent was covered by the heavy aromas of the burning incense and scented candles that dripped wax onto the stone floor from their holders. A table had been set up in the middle of the room. Its four dark wooden legs each carved by hand, the details were precise and intricate.

A velvet purple cloth covered the surface of the table and hung over the sides, spilling onto the floor. Bowls of meats and fruit had been placed across it, still steaming and fresh.

My stomach rumbled as I moved closer to it.

Hadrian was behind me, pulling a chair out from the table and gesturing for me to sit. "Please…"

Once I sat, Hadrian pushed me from behind until I was eased beneath the table. "I hope you like figs and duck. It is my favorite combination, so I requested it for tonight."

"I can't say I've ever tried a fig, but duck is a favorite of mine." I'd only had it once before and I could still conjure the memory of its pleasurable taste.

Hadrian moved for his own chair, a smile still plastered on his face. "Well, I hope this exceeds all expectations." He lifted the metal cover off two plates and the most incredible smell washed over me.

I looked at him, really looked. He was handsome, more so than I had cared to notice before. The side of his face was pink from the sunset, extenuating his sharp jaw and high cheekbones. His dark, wavy hair had been tucked neatly into a ponytail. The same circlet I had seen him wearing before held his hair in place. It was the first time I noticed the faint scar that ran through his left brow. It was subtle, but now that I'd noticed it, it was hard to miss.

"Where do we start?" Hadrian questioned, pouring a deep, red liquid into a crystal glass and pushing it over the table towards me.

I coughed, clearing my throat. "Anything but what happened with Petrer. I'd be glad to forget about it for now."

Hadrian lifted his full glass, "Out of sight, out of mind."

I relaxed at his response and lifted my glass to his until they clinked together. We both took a long sip. The liquid graced my tongue and my cheeks clenched from the sour twang of the drink.

Hadrian chuckled from his seat, "Never tasted wine before?"

He already knew the answer. I wiped a drop of wine from the corners of my lips. "No, never. What's it made from?"

He swirled his glass before him, allowing the red liquid to dance in his glass. "It is made from a fruit called grapes. It is not common in Thessolina but is from the lush jungles of—"

"Eldnol, I know. Your father showed them to me when I had the audience with him. But I had no idea they could be turned into a drink."

"Father has a way of getting what he wants…" I caught his eye roll. "As I am sure you are aware."

I nodded, "Still, I don't understand why he would lie."

"I am finding it hard to process what you have told me. But I believe you, something is off about all of this." Hadrian began to eat and I did the same. I just didn't want to be the first to start. "But it seems that father has not been the only one to lie about something. What about your little secret you have kept so hidden until Nasamel?"

"And yours," I replied, stuffing a forkful of duck into my mouth.

"It would seem we are a kingdom built on lies. But from today I would like at least for us to be entirely honest with one another." Hadrian didn't look up as he spoke. "Do you think you could do that?"

I played with the food on my plate. Pushing a pile of buttered beans around whilst I looked at Hadrian stuffing food into his mouth, his lips stained red from the wine. I didn't know what to say. How to respond. I wanted honesty, at least with someone. I was built on lies and half-truths, since childhood I'd hidden a big part of me. Even with Petrer I was never truly honest and open. I couldn't help but think that was why he did what he did. A punishment for my deceptions.

I nodded, focusing on my plate. "I would like that."

"Good," Hadrian replied, "So let's start with your secret. I will ask you again, what are you?"

I almost laughed. "Despite everything, that has been the one truth I can stand by. I don't know what I am."

Hadrian looked puzzled but then smiled. "I believe you. Since that is part of our new pact. How long have you known about your power?"

"For as long as I can remember. It's always been a part of me."

"And your parents, they never told you or gave any indication they knew what it was?" he asked.

"No. It was a conversation that was never allowed. I gave up on answers a long time ago. What about you though?" I changed the direction of attention back to him, "You were going to tell me this morning what you are before we had to leave the tavern."

"Ah, yes. I have something that may help with that explanation." Hadrian's chair screeched across the floor and he stood from the table. I watched him with intent whilst he moved over to the right of the room, closest to the desk and the wall of bookshelves. He riffled through the stacks of books, muttering to himself whilst he searched.

"What are you looking for?" I asked, staring at the back of his head from my seat.

"A book," he said, not turning to address me. "Do you enjoy reading?"

"I suppose, although it was rare for me to get books back home, they usually cost a pretty coin."

Hadrian scratched his head and he released a pleased sigh, pulling one book from a pile that almost toppled over. "That is a shame. I enjoy it very much, as you can tell. This book is one of my favorites though and is an essential read. It depicts our history all in a thousand or so pages…"

Hadrian pulled a thick book from the shelves and moved back to the table. With one hand, he pushed my plate to the side and dropped it before me, dust billowing from its cover. "As you can tell it's been a while since I've read it."

I ran my hand over its worn leather surface. It was bigger than any book I'd seen before. Its face was bare, not a single word or mark to be seen. Whereas on its spine, silver thread covered it and three pressed letters stood out against the worn surface.

S. T. H.

"It's... huge." I said, running a finger over the three letters.

"That's not the first time I've heard that. Oh, you're talking about the book, my bad." He winked. I shot him a look, trying to keep my face straight, but failing.

"Is it impossible for you to not make jokes at the most inappropriate times?" I had to bite my lip to stop myself from laughing.

"You know the answer to that," he replied, sitting once again and taking a swig of his wine. "Open it."

The first few pages were blank, yellowed and faded at the edges. I flipped through until I reached the first page with the neatest handwriting I'd ever seen.

I read the words aloud. "Dalibael, A history. Has someone written an entire book about the Goddess?" I asked, "I didn't think there was this much to know about."

"Yes, S. T. Hallis was believed to be a druid historian. Well, that is the only information I have worked out from the book. Not much is known about her as this is the only book of its kind and I am not willing to give it over to historians to study. It was passed down from my mother to me. It is special."

"But the druids died out hundreds of years ago. There hasn't been mention of them since the great war. I thought the peace treaty eradicated all documents and artefacts about them?" I said, imagining her rune covered face.

"Correct, that is another reason why I have not passed it on. It would be destroyed straight away," Hadrian said.

"So, why is a druid writing about our Goddess? I would think they would focus on their own God, since that is who created them."

"Not all the druids followed their creator just like some elves do not accept Dalibael as their Goddess. Don't be so quick to assume."

"But how does this explain what you are? Are you a druid?"

"Not quite, although what I am is a product of their existence." He reached over the small space between us. "Let me help you find the right page."

Giving up on looking over the table he stood once again and came to stand behind me.

Hadrian bent over my shoulder, his face close to the side of mine. He flipped the pages over until he found what he was looking for and pointed to the first line and read aloud.

"When Dalibael, Goddess of Light, created life in the form of elves, death was also created to keep the natural balance. They called him Vorlcas, the God of Shadow, or night depending on the translation. Vorlcas was jealous of Dalibael's creations, each a reflection of her image so he created the druids, masters of dark power and shadow in his image."

"I know this story…" I said, looking over the drawing on the page before me. A towering shadow of darkness etched into the yellowed page.

"For years, since the eradication of the druids, the three elven continents have worked hard to erase all mentions of Vorlcas from our history. Although the druids have all been killed, how can you destroy death itself? For those who believe, Vorlcas still reigns in the dark, just like Dalibael still rules in the light."

"But what has this got to do with you? I don't understand."

I was even more aware of how close Hadrian was when he ran his finger over the lines of the book and turned to the next page.

"During the great war, the druids worked with dark magick to create creatures to aid them in victory. Although the creatures and their magick ultimately backfired on them. Druids, like their creator, are masters of death, *not* life. So, in creating these beasts they used magick aligned with Dalibael thus meaning she owned these beasts and had control." I followed his finger to the word that stood out more than any other on the page. The ink darker than the rest around it.

My voice didn't sound like my own, the word twisted and awkward in my mouth when I read it aloud:

"***Dragori.***"

CHAPTER

TWENTY-FOUR

THERE WAS SOMETHING familiar about the word. As I repeated it under my breath I filtered through the haze of days that'd passed, searching for where I'd heard it.

My finger went white under the pressure whilst I pressed it onto the page, my mind lost to the word.

"You have heard of *Dragori* before. I can tell by your face," Hadrian said, the name sounding even more beautiful coming from his lips. His slight accent extenuated the vowels, giving the word more meaning than it did on the page before me.

I knew I had, but I couldn't tell if it was exhaustion or confusion that prevented me from reaching the stored memory. "I believe so, but again, I am not sure. Everything is a little overwhelming." I gestured to the book. "This Dragori, it that what you are?"

He nodded, whispering, "Yes."

"And what exactly is a Dragori? You said it had something to do with the druids and a curse, but they died long before you were born so how could you be cursed?" A headache was brewing in the back of my mind, I could feel its presence growing as I spoke.

"So many questions."

"Just tell me, Hadrian, less of the cryptic bullshit and more answers!" I slammed my palm on the table.

I cringed at how harsh I sounded, but my want for answers was too great to care about how I got them.

"Dragori are very similar to shifters. The druids created them but could not control them." He took a breath, "The book suggests that the Goddess took them under her power and blessed them each with a gift. The four Dragori were linked to the druid's powers because they were created from it, and thus were the only beings able to destroy the druids. A magick matched in power to that it was born from. These four protectors each represent an element of the Goddess, magick to aid them in her fight to destroy their ever-spreading darkness."

I looked over the page again, passing my eyes over a new drawing.

"I still don't understand. If you are a Dragori, how old are you? The end of the war was hundreds of years ago."

I looked at Hadrian, searching for any hidden signs of old age.

"I am no different from your age, Petal. Those four guardians have long passed. Elves may have a longer life span than druids, but we still die, that cannot be prevented. Truthfully, I am not sure how I came to be cursed, the book doesn't explain the passing of the gifts. But I do know I am one of four."

"How do you know though? I've heard of the great war, but never the Dragori, it sounds like nothing but a story."

If my mind was not full of overwhelming information before, this really tipped me over the edge. A deranged laugh slipped past my lips. I fell into a fit of giggles, my entire body shaking in the chair. "You really had me for a moment." I closed the book and pushed it away from me.

Hadrian didn't laugh back. I jammed my fork back into my food and began to eat, ignoring his glare.

"If you are not going to take this seriously then what is the point?" His disappointment cut into me like the knife strapped to his belt.

"I am taking it serious Hadrian, but it all sounds like a made-up story. Fiction. A story told to younglings like that of the beasts living in the forests and the monsters in the sea."

"It is no story, Zacriah." I didn't like how he used my full name. "And if my suspicions are correct, it explains your power as well."

"You really are joking with me. I'm not cursed or blessed or whatever a *Dragori* is."

"It's the only explanation for your magick and there is a way to check."

"Feel free to elaborate."

Hadrian moved from the table and I kept my eyes on him as he walked to his desk. I couldn't see what he was doing beneath it, but I heard a drawer slide open and the rustle of something as he reached within.

He held something in his hands. I squinted at it but saw that it was nothing more than a bundle of white silk. Hadrian threw the bundle toward me, but midway through the air the white silk fluttered away and the object concealed in its folds was headed straight for my face.

My reflexes kicked in and I caught the unknown object before it hit me.

I gazed into my open hand and admired the chain I'd caught, heavy and cold in my hands. A large circular pendent hung from the end, etched into the surface was the Niraen emblem.

Gold.

Pain shot, hot and sharp, across my palm. I dropped the chain to the floor but the scent of burnt flesh wafted into my nose. I looked to my palm, gripping my wrist to block the pain, to see a burn mark. Hadrian was already next to me, a dripping wet cloth in his hands ready to press onto my palm.

"What in the Goddess was that?!"

"I think I may be right…" he whispered over my shoulder, holding my hand out to press the wet cloth onto it. The chain lay next to my feet. I kicked at it, sending it skirting across the floor away from me. "Pure gold is toxic to Dragori. That's what I gather from the book. And because I also have the same reaction."

"So, thought you would risk it and check by giving me something that might hurt me?" It was more of a shout than a question.

"You're right, I shouldn't have done that." Hadrian look displeased with himself.

"That's what happened in the corridor with the elfin woman," I said, "The gold band she wore, it hurt you."

"Yes. I panicked when she got close." The necklace was his mother's. I looked beneath the table, to where my kick had sent it and apologized.

"I didn't know it belonged to her," I said, but Hadrian only shook his head in dismissal.

"You said Dragori are like shifters, but I've never been able to shift. Ever."

"I don't know what that means. I agree it is odd, but I know someone who may be able to help us out with our questions," Hadrian said.

"Who?"

The door to the room swung open and Alina emerged from the shadows of the corridor beyond. My body ran cold, just like it had with the phantom I saw in the bath.

"Prince Hadrian…" She bowed, shooting me a quick glance before she closed the door.

"How can we help you, Commander?" His voice had lost all edge of concern that had laced it only moments before. He still held my hand, not once letting go as he addressed her.

"I apologize, I was unaware you had company. I have been told to pass the news that King Dalior has requested an audience with you, the matter is urgent." The side of her thin mouth twitched into a smile.

"You can tell my father that I will be there in a matter of moments, after I finish up here."

"But—"

"Please leave us and report back to Dalior immediately. Tell him I am on my way."

"He would prefer if I waited with you."

"Immediately."

His words were final. Alina's face lost all hint of her smugness. Hadrian's request was clear, her presence was not wanted for another moment. I looked to my feet, trying to force the smile from my face.

"As you wish," she replied and turned for the door, but paused with her fist clenched around the threshold. "I notice your guards have been sent away. I will ensure they are returned immediately. I know it will put King Dalior's mind at ease."

I looked up to Hadrian to see him smiling.

"Thank you, Commander. They must have lost their way."

I was sure she muttered something under her breath when she turned, opened the door and left. She didn't close the door behind her so we could both hear her footsteps fade into the dark corridor.

"Well thank you, Zacriah, for joining me this evening, I was happy to show my appreciation for your actions at Nasamel." I caught the wink when he spoke, his tone still heavy with every word. He flickered his eyes toward the open door and mouthed Alina. *She could be out there listening.*

"You are more than welcome, my Prince. I do hope that will be the only time your life is put in danger."

"I am aware that my father rewarded your actions by revoking your morning duties, but I too have something to give you."

He pulled me up and guided me out the door. If I looked away from him I would have missed him slip the book from the table into the folds of a spare cloak and place it under his arm.

Really, I mouthed. Nothing but a hush of air leaving my lips. His nod was enough to tell me he was being truthful.

"Thank you, that is awfully kind."

"Please, follow me." He passed the folded cloak to me, the weight of it heavy from the hidden book.

We left his room behind, moving down the corridor. Flame lit candles hung from holders in the walls, giving enough light to clear the darkened path ahead. Hadrian didn't utter a word, but I understood why. I could too feel a slight presence lurking in the shadows, Alina was still close by. He only reached an arm behind him when he walked, his hand grasping mine.

We reached our destination in a matter of moments, it was only down the corridor from his. Stopping before a dark oak door, he finally spoke.

"This is your new sleeping arrangements. My gift to you as thanks for saving me. And after the way I saw your *friend*, Petrer, react to you back in your old room, I think it best you keep away from him for now. It is only down the way from mine so please do call on me if you ever need me."

I knew not to complain or ask any questions, not with Alina's presence still creeping at the back of my mind.

He turned the brass handle of the door and pushed it open. "I hope it is up to your standards…"

The room was large, twice the size of the sleeping quarters I'd been sleeping in. A four-poster bed took up most of the space toward the far-left wall. White silken material hung from each poster, billowing in the stream of wind that blew through the pair of large windows on the main wall of the room. A small dresser sat beside the bed and a large wardrobe against a wall to the left, leaving a vast open space big enough to store five, fully grown elks. The vaulted ceiling cast slight shadows across the marble floor that we walked across. It was more than I could ever have imagined.

The click of the door being closed behind me sounded and I turned to Hadrian who held a finger to his lips.

I turned back to the room and walked to the window closest to me. The view beyond made the one in the previous room look pathetic. I was sure on a clear, sunny day I would be able to see the two other continents even from hundreds of miles away.

"I knew you would like it," Hadrian whispered in my ear. "It is safe to talk now, the stone walls are thick, oak doors prevent those who listen from hearing anything." He reached both hands around me and lifted the bundle of cloak that held the book from beneath my arms before moving off in the direction of the dresser to place it down. My skin prickled from the lack of space.

"I hope the same applied when we were in your room," I said, turning from the window to face him. He sat perched on the edge of my bed, the sheets crinkling beneath him.

"Absolutely, Alina would not have been able to hear a thing."

"Good." I yawned.

"I think it would be best if we cease our conversation and return to it tomorrow. Would you feel up for going on a little trip with me in the morning? I would like to begin testing out your magick to see just how much control you have over it."

"Will we be visiting the person who can find out what's wrong with me?"

Hadrian's laughed. "Nothing is *wrong* with you. And no. Unfortunately, he is out of town, but will be back in a few days. Until then, do not worry about what I have told you about the Dragori. Your late age and the fact you have not experienced a shift suggests it is likely your magick is not a result of you being one. But it will do no harm for you to read up about it in the meantime." He gestured to the mound on the dresser next to him. "Get some rest. And I shall see you in the morning."

"Thank you for supper," I said as Hadrian moved to the door, and I to the bed.

"It was my pleasure. Sweet dreams, Petal."

I watched him leave, already anticipating the comfortable sleep that waited for me. I felt the soft mattress beneath me and knew I was going to experience the best sleep yet. But when I slipped into the sheets and pulled my hair from the bun, part of me wanted to see Hadrian come back.

Tomorrow couldn't come soon enough.

CHAPTER

TWENTY-FIVE

I KNOCKED MY feet against the side of my elk, urging it to move faster. Hadrian rode ahead on Elmirr who sprang up the hill before me. Compared to Elmirr, my elk was slower. It may have been due to the fact that it had shorter legs and a rounder frame. But I didn't mind, it was just nice to be away from the palace.

The sun beat down on my face, wrapping me in cocoon of warmth. My arms tingled from its rays and I was sure that by the end of the day more freckles would show themselves across my arms and nose.

My new brown leather boots felt stiff on my feet, unworn. I felt the bite of a fresh blister on my ankles with every movement. It was Hadrian who'd suggested before we left that I dressed like one of the royal guard, rose gold-plated shoulder armour above a purple top and leather slacks. His argument was that I would blend in, no one would question the Prince leaving with one of his guards.

It made sense, I couldn't blame him for his cunning thinking. He'd dodged the two guards that had been stationed to watch over him today before he came to get me. He'd then used me as a decoy whilst we left the palace. It would last for a while, but it wouldn't take long for word to get around. No matter how authentic I was.

"They are still going to notice that you're missing!" I said, kicking my elk into a trot to catch up with Hadrian. "And as soon as someone notices that I'm also missing, they will put two and two together and come looking for us."

He turned and smiled down at me, Elmirr towering over me. I looked up to him, squinting at the light that cast a halo around him. "Has anyone ever told you that you worry too much?"

"They hate me. I don't think it's wise that we add more fuel to their burning fires," I replied, ignoring his comment.

Hadrian flicked a finger and pointed it to the sky. A burst of flame shot to life and danced across his hand. "Have you forgotten about me and fire? Even if we do add *fuel to their fire* I will just have to be there to put it out. Won't I?" Hadrian chuckled, closing his hand into a fist and extinguishing the flame.

"It comes so easily to you," I said, hoping he would do it again.

"I am glad you are impressed." Hadrian leaned forward and whispered into Elmirr's ear. She had been startled by the flame and was twitching all over the place.

"I am."

The view from the top of the hill was incredible. We walked in tandem across a worn path in the grass, Hadrian up ahead and me behind. I peered to the left and all I saw was the endless cliff face of white chalk. My stomach jumped but I still peered over, enough to see the sharp drop into the ocean and the many birds that flew in and out of the cliff face.

"I would not get so close, *Petal*, many before you have given into the lure of the view and ended up becoming a part of it." Hadrian's words sent shivers across my arms.

"I'm pretty good with heights, and plus, I don't think the many before me had the same abilities as me." Saying it aloud felt strange. The kind of strange that I could get used to. It was so easy to be open with Hadrian, to forget the years of hiding in one evening and be honest.

Hadrian turned to look at me, taking his eyes off where he was going. I cringed when Elmirr tilted close to the edge, sending dirt flying into the abyss.

"I have been wondering about how you ended up outside of the palace on your first night, I think you may have just answered that for me." Hadrian twisted his entire body around to face me.

"Would you watch where you are going?"

Elmirr's hoof slipped again, a shower of dirt falling into the depths below.

"And yes. Like I said, heights have never bothered me."

"Good to know…" Hadrian replied.

It was the first time I'd been to the southern part of Olderim, its beauty was paramount.

I looked around and saw endless hills and long grasslands. The view was dotted with buttery dandelions specking the ground like the stars in a night sky. The occasional tree stood proud amongst the scenery, bent and beautiful like a statue stuck in time.

I turned behind, looking back at the city we'd left. From this high up, it seemed miniature, small enough to fit in the palm of my hand. As I looked around I couldn't help but think of Mam and how she would love to be next to me. She'd always spent her days painting scenic views on faded parchment.

My chest tightened when I thought of her, but I didn't dare complain. Not with Hadrian close by.

Considering King Dalior's threats of the Morthi invasion, it was odd to see no protection over the seas. Not a single ship or boat to guard Olderim. It only added to the worry that his entire accusation was a lie.

"Come see this!" Hadrian shouted ahead. My elk moved forward to Hadrian's call, not needing my guidance. I reached the crest of another hill where Hadrian waited atop and looked down across the sea of cream tents below.

"Is this what I think it is?" I asked, unable to count how many there were.

"I had heard father petitioned for a camp to be created, for those who signed up to join his military. Looks like his response was successful."

The small bodies of hundreds of elves weaved amongst the pitched tents below. They looked like ants from here. Small moving dots shifting amongst burning fires, hundreds possibly thousands of them.

I couldn't take my eyes off the camp; I was lost in the vision. Hadrian had already moved away but I didn't notice, not until he shouted my name. I turned to see him, not expecting that he had dismounted. He'd tied Elmirr to a tree close by and helped me down from my elk to do the same.

I leaned against the tree and rubbed at my feet. As I fussed, pink blossoms fell from a branch and scattered across the ground around me. They stood out on the green ground like droplets of fresh Niraen blood.

I pulled a skin pouch of water that hung from my belt, and tipped the contents into my mouth, spilling some down my chin. The water was warm and the moment it touched my stomach an empty ache spread across me. *I shouldn't have missed breakfast.*

Hadrian turned for me, his hand outstretched. "May I?"

I nodded and passed the water to him, watching the lump in his throat bob whilst took large swigs.

"Are you going to tell me where we are going?" I asked.

"We still have a small walk before we get there so you can just wait and see."

"But why? There's nothing for miles around here. What is possibly that exciting to be kept such a secret?"

"It is less what we are going to see and more what we are going to do. And plus, the further we are from prying eyes the better."

~

FIRST, I WAS to lift the leaf from Hadrian's open hand and bring it towards myself. It was easy, a trick I'd practiced many times as I waited in trees and hid in bushes during a hunt.

Without much concentration, I allowed a sliver of magick to escape from the cage. I lifted a hand, calling for the wind to respond to my plea.

And it did.

The leaf levitated and held still in the air inches above Hadrian's hand. Being one for dramatics and because I felt excited that I was finally able to share my power with someone, I decided to complete the task with a flare.

I narrowed in on the leaf, creating a small cyclone around it. Hadrian tried to keep up when the leaf jumped to life and spun up into the air.

I could sense the stream of air as well as feel my own heart beating. It was natural, easy. My mind whispered to the wind, urging it to spin the leaf faster. I waited for the right moment and just when Hadrian reached out for it I changed its direction, urging it to dive between his legs.

In seconds, I plucked the leaf from the air before it flew past me. I looked back to Hadrian who clapped, his face full of glee.

"Incredible, truly remarkable!"

"I've had a lot of practice and time alone to perfect simple parlor tricks. I *do* hope you have something a bit more challenging for me. That was piss easy." I winked, waiting for his next instruction.

It seemed my taunting had knocked the tasks up a notch.

Hadrian walked away from me and stopped in the distance. He was so far away that I couldn't see the details of his face, but didn't miss when he reached for his bow.

He notched three arrows and held it ready to fire.

The task was simple enough, but not something I'd had practice in. Before Hadrian had walked off, he explained that I was to stop the arrows just like I had in Nasamel.

One was easy, but three, not so much.

I opened my legs into a wider stance, raising both hands before me and I waited.

Bring it on.

I closed my fist, urging my magick to harden the air around me.

I stilled my breathing and reached a hand of magick for Hadrian. He stood, holding the arrows and bow ready, but not releasing them. I held onto my concentrations and power, just in time for the arrows to be released at me.

I moved with speed. I threw a hand up, slicing a beam of air at them. I met one, throwing it downwards into the ground. One down.

That left two. I pushed more magick from my cage. The second arrow went down to the ground. Two down.

The final one was a blur. I panicked, and threw a blast of air at it. I closed my eyes as an explosion of flames scattered across the arrow and it connected with my shield.

I looked up, cringing from the heat encasing my shield. Fire spreading rapidly over it. The air fed into the fire, urging it to burn stronger in hues of blue and purple. Unnatural.

Panting, I clenched my fist, dissipating the wall and the fire with it.

Hadrian's form came into view when the flames disappeared, his mocking smile spread from ear to ear. "For someone who does not know what they are, you sure know how to use your magick."

"I didn't expect you to pull a stunt like that …" I replied, stuffing the power back inside the cage against its will. "I thought it was my magick you wanted to test, not your own."

Fire danced in patches across the grass around me. Hadrian only looked at it and the flames ceased their burning. "You should know by now, always expect the unexpected with me."

"Oh, I do," I whispered, trying to catch my breath.

"I think it's time we move on but before we do I have to ask. Did you get to the book I left with you last night?" Hadrian asked, dropping to the bow to the ground.

"No, it's not exactly the most interesting bedtime story," I replied. "But I have been wanting to ask you something."

"Ask away, I'm *all* yours."

"When did you find out you were a Dragori?" I asked, biting into a plum I'd packed in my sack and passing one to him.

"When I was six moons old, it was during a temper tantrum. I had scared my nanny close to death when I set her dress on fire. Mother managed to bribe the nanny not to tell. She feared the rumours that would spread. The accusations of me having power that should not be possible for a Niraen." It was clear that Hadrian felt troubled when reliving the memory. "Mother took me to a local empath, a man who lived in the outskirts of Olderim. In fact, the same man I will be taking you to see when he returns from Eldnol. He confirmed what I was, after diving into my mind through his mystic ways."

An empath, I knew that was something I would be bringing up again, my promise to Nyah stuffed at the back of my mind.

"He informed us to keep it to ourselves, promised that he would provide us with information on my aliment that came in the form of the book I have lent to you."

"And your father, King Dalior, what did he think?" I asked.

"He does not know. It was my mother's and my little secret. I suppose holding onto that makes me feel like I still have a grasp on her, even though she is no longer here."

"I'm sorry for bringing it up. I couldn't imagine how hard it must be to lose a mother." I reached out across the empty space between us and rested my hand on his crossed knee.

"Nothing to be sorry about. It feels good to talk about her, I am not able to do it often. Father has not spoken about her since she died, it is almost like that part of him died with her."

I rubbed my thumb in circles on his thigh, hoping it filled him with some sort of comfort. "I am honoured you feel like you can talk to me about it."

Hadrian didn't reply with words, only with a subtle smile.

"I did read about something…" I added, deciding the best thing to do was to direct the conversation away from painful memories.

He looked up with a glint in his deep, golden eyes. "Go on."

"It didn't say much about what it is you can shift into. But there was a drawing that caught my attention."

Hadrian stood, "I know the image. Would you like to see it first hand?"

"But what is it? There was no explanation nor description for what the image showed, and even that was faded and poorly drawn."

"Not many elves have seen the Dragori in its true form. I think it's best if I just show you... Now you are going to have to be patient with me, it has been a while since I have shifted." Hadrian rolled his shoulders, stretching his head from side to side.

There was no scent, no smoke and no sign that the shift had even began. Not like what I was used to seeing with Petrer.

His skin rippled from the ground up. His hands changing first. His fingers lengthened, his nails growing into sharp, claw-like points. A shadow separated from his back and hung in the air before solidifying. Wings protruded behind him, a dark web of thick membrane, vein-like marks visible from the sun that shone through them.

Hadrian flexed, bringing his wings wide and relaxing them like he was a child learning to walk. Their span was great, almost six feet wide on both sides.

I looked at him, my mouth had dropped open. Two horns stood proud on his head, rounding into a spiral. As well as the wings, horns, and sporadic scales that seemed to cover random sections of his exposed skin, I also noticed his height. He was a monster. Two fangs lapped over his bottom lip and his nose had seemed to flatten on his beast of a face.

"If you could only see your face." Hadrian voice was deeper than before. He rested his clawed hands onto his hips, and I noticed how his clothes had stretched and ripped during the shift.

"I-I—" I couldn't seem to find the words to reply.

"Do not worry, Petal, I only bite when asked."

TWENTY-SIX

"YOU LOOK LIKE…"

"A dragon?" he answered for me, his wings flexed behind him.

"I was going to say something more along the lines of a bat-goat hybrid, but sure, dragon works."

The drawing in the book was the spitting image of what Hadrian looked like.

"But how? Dragons are story book creatures. Not real," I said, stunned into disbelief.

"Where there is smoke, there is *always* fire. Dragons are not real, they are a product of whispers that have mutated over the years. The Dragori, as the book explains if you actually bothered to read it, are very much the fire that caused the smoke of dragons."

"But what if someone sees you?"

"Do not worry yourself, in this form I have better senses than even the best Alorian elf. I will hear anyone before they even get close enough to see. No one ever comes this far up from Olderim anyway."

I couldn't take my eyes of him.

"Impressive, right?" Hadrian said, his wings moving behind him, as if they had a mind of their own.

"Very." It was the most incredible thing I'd ever seen. I stood up and walked to where he was. I ran a hand down the side of his face, my fingers brushing over the overlapping scales patched on his jaw. "Does it hurt?"

"Not at all. Not since the first time I shifted, even the memory of that is painful."

"Well, I can honestly say this has never happened to me. Ever." I couldn't take my eyes off him.

I had so many questions. I couldn't believe what stood before me.

A deep growling sound came from the base of Hadrian's throat. I looked at it and there seemed to be a glow of red fire coursing beneath his skin.

"Was that what I think it was?" I asked, flickering my gaze between his eyes and neck.

"In this form, I am connected more to my element than normal. I can do all sorts, just you wait and see."

The force of his wings knocked me backwards. I stumbled and in one strong swoop, Hadrian shot into the sky, moving into the blue expanse with ease. I shielded my eyes from the sun that beat down above us to see him dancing above. His hulking body trailed effortlessly beneath his wings whilst they kept him aloft.

Hadrian change direction and flew directly toward me. I released a gasp and stumbled back. In one move I was lifted in his arms and taken up into the sky.

The air rushed around us, screaming in my ears. I felt weightless, a feeling I loved. I laughed out loud, my voice lost to the rushing winds so high up. I could see the grass land fields below, far, *far* below. Our elks looked miniature, almost toy-like from this height.

I was so close to Hadrian's face, but his gaze was kept on the horizon. I held onto him, tightly and felt safer than I'd been in the past week.

My eyes streamed from the constant batter of the wind, but I didn't care. Heat radiated off Hadrian, encasing me in comfort. I should've been cold this high up, shooting between clouds, but I knew Hadrian was manipulating his power to warm me. I felt it cover me like a blanket.

∽

WE FLEW UNTIL the sky changed. The sun melted into the horizon and the moon rose high. I couldn't tear my eyes off it, half formed and large before me. I felt as though I could run my hands across it from so high up. My stomach flipped when Hadrian guided us back to the ground. But as my toes landed, I almost fell, my legs unsure and weak from the hours of flight. I looked around us, but didn't recognize where we landed. We'd flown far from our elks.

"I am exhausted!" Hadrian said, catching his breath, his wings held tight against his back. "Yet I wish I could carry on. It has been a long while since I have felt so… free."

His skin was pale. Two dark circles laced below his eyes.

"You'll have to promise me we can do that again sometime," I said, a rush of euphoria filled my whole body.

"When you win the duel, I will take you as much as you want," he replied.

The mention of the duel dampened my mood. "*If* I win."

Hadrian's stomach rumbled so loud I thought it came from his throat. He looked up at me, biting back a laugh. "We have plenty of time. Let's focus on finding the elks and getting back. I am worried if I don't eat soon… I'll have to eat you."

He snapped his fangs at me, his eyes wide.

"Let's hurry then." I replied, jumping back from him as a joke.

"I do not fancy lugging these the entire walk back." His wings shook behind him. "They are heavier then they look."

The ripple started on his horns and by the time it reached his feet he was back to his usual self. His clothes hung off him in tatters, exposing his hard stomach and smooth chest.

Hadrian followed my gaze and looked down over himself. "Well, I cannot go back to Olderim like this. Just imagine the stories. Prince comes back from day with mystery guard with no clothes, or modesty left. I have left a spare set of clothes in my sack, when we find it I will have to change."

"Good idea." I pulled my gaze from his exposed, hard stomach and began to walk off.

It took us a while to find our sacks. Once we did Hadrian changed like he said he would and I packed our belongings to keep myself busy.

We both looked at each other when an animalistic scream lit the sky.

I ran towards its origin, not saying a word, Hadrian close behind.

We passed through the night, our boots slamming against the ground. We both knew what made the noise without having to say it aloud. We ran through the field until the tree that our elks were tethered to came into view.

I looked straight at them.

I saw nothing but blood.

CHAPTER
TWENTY-SEVEN

BLOOD FLOODED THE grass and covered the bark of the tree in splatters. Even the pink blossoms were stained red.

I ran fast for them and tripped, landing on the ground. The fall knocked the wind from my lungs. It gave Hadrian time to pass me and he reached the destruction before I even caught my breath.

I could hear his angered slur from where I was. It urged me to pick myself up and catch up to him. Between the details that greeted me and the pain in my chest, tears blurred my vision and spilled down my face.

The horror of what I saw next sent my stomach turning. Hadrian was sobbing, walking back and forth before Elmirr's body, his hand covering his mouth and the other tugging at his hair. I hung back, shocked by the true state of her.

Goddess, no.

Elmirr had been gutted. From the base of her throat, to the bottom of her stomach.

Her innards had been flung across the ground, some still falling from the open gash. Deep slashes covered her sticky hide, her entire body mutilated beyond belief. Whatever had done had been rushed. I scanned the horizon, reaching for my power, to look for what did this. I saw nothing but the night, I couldn't even see where the grassland ended and the cliff started. The only light was from the moon and the ball of fire that erupted in Hadrian's hand.

My knees slammed into the ground, a jolt of pain crawled up my spine from the impact. I leaned my palms on the ground and vomited. Once my stomach had stopped cramping I could see why my hands felt wet. The ground beneath them was covered in Elmirr's blood. I wiped my hands across my slacks and top, wanting to rid of the blood but it just smudged the stain even more.

There was a whimpering noise and I looked up to see my own elk, hidden behind the tree, its eyes glazed and confused. I pushed myself towards him, stepping over a red bulge that had been scattered on the ground.

I pulled the dagger from my belt, wishing my claws hadn't been left at the palace, and brought it down on the leather strap that connected my elk to the tree.

The strap snapped, and I held firm to the tether and guided my elk away.

My arm screamed whilst he yanked on me, trying to free from my grasp. I could feel the waves of his panic roll off him.

"Who would do this?" My voice shook.

Hadrian still paced, the whites of his eyes red. Blood red. "Not who, but what." He smudged his hand to wipe his tears, only to spread dirt across his face. "Look at the marks... this was an animal attack." I couldn't look at Elmirr, or what was left. "No knife could make such deep, large wounds. Look at her neck..."

I bit my lip and looked, the mark on her neck could only be caused by a creature with large jaws.

"There is no beast around these parts that could do this." His voice shook. "But in Olderim, there are many..."

I didn't have to elaborate. I know what he was suggesting. The shifters.

"It doesn't make sense." My elk was still pulling hard on my arm. I raised a hand to its muzzle and rubbed it in hopes it would help.

"No, Zacriah, it makes perfect sense," he shouted, walking over to me and taking the reins from my hand.

"What are we going to do with her?" I asked, watching him mount my elk.

"We leave her," he replied, reaching a hand for me to climb up behind him.

I wrapped my arms around him, there was not much space on my small elk for two. Hadrian punched the air and a ball of fire spat towards Elmirr. In moments, the entire area was on fire.

I cried into Hadrian's back the entire ride to Olderim, trying not to make a sound. Tear stains pooled on his shirt, but I didn't stop.

Most of the ride I kept my eyes closed, and only opened them when Hadrian cleared his throat. Olderim's main gates were ahead.

We stopped beside the gates and Hadrian whispered to the guard who greeted us. He must have felt me move because he ceased the conversation and carried on through the opening gates.

It was Fadine, I would recognize the helmet anywhere. When I looked back at her ,she was not looking. Her face was staring in the direction of where we'd come from. I looked, following her gaze to see a red glow in the distance.

"I am going to need you to do me a favour," Hadrian whispered. "You must promise me not to mention what has happened to Elmirr."

"I promise."

"Not until I find out who was behind this. And I *will* find out." Hadrian only stared ahead into the dark streets of Masarion when he spoke.

"You think a shifter did it, don't you?"

"I know they did."

"But why?"

"Because whoever it was had been given a command to follow. And there is only one person in charge of the shifters who would be able to conduct such a thing."

⌒

HADRIAN INSISTED ON finding Commander Alina himself. After taking me back to my room, he promised to return as soon as he could.

I paced from one end to the other, unable to stop replaying the haunting thoughts of what had happened.

I'd tried losing myself in the view from my window, but failed. I even picked up the book Hadrian had given me, but was unable to make it past the first page before I gave up.

There was a tap at my door. I ran for it, hoping it was Hadrian who was on the other side. It wasn't. I threw the door open to see Nyah, her face red and hair frayed.

"You can at least pretend you're glad to see me," Nyah said. She walked passed me, into the room without invitation. "So, this is where you've been hiding all day. I don't blame you for not leaving, it's so… fancy."

"I was actually expecting Hadrian."

I looked down the corridor, but saw nothing. I closed the door behind me and turned to Nyah. She laid herself down on my bed, both her boots resting on my clean sheets. "Well, it's taken me ages to find you. Trying to get directions to your room was like drawing blood from a stone. I suppose I'd be hiding up here though too, everyone is talking about it."

My heart stopped. "Talking about what?"

"Tomorrow…"

"Tomorrow what?" I asked. Nyah looked at me like I was crazy for even asking.

She leaned up on her elbows, one eyebrow raised. "Are you kidding? You haven't even been told?"

"Nyah," I shouted, frustration taking hold. "Told what?"

She raised both hands in defence, "I can't believe I'm the one telling you this. We were all told during breakfast that the duel has been brought forward to tomorrow."

Everything stopped.

I stumbled for something to grasp onto. Nyah was already by my side, hoisting me up and directing me to the bed. I couldn't think. I couldn't breathe. Panic constricted around my legs and black spots covered my vision.

This couldn't be happening. Why is this happening?

On cue Hadrian burst through the door and looked to Nyah first, then to me. I saw three of him.

"She told you…" he said, closing the door behind him.

I tried to listen but the loud rush of blood in my ears muffled everything Nyah said to him. My eyes were focused to a spot on the stone wall beside Hadrian's head.

"I could not find her, no one knows where she is. It was father who told me about the duel, it was his idea. I am so sorry, this isn't right. Everything is just so *fucked* up." He was talking about the Commander. But still his words were nothing but a jumble in my mind.

I pressed the heels of my palms to my eyes, flashes of light burst behind my lids. Neither Nyah nor Hadrian said another word, not until I spoke.

"It's all just so convenient." I said.

"What do you mean?" Nyah leaned forward and rubbed a thumb into my shoulder.

I trusted her as much as I did Hadrian, but I could tell by his eyes that he didn't want me to tell her.

Hadrian cut in, saving me from having to lie to Nyah. "I shall attempt to speak with father and see if I can prevent the duel or at least put it off until the original date. But do not expect it. I can promise you, I will try everything in my power to stop this." He turned to Nyah. "Stay with him until I return. He is going to need you."

I wanted to tell him to stay. To stop him from leaving me, but I couldn't muster the words.

～

NYAH HELPED ME change out of my clothes. I relaxed into her silence, thankful for her presence.

"On another day, I might ask why there is blood on your shirt and hands..." she said, guiding me to the bed. "But I shall not pry tonight. Give me your hand. You are going to need to get some rest so let me help you. Just close your eyes and give into me. I'll wake you if Hadrian returns." Her voice was soft, like a lullaby.

I didn't have the energy or the want to refuse. In fact, the idea of sleep was too inviting to ignore. I gave her my hand and in moments it was alight with her deep glow.

I gave into her magick and felt my mind melt into a forced sleep.

"Stay with me," I murmured before I gave into the wave of sleep.

CHAPTER

TWENTY-EIGHT

THE WORLD CREPT into life as sleep left me. I felt weightless of worry. Light brushed against my closed lids, urging to me greet it. I peered around my room, dazed and eyes heavy. Then, the events of yesterday came crashing down over me.

I shot up. Nyah choked on a snore beside me where she was laying above the sheets. I nudged her feet resting on the pillow next to my head, but she didn't wake. I looked at her, rubbing the sleep dust from the corners of my eyes, her face covered by her mound of red hair. She'd stayed with me, I remembered asking her to.

It was bright outside, a beautiful clear day, different to the dark clouds in my mind. In a matter of hours, I would be put on display for the entire palace. To duel, when I was not prepared. Not in any sense of the word.

I forced myself to sit over the side of the bed. Hadrian hadn't returned, which meant he had no news regarding the duel being postponed. It was going ahead, the thought sickened me.

Nyah groaned behind me and I felt the bed shift as she rolled over. It must have been the first time she'd stayed asleep this long. Morning service in the kitchens must've been called off. I'd let her sleep a while longer, she needed the rest.

I decided to pass the time by shuffling around the room. The cold stone nipped at my bare feet, but was not enough of a distraction whilst I waited for Nyah to wake, or Hadrian to turn up.

The call of seagulls greeted me beyond the window. It sounded like laughter, mocking me. I pulled the doors open to my wardrobe, trying to find the most suitable outfit for the day. If I wanted any chance, I would need something flexible and tight fitting. Whichever guard the Commander picked would be well skilled and I didn't want them to have any more of a chance.

I decided on a plain, black top and the same slacks I'd worn to the Antler & Cart. They still stank of smoke; the smell was rancid.

I pulled the clothes on and something soft fell onto my foot. My breath caught when I glanced down at the bloodied cloth, stained grey and red.

I picked it up, studying the cloth for what must have been the millionth time since Nasamel.

"What you got there?" Nyah squeaked, stretching her freckled arms and clicking her neck from side to side.

"Just another reminder that I'm completely fucked and even the Goddess is against me."

"Good morning to you too," Nyah replied, brushing the hair from her face. "You really need to stop this pity party you're having for yourself. I'm not buying into it."

"Do I sound that bad?" I slunk over to the bed and sat beside her.

She took the cloth from my hand and rocked back. "This is what you showed the prince…"

She ran her hands over the cloth, studying it carefully.

"Do you think you could work your empath power on it?"

"Usually not, but the blood, there is a slight residue of emotion trapped to it. Like a mark or memory." She shrugged her shoulders and held it out for me.

I thrusted it back at her, the excitement of getting some answers was too much to pass up. "Try again, see what you can find out from it. I know it doesn't belong to the Morthi, but if there is a possibility you can find out whose blood it belongs to then—"

"Zacriah, even if I did that how in hell am I going to know who it belongs to? It could be anyone's or anything!"

"Please, just try."

There was a knock at the door. Without needing to be told, Nyah shoved the cloth beneath her and we both looked up as it swung open.

Two guards walked in first, sending my nerves a blaze. Hadrian followed in close behind, his face showing no sign of good news.

He was dressed in the finest of clothing, richer than anything I'd seen him in. He had a light lilac tunic with the most intricate beading across his chest. The velvet cloak dragged on the floor behind him, shrouding his silver linen slacks. The circlet on his head held back his hair, a single aqua gem placed in the centrepiece. He didn't smile when he looked at me.

"I have come to personally collect you." His voice was stern and formal, "You are to follow me to the throne room where you are to prepare for the duel. In an hours' time, when the great bells are rung, the duel will begin. Please fetch anything that may aid you. I shall be waiting to escort you outside." In the next breath, he stepped away and clicked with his tongue for the guards to follow.

I was almost certain Hadrian's cold tone was due to the guard's presence.

The moment the door closed behind them Nyah sprang from the bed. I pulled on my new boots, already aware of how stiff they would be during the duel, and snatched my claws from my bedside cabinet.

Nyah waited by the door. Her hands were empty of the cloth, but she gave me a quick look and flicked her gaze to her boot where I saw a small patch of material sticking out. She pushed it down with her long nail, until it disappeared inside.

∽

I KEPT MY eyes ahead of me, not looking at the many elves who stood watching me pass. I heard some whisper words of luck, but others didn't.

Hadrian stayed ahead of me and Nyah behind, both their presences appreciated whilst we passed through the throne room. By the time we reached a room off to the side, my entire body was shaking.

Nyah reached for my hand and squeezed before whispering into my ear, "Good luck." She was ushered away by one of the guards before I could thank her.

The remaining guard waited beyond the door, leaving me and Hadrian alone inside.

As soon as it closed Hadrian turned to me and engulfed me in a hug. His hard arms pressed in on my sides, his face nestled into the crock of my neck. I first felt stiff, shocked by his affection.

Hadrian let out a large breath that warmed the side of my neck, "I am so sorry this is happening."

"Don't be, it's out of your control."

Hadrian pulled away, but still held onto my shoulders. His eyes trapping me in his stare. "Did you sleep well? Or is that a silly question?"

"I slept fine, considering."

"I would've come back for you last night, but father kept me until the early hours. I tried to get you out of this but no matter how hard I pleaded he refused to call it off."

I shook my head, "Did you find the Commander?"

His faced darkened. "No."

He dropped his hands from my shoulders and I dropped his gaze.

"No matter what happens out there, I *will* stop the duel if I see it getting out of hand."

I forced a smile.

"I want you to do something for me," Hadrian said.

He directed me over to a mirror that hung on the wall across from us. It was a gilded masterpiece of carved wood and flawless glass. It was mounted to the wall by a long, thick chain nailed into the stone.

He placed me before it, standing behind me. It was the first time I'd seen my reflection for a long time. My body had filled out from what I could remember. The shaven hair on the sides of my head had grown out more than Mam would ever allow. The gaps between my braid and roots displayed just how much it'd grown since I left home.

Freckles had blossomed across the bridge of my nose from the sun, just like I knew they would.

"I want you to look at yourself, really look at yourself…"

I flickered between him and my reflection, his tone soft yet commanding.

"And I want you to repeat what I say."

I must have pulled a face because he added, "Do you trust me?"

He didn't wait for me to respond.

Of course, I thought.

"I am strong, I am brave, I am fierce..." he began to chant and I almost spat out with laughter. I paused at the look Hadrian gave me. He was being serious.

"I am strong, I am brave, I am fierce..."

On and on he repeated the chant over my shoulder, his gaze trained to my reflection.

I looked at myself again, deep into my light grey eyes and followed his instructions.

At first it sounded odd, like I was trying to convince myself that I was something I wasn't. But I carried on and the words began to ebb together into a mantra that vibrated through me. It was as if everything disappeared and it was just Hadrian and me. The words began to have meaning, like they were tricking my mind into trusting them. Believing them.

I didn't notice when Hadrian stopped chanting, leaving me to sing the song to my very soul.

Hadrian spoke up, interrupting my song and stopping me.

"My mother used to do this with me every night before I went to sleep. Stand me before the mirror in my room and repeat those very words with me until I believed them. It took a while, and sometimes I still doubt myself. But she would tell me that our only enemy is within and once you overcome it, you can conquer anything."

"She sounds like a wonderful person." His smile warmed me.

"She was."

I turned from the mirror to face Hadrian. He ran his warm thumb down my left cheek and across my jaw, stopping beneath my chin. All I could do was stare into his eyes, his gorgeous, powerful golden eyes.

In a trance, I leaned into him and pressed my lips to his.

At first, it was only me behind the kiss. But it didn't take long for us to melt into one.

His warm lips danced with mine, tugging and nipping. I gave into him, moaning when his hand dropped from my chin and both his arms wrapped around my waist. I could feel the cold glass of the mirror press into my back, but I didn't complain. We pushed and pulled each other, the kiss intensifying. His tongue brushed against mine, checking to see if I would allow him in.

He pulled back, not by much, but enough to whisper, "I vow to keep you safe..."

My stomach flipped and goose bumps spread across my hands and arms. He nestled into my neck, and kissed me over and over. I tilted my head to the side, allowing him to get closer. "Why do you care so much?" The words flew out of my mouth. I drowned in the pleasure of his closeness. The kisses on my neck ceased and he pulled back, his lips red and swollen.

"Because for the first time in a long time, I have met someone who treats me as an equal on all levels. I have experienced and shared things with you I thought I never would. I am still not sure why, but I know more than anything else that I would do whatever you asked of me."

I was stunned into silence. I nipped at my own bottom lip, absorbing his words, but wishing he would take me again.

He placed another kiss on my palm and then on the back of my hand. "So that is why I care. I care because that is what you deserve. I care because every morning I have woken up and my mind passes to you. It also helps that you are one of the most beautiful creatures I have ever had the pleasure of standing before."

I grabbed his face and planted another kiss on him.

We pulled apart when the bang of a bell rang out in the hall. My heart sank and we both gazed to the door.

The duel was about to begin.

TWENTY-NINE

"WELCOME ALL. I see you are all as thrilled as I am to see the display of two new recruits and the results of their training." King Dalior spoke with confidence, walking around the empty square space in the middle of the crowded room. A long, deep silver robe dragging across the floor behind him. His choice of clothing spoke volumes, diamonds and crystals glittered across his bodice when he walked.

I spotted Commander Alina and Illera who stood behind King Dalior, both their eyes glued on me. *Why is Illera here?* I was confused to why she was dressed, ready to fight. Where was the guard?

Gentle hands brushed against my back and shoulder, someone even grabbed my hand as I passed through the crowd. It was hard to see who it was through the blur of faces that pushed to the front of the crowd to get a better look.

I decided to keep my focus on the Commander and her alone. I wanted her to know I wasn't afraid. Even when I really was.

Hadrian's hand was pressed into the curve of my lower back and he directed me forward. He didn't drop it. Not even when King Dalior looked up to us and spoke.

"Welcome my son, Hadrian, Prince of Thessolina." King Dalior lifted his hand towards us, the numerous rings that covered each finger winking. "And Zacriah Trovirn."

Whispers from the crowd erupted, some pointed at us and giggled. Unlike Hadrian, I scanned over them all, hoping my sharp glare would stop their laughter.

When we reached the empty space in the middle of the throne room, King Dalior stretched out his hand for me to take. I took it, noticing just how ice-cold King Dalior's was. He pushed his own hand towards my lips, forcing the largest ruby ring bit into my mouth.

King Dalior held it to my lip then he ripped his hand from mine and walked back to the Commander. His face burned with disgust.

"Please welcome Commander Alina and her chosen competitor, Illera Daeris. Illera has joined our Rank Mamlia and is one of the most powerful shifters we have had the pleasure of hosting at Olderim." He wrapped a jewelled arm around Illera's shoulder to show her off to the crowd.

It was clear who his favourite was, and it didn't go amiss to the crowd. Eyes were trained on Illera and the Commander, some even going so far as to throw an assortment of petals their way.

I looked at Hadrian for comfort, but he was ashen. His tense body watched his father hug Illera. He didn't take his eyes off him, but instead leaned into my ear and whispered, "Alina has gone against my request and picked a shifter not a guard…"

I couldn't respond. I looked back to King Dalior who carried on his conversation with the crowd.

"The rules are clear. The duel will last for as long as *I* see fit. Both competitors are to stay within the space provided, and as both are shifters they are able to use their ability if necessary."

I yanked on Hadrian's hand as he stepped forward. "Don't," I hissed.

"Guards," King Dalior shouted, clapping his hands. All around us the room burst with movement. Within seconds, guards pushed through the crowd and began to line the square space we stood within. They each held a short spear out in front of them, blocking the crowd with their weapons.

"Illera Daeris, Zacriah Trovirn. You are to stay within the area provided. The guards are there only to protect the crowd in case you become... enthusiastic. I wish you both luck and for the Goddess to look down on you as a spectator to see just how powerful her children can be. You may take a moment to prepare yourself before the duel begins." And with that, he swept from the duelling space and filtered into the crowd.

The crowd erupted in cheers. Their claps of thunder echoed across the large, stone room, matching the frantic beat of my heart. I didn't know what to do. I tried to catch Illera's gaze, but she wouldn't look at me.

Hadrian took me into his arms and pulled me into a long embrace. His action didn't go unnoticed, the crowd's calls lost their volume of noise and were replaced with gasps.

"I have promised that I will keep you safe, and I will."

"I'm going to lose, Hadrian."

"Just focus, and try your best." He placed something into my hands and planted a long kiss on my forehead, "Either way, show her hell."

"Thank you," I mouthed back.

He walked away in the direction of the wall of guards who quickly let him pass. I watched him leave me, longing for him to come back.

A cough sounded behind me. Illera was ready.

The King's voice rose above the crowd from his hidden position amongst the crowd and shouted, "Let the duel commence!"

Everything slowed down. I opened my hand to find a single petal resting in my palm. Hadrian. My cheeks warmed and my heart slowed enough for me to focus.

I stuffed the petal into my sleeve and turned to Illera who was already in position, waiting.

I bent my knees and tensed my core for balance. Keeping both my fisted hands before me, I watched Illera juggle a short dagger between both her hands.

A long blow of a horn sounded around us and Illera wasted no time in making her first move. She leapt across the space between us, thrusting the dagger at me. Lightning fast jabs. I dodged, stumbling backwards. I was already losing my balance, aware that Illera was moving me towards the spikes of the guard's spears. I was waiting to make my first move, calculating the best choice. She swung the dagger. I felt it brush inches before my stomach.

I dropped and rolled to the side, needing to get out of the corner she forced me into.

I found my footing against the slick floor and loosened my claws from their holders. I lifted my hands up, the light catching the tips of the metal.

Time to dance.

They sang as I slashed through the air, aiming for her face. I revelled in her surprised expression, but she moved just in time before my claws caught her.

Adrenaline burst within me, filling every muscle with fire.

I almost fell when her leg connected with my shin, but I caught myself in time to slam my forehead against hers. She stumbled back, her hand pressed to her nose. Blood oozed between her cupped fingers, droplets escaping and falling to the floor.

The crowd's sounds changed with each move. Their shouts mutating from ohhs and ahhs to screams and shouts. Hearing their joy over seeing blood sickened me.

I heard Hadrian over them all.

Illera straightened and dropped her hand, revealing her nose and bloodied mouth. She ran her tongue across her teeth, making a wet smacking sound. "Want to see my claws?"

My body chilled.

She wouldn't dare.

I moved quicker, aiming for her arms, legs and face. Anything to stop her. She smiled and dodged my advances, one after the other. I knew what she was thinking, what she hinted at. I couldn't let her shift.

I swiped again, catching her with my claw. I retracted, then pain exploded on my side. I looked down to see an open gash and Illera yanking her dagger back. She'd stabbed me.

It was ice cold and burning hot all at the same time. I was transfixed by the gushing blood and Illera took full advantage. One moment I was looking in shock, the next I was screaming as Illera jammed two fingers into the cut.

Pain raced up my left side and my vision faltered. I crumpled, wanting to get away from her. I pressed a hand to my side and rolled, dodging a foot as she kicked out.

I was blind with panic.

My magick stirred.

A fist connected with my face.

 A foot smashed into my leg.

I screamed.

She stabbed at me again. I slapped my metal coated palms onto either side of the blade and with all my strength, I twisted. The dagger fell from her grasp and I threw it behind me. I didn't know where it landed, but I heard a gasped scream of someone in the crowd followed by the dull thud of the dagger. I didn't care.

Illera's face twisted in rage and she pounced forward. She went for my throat, both hands reaching out. I swung a fist into her throat and she stumbled back.

I lifted my foot again and aimed for her chest, but she grabbed it and turned with it in her grasp. We both went down to the floor. The back of my head smacked into stone, sending a spark down my spine.

She lay on her stomach, my leg beneath her and she sank her teeth into my exposed ankle.

"BITCH!" I screamed.

In blind rage, I dug my claws into her back until the tips had disappeared beneath her clothing, into her warm flesh.

She roared. But it was not a normal sound, her beast was waking.

She let go of my leg and I pulled it from under her. Scrambling backwards against the floor.

I turned to find Hadrian, hoping someone would call off the duel and announce me victorious. Then, I smelled the shift.

Within seconds Illera was no longer behind me. The lion was bigger than I remembered it to be. It wasted no time to pounce.

I opened my mouth and froze. Illera placed a paw on my shoulder and held me down.

She opened her jaws, strings of spit connecting each pointed tooth. *This was it.*

A loud horn blew. I opened my eyes and saw Illera looking in the direction of the sound. Hadrian was shouting, running through the wall of guards, his sword drawn and pointed at her.

"Get off!" His scream matched the purr that vibrated in Illera's throat. He stood his ground, pressing the tip of his sword onto her muzzle. "NOW!"

"Stand down, Hadrian." King Dalior's voice burned with anger. Even Hadrian faltered at the rage that oozed from him. I rolled my head to see King Dalior walk through the crowd, the Commander following behind.

"It is an unfair match, you cannot allow duel between a lion and a simple elfin."

"I can *allow* whatever I deem fit; I am your King! This is not over, not until I say it is."

"But—"

"You have spoiled this event for your own selfish emotions. Stand down."

Hadrian dropped the sword from Illera and stepped back. "I request a break."

King Dalior kept Hadrian's gaze, cocking his head to one side. "Is that so?"

"Allow Zacriah a moment to prepare, please. Father, please!"

King Dalior recoiled at the word.

"Fine. Both competitors have until the horn blows to compose themselves. Believe me, if you interrupt the duel again you will be removed from the room, Prince or not."

King Dalior turned and walked back through the wall of guards. I didn't notice how silent the room was until he left from view.

I fell into a fit of coughs when Illera removed her paw from my chest. I rolled on my side, keeping my eyes on her as she padded toward Commander Alina.

Hadrian knelt beside me and pushed his hands beneath me to help me up. "Let me get you some water and clean you up. We do not have long."

A stool had been brought forward and Hadrian placed me on it. A chalice turned up and I took the first gulp, swigging it around my mouth and spitting it onto the floor. Blood and water covered the ground before me. I repeated the process until the coppery twang left my mouth.

"You shouldn't have done that," I said. The cut in my side stung when Hadrian held a wet cloth to it.

"I do a lot of things I should not do. I promised I would stop if it got out of hand and from where I was standing, it looked like you were about to have your face ripped off."

He was right, but he was only delaying the inevitable.

I followed his gaze to where Illera was, still in her shifted form, prowling back and forth.

There was shuffling behind me and a familiar soft voice. Nyah apologized, pushing her way towards us. I could hear those around her complain, but she caught our attention and waved.

"Let her through," Hadrian commanded.

The guards moved their spears and allowed her to pass. She fell to her knees beside me, her face pinched with concern. She lifted my hand to see the cut on my side. "If you don't get this looked at you are going to be in serious trouble."

"You don't happen to have some of that healing water with you? I could do with some right about now." My attempt at breaking the tension didn't work. Neither Nyah, or Hadrian laughed.

She shook her head. "I don't. I have been too busy, with… you know."

My heart skipped a beat as I studied Nyah's face. She knew something.

Her eyes flickered to her boot. "Zacriah, I know whose blood this belongs to…"

CHAPTER
THIRTY

ILLERA'S MIGHTY ROAR drowned out what Nyah said next. But it didn't stop me from reading her lips. Until a single name rang in my head.

The name melted my control.

The name was the hammer that smashed the cage open.

The name broke down every wall.

The name allowed the world around me to burst into wind and magick.

I heard Nyah shout, but I could no longer see her.

I opened my hands and the doors to the room burst open. Wind screamed against the stained-glass windows until they too burst, sending shards across the crowd. Screams of confusion and fear filled the room, elves cowered to shield themselves from the raining glass and onslaught of wind that roared around them.

I didn't care.

I threw my arms forward. The torrent of air reached Illera first.

It was so easy. I was unstoppable.

I flicked my hand and she flew. I needed her out of my way. She skidded across the floor, nothing more than my toy. I giggled, watching her flailing body slam into a set of guards who had been moving closer to me, spears up, sending them toppling over one another.

I pushed both hands to the floor, spending a burst of wind away from me on all sides. It reached the guards that walked for me. They each went down to the ground and toppled into the crowd.

Illera whimpered. I turned my gaze to her and brought my hands down, sending my magick on top of her feline body until it crushed down on her. The bones of the guards beneath her snapped, it was music to my ears.

Illera shifted back and gasped for air, stumbling from the broken bodies beneath her and running. *She will not bother me again.*

Arrows rained down on me but never made it past my shield of spinning air. Like twigs, they bounced off my wall and fell to the floor. Many guards attempted to run for me. I slashed the wind at them and sent their bodies smashing into the walls.

I was their hurricane.

I turned for Alina who stood before me. Her sword drawn. Pathetic. The name, her name, still rang across my mind fuelling my storm. It was her.

"Why?" my voice thundered across to her.

She only smiled.

It would be her last.

A part of me wished for answers, to find out why she had done it. It was her in the forest who'd tried to kill Hadrian. But the overwhelming emotion that filled every cell in my body only wanted one thing. Death.

I lifted a single finger and pointed at her. I wrapped my air around her sword and yanked it from her hands. She was a chicken in my pen of air, and I was the fox.

Her mouth was forced open by my magick and my tendrils of power flowed into her. She clawed at her throat whilst I winnowed all remnants of air from her lungs. She would no longer need it. Her cheeks began to cave in, her eyes red and bulging.

I laughed at her attempts to make any sound, taking pleasure in every gasped cough and gurgle of spit that flew from her mouth.

I held her from the floor, my little doll.

A familiar beacon of warmth hit my shield and I turned to see Hadrian, his red face mid scream. He was beautiful awash in his own flames.

This was for him.

I yanked hard at the invisible strings that held me tethered to Alina. They pulled her arms and legs in different directions. Her face contorted in pain and terror.

Hadrian slammed his fiery fists, hitting my wall of air. It irritated me.

I pushed more power into my shield and turned back to Alina.

It took me a moment to realize she was dead. I was disappointed, I wanted her pain to last a life time.

I no longer had a need for her. I closed my eyes, pulled at my cyclone of power and sent her lifeless body flying. Her body spun around and around until she fell from view outside of a half-smashed window.

As soon as her body disappeared, everything began to falter.

What was I doing?

Hadrian took full advantage of the slack on my shield and pushed through, ripping it open with flames burning from his hands. I squinted from the heat and he grabbed me.

I hated him for it. I tried to push at him, but his strength was too much.

Why was my magick not listening to me?

He was whispering something in my ear, but my power ran wild. Something fluttered beside my head, a small emerald body with pulsing wings. Nyah. I blinked and she had shifted back and placed a hand on my neck. I wanted to scream the moment she invaded my body with her glowing existence. I couldn't get her off.

I screamed and screamed. My magick pushed at her invasion, but against my will, I began to lose my hold. The wind died and my mind fell black.

Nyah kept her hand pressed to me, her face twisted in concentration. The air ceased and the view of the room was spinning in front of me. The great hall was destroyed. Glass and stone layered across bodies of unknown beings, ruby blood puddled beneath them.

"Help me!" Hadrian's voice was filled with panic.

He moved fast, lifting me into his arms. He ran to a door. I couldn't be sure. My mind was focused on the lifeless bodies littered across the throne room floor.

I did this.

I looked up to the main throne room doors where shouts met my ears. Guards flooded into the room, pointing our way. Right at me.

"I killed them," I whispered.

Neither of them responded.

Nyah swiped up a spear from a fallen body on the floor. Her knuckles white when she held onto it.

We reached a door.

"I killed them."

The shouts were growing louder behind us. Hadrian thrust a fist at the door we'd passed through, sending a ball of fire towards it. Flames licked up the doorframe and blocked the view of the throne room.

"It will hold them, but not for long." He was talking to Nyah, not me.

"I killed them."

He ran fast. I pushed at the burning in my chest and fought through the exhaustion that battered my mind. We moved through the darkened rooms, corridors, and down a set of stairs until we were in the belly of the palace.

The guards had made it past Hadrian's inferno, I could hear their feet pounding on the ground after us.

"I killed them."

My mind drowned in exhaustion and it was a struggle to keep my eyes from closing.

Light shone ahead, blinding me for a moment.

We were outside. I felt the fresh bursts of sea hit my face and heard the loud clash of water against rocks.

Hadrian dropped me from his arms. I tried to stand, but wobbled to the ground.

I squinted to where Hadrian was running to. I spotted two shapes who stood in the distance. One was waving their arms to catch our attention. Hadrian noticed I wasn't following and turned back. He shouted something. I couldn't hear.

The arrow surprised me at first.

There was no pain.

I looked down at my chest to see the metal arrow head poking out from my shirt. I poked my finger on its bloodied point, my metal claw clanking against it. I looked from the arrow to Nyah whose face was a mask of a silent scream. I turned behind me in time to see the next arrow fly at me from a window in the tower closest to us. It struck my leg, sending me to the floor from its strong force. Still no pain.

I opened my mouth to call for her, but choked on the sudden bubble of blood.

The world tilted and I fell to my side. Then there was only water.

CHAPTER
THIRTY-ONE

THERE IS ONLY PAIN.

I am pain.

I breathe it. I live in it.

Fire courses through me. Water drowns my ability to move. There is no air. I am buried under mounds of earth.

There is no light. I don't see the blessed tree of life. Only black.

Hello? No response.

I give into the lull that rocks me like a lullaby.

Goddess, take me.

CHAPTER

TɊIRTY-TWO

I HEARD VOICES around me but no matter how hard I tried to open my eyes, I couldn't. Hadrian was next to me, I could feel his hand in mine. Its warmth, like dwindling fire and the midday sun.

The room smelled odd. I couldn't place its scent. Wet leaves, earth and… the sea. I could smell the sea.

Hadrian squeezed my hand again.

My name. I heard it being called, but it sounded distant. As if it was being screamed underwater.

I wanted to open my eyes, to respond to them. But sleep was easier to face.

❦

"I SWEAR TO you, if you don't wake up right now I'm going to drag you out of bed myself!"

Nyah's voice pulled me from my deep sleep. I peeked my crusted eyes open and peered at her. She towered beside me, both hands on her hips. There was a graze, half-healed on her cheek and her hair was limp over her shoulders. It was hard to see much else from the overwhelming light behind her. "It's nice to see you're finally up."

I opened my mouth, but my jaw screamed from the tension. My mouth was too dry to respond, my lips too cracked. I tried to lift my head to still my confusion, but my neck resisted. My entire body ached with sores and pains.

I heard water being poured into a cup from somewhere in the room. But Nyah was still beside me. Whoever it was had heavy footsteps as they walked over to me. My eyes had still not adjusted to the intrusive light that reflected off every part of the mysterious room, so I couldn't make out who it was. A glass chalice with silver decorations was passed to Nyah who then held it to my lips, her hand lifting the back of my neck.

She tipped it up and water poured into my mouth. The water soothed my aching throat and quenched my thirst. I took the first two sips with caution, but finished the chalice in hulking gulps. I couldn't get enough.

"How are you feeling, Zacriah?" The mysterious figure asked.

"Do I know you?" I rolled my head, ignoring the scream of pain, and caught a glance at the speaker.

I recognized his face, but I couldn't place where I'd seen it before. There was a large scar that ran from the bottom of his right brown eye down to his lip. It was thick against his deep bronze skin and disappeared under the long thick beard that was peppered with grey. His face was weathered and covered in deep wrinkles that pinched on either sides of his eyes and covered his forehead. Besides the thick beard and equally bushy brows, he had no hair on his head.

"It's been a long while since I last saw you." He placed his rough, calloused hand on the sheets above my chest and smiled, showing off his missing teeth. "Do you remember my name?"

I shook my head.

"Good. It means my power worked well on you." He winked.

"Gallion, I think we should wait for Hadrian to return before we…explain," Nyah interrupted.

Gallion. I repeated his name in my head, as if it would help bring back my missing memories.

"What happened?" I croaked.

Gallion pushed on my shoulder, stopping my attempt to sit up.

"You need to rest," he said, holding me down.

"Would you go and fetch Hadrian? Precious time has already been wasted waiting for Zacriah to wake."

"I'll be back as soon as I can," Nyah whispered, running a hand down my frozen arms. "Don't worry about him, he's harmless."

I didn't want her to go. I tried to reach for her, to pull her back, but I was too weak. She slipped out of my grasp and left, closing the door behind her.

I was thankful for the sudden darkness as the door shut out the light. It was easier to make out the details of my situation.

Gallion stepped forward, taking Nyah's empty space beside me and leaned in close.

"You've been through a shit storm and it's going to take you a few days to get back to normal," Gallion said.

"Where am I?" I asked.

"I will answer all your questions as soon as Hadrian gets here. You've been out for three days and he's gone mad waiting for you. He'll be fuming when he hears you are awake and he wasn't here when it happened."

I raised a hand, moaning, and pressed it to my eye. Everything sounded so loud. I closed my eyes, trying to focus on stilling the overwhelming noises around me.

"Are you in pain?" Gallion asked.

"Everything is too loud. Why is it so loud?"

Gallion didn't reply.

"What's happened to me..." Pressure was building in a cavity in my chest. Gallion dropped eye contact and placed a thick finger to my lips. "Hadrian will be here soon and then we will explain."

"But why can't I remember?"

"I've placed a barricade on your memories. Trust me, you will thank me for it." His reply was simple, short.

With every passing moment, the sounds grew louder around me. I heard a pounding, someone beyond the room. So loud, my head screamed with pain.

The door was kicked open and the wash of blinding light filled the room once again. I squinted past Gallion to the doorway to see a silhouette.

Hadrian. One moment he stood in the door frame and the next his arms were wrapped around me. Gallion fussed over Hadrian's shoulder, but he was ignored.

"Be gentle, boy, he's still in pain!"

I didn't know why I was crying. But tears streamed down my face and smudged across Hadrian's cheeks. My arm ached as I lifted it to wrap around his shoulder.

"Are you feeling better?" Hadrian asked, holding my face in his hands and looking me up and down. A shadow of a beard covered his jaw and neck. Beneath his eyes, two large dark bags stood out in contrast to his pale skin. He looked exhausted.

"You suit a beard." It was the only thing I could say. Hadrian took my hand in his, running it across his beard.

"I grew it just for you," he replied, his smile not reaching his eyes. "I am sorry I was not here when you woke. Blame Gallion, it was his suggestion I should go herb picking with his sister to pass the time. I would never have gone if I knew."

"What a reunion." Nyah came and stood to the other side of my bed. "I'm just glad Hadrian has someone else to talk to now your awake."

Hadrian shot her a look then turned back to me.

"You look like you are in pain."

"I'm fine. Is anyone going to tell me what is going on?" I looked to Nyah first, then to Hadrian who was already looking at Gallion. They each seemed stressed by my question.

Gallion placed a hand on Hadrian's shoulder, a single crystal ring on his middle finger. "I think it might be best if we take this slow."

"I agree," Hadrian said.

"What he said," Nyah agreed.

"Zacriah, if at any time you become uncomfortable, we can stop. You may feel some pressure first, but it will ease in time." If Gallion's words were meant to calm me, it didn't work.

"Just be careful," Hadrian cut in.

I was surprised at just how warm Gallion's touch was. He splayed his fingers across my forehead, "Hadrian will ask you questions whilst I remove the barrier. Take your time and don't panic. Once the barrier is down, I will not be able to put it back."

I reached my hand out and Nyah grabbed hold of it. "I'm right here, Zac. Breathe."

My vision filled with a glow of opal. I felt the tickle of power radiate from Gallion's hands and fill my mind.

At first it didn't feel like anything. Then I felt it. The barrier. The strong wall of pressure was alien to my body.

"Do you remember the duel?" Hadrian asked.

I didn't, not at first. But slowly the memories of the crowd, and the throne room seeped back into my consciousness. I could see the Commander, Illera, and King Dalior.

"Yes," I replied.

"Do you remember when I stopped it?" Hadrian asked.

His words were the key to unlocking the door of new memories. As soon as he asked I saw Illera shift and pounce on me. I wanted to scream. It was all so real.

"Yes." I could hear the panic behind my reply.

"Do you rememb—"

Anticipation took hold of me and I ripped down the barrier. I felt Gallion's surprise through our connection.

"Yes," I sobbed, "I remember everything."

All at once the memories flooded over me. The wind, the magick, the fire. I saw the bodies of those I'd killed every time I blinked.

"It was Alina. She was the one in Nasamel forest. The one who tried to kill me." Hadrian's voice shook. From sadness or anger, I didn't know. "You had been right all along. It was never the Morthi."

"I killed her." She'd hung in the air, her body lifeless and under my control. I had killed her.

"...As we escaped the palace, you were shot. I thought we had lost you."

There was a phantom pain tingling in my chest, then in my leg.

"You died," Gallion said. I hadn't even noticed he'd removed his hands from my head.

"I remember." It was all I could say.

"You lost control of your mind, your magick took over. That, is my fault," Gallion added.

I looked at him, "How? I still don't even know who you are. How could you be at fault for my actions?" It was hard to see him through my tears.

"You still have a lot to learn," he responded.

"Where are we?"

"A small Island off the coast of Eldnol," Hadrian added, taking my hand and squeezing. "After the archers got you,

you fell off the walkway into the ocean. We lost you. It was Browlin who saved you."

"She jumped in after you, found you, and brought you out of the sea." Nyah said.

"My sister has her uses." Gallion shuffled. "Speaking of the witch…"

It was hard to miss the light popping sound from the left side of the bed. I turned my head and saw her, Browlin, bent over to the bed.

I recoiled from her.

"He fears me," she said.

"He has been through a lot," Gallion replied to her, then turned back to me. As they stood beside each other it was clear just how similar they looked. Both shared the same beautiful skin and eyes. She smiled, although I still didn't trust her.

"She's your sister?"

"Yes, that she is. Amongst many other things," Gallion replied.

"He should be more thankful," Browlin said.

"I think that is enough talk on this matter for the day. It's time we all leave you to get some rest," Hadrian added.

"You can't! You've got to tell me what happened. How do you expect me to rest?" I shouted.

"I can help with that," Gallion said whilst he leaned over me.

Hadrian blocked Gallion with his outstretched arm, "I am telling you Gallion, do not do this."

"I have to."

"I will not allow it."

I looked between them as they argued over me like I wasn't here.

"You don't rule over me, boy," Gallion seethed, "Now, move."

Hadrian dropped his arm, defeated.

"You need to sleep, son. We will continue this conversation when you wake."

"Sleep... sleep... sleep," Browlin sang.

"But—"

The world slipped from my grasp as Gallion touched me and I fell into his waiting magick.

THIRTY-THREE

I STUDIED THE map of bruises that hid beneath the surface of my skin. Faint blues and purples shadowed the side of my face all the way past my collar bone. Both my eyes were bloodshot, no remnants of white left. I held the mirror before me, although my arm still ached from such a small task, and examined myself.

I looked like a monster. A title I matched in every sense.

I had begged Nyah in the early morning to put me to sleep the same way Gallion had days ago. It was the only time I had a release from the guilt that ate away at me. But she refused.

No matter how many times I went over it, I shouldn't have killed Alina.

Nyah was draped across the wooden chair behind me, mouth open and snoring. I contemplated waking her, but decided against it. She'd spent the past few days with Gallion, training her empathic abilities and was tired. I'd guessed that Gallion was an empath, but there was a part of me that already knew. Deep in my mind I had a feeling I'd met him before. Yet every time I brought it up, the conversation was changed.

I drifted through the endless meetings with Hadrian and Gallion and healing with Browlin. All my time had been occupied and I'd spent no time with Hadrian alone. I was glad; I couldn't take his pitiful stare. Every time he looked at me, it was all I could see.

My strength had returned, but my magick didn't. I put its absence to exhaustion, but with the time that passed, I knew it was something more. I felt the gaping empty space within me where I used to keep it buried. There was not a single part left.

I took comfort in its loss. I didn't deserve it.

Anxious to leave. I tiptoed from the room. I turned a final time to check on Nyah, opening the door carefully so I didn't wake her. It would be a while before she'd wake and notice that I'd left.

∽

I'D GROWN ACCUSTOMED to the sounds and smells of the island. The earthy scent was a result of the dense forest covering most of the island and the daily hot showers that passed over. It must have rained recently for my bare feet were damp as I stepped onto the walkway beyond the room.

For as far as I could see there were only trees, the view was breath taking. All around me were small buildings raised in the treetops and nestled in the dense foliage. It was a village in the sky. Although they were all empty of life, I could imagine how it once was full of it. *I wonder why they're not anymore.*

Birds I'd never seen before hopped across branches, singing to one another. I walked to the edge of the platform to get a better look but my stomach spun as I looked down. I was a far way to the ground below. With the lack of my magick the height made me nervous.

I'd heard about the Alorian way of life. It'd interested me. I knew they lived in settlements above the ground, but never imagined it to look like this.

I began to walk from the room, around the pathway. I brushed my hand against the banister beside me, my legs still weak from the days of disuse.

I reached out my hearing, still not used to how sensitive the world became. I heard the scurry of small feet and rustling of chewed leaves, like it was happening within my own mind.

It took me a moment to pinpoint Hadrian's location. When I did, I recognized the familiar beat of his heart, something I'd listened to the past nights to help me sleep.

I walked the winding walkway down to the ground, regretting my choice to leave boots back in my room. The mossy floor was wet and covered in sharp leaves and twigs.

The closer I got to him, the louder the beat of his heart became. I found the closed door to his room and paused. *What, if after all this, he doesn't want to see me?*

I pushed that worry to the back of mind with the rest and opened the door.

He was asleep when I walked in. I padded across the floor to his bed and sat beside him. He looked so peaceful, his face relaxed, not a line of worry etched into it.

"Can I join?" I whispered, wanting nothing more than to curl up beside him.

He opened one eye, dark lashes pulling apart from one another. His stretch was colossal and his arms reached for me and pulled me close to him.

"I hope this is not a dream." His voice was raspy.

Hadrian stroked my head. His breath had a twang to it, but I didn't mind. I was happy to be in this embrace.

"Where is Gallion or Nyah?" he asked.

"Nyah is asleep and Gallion is scouting with Browlin. News is King Dalior has ships out looking for us."

"Sounds like something he would do," Hadrian replied.

"What happens when they find us?" I shivered at the thought. Nyah had promised me he wouldn't, but the worry of what he'd do to me if he found me made me sick. *Maybe I deserved the punishment.*

"He won't, not here. This island is not on any map in Thessolina and I have studied them all. Gallion is just being cautious before he decides our next move." Hadrian squeezed me tighter.

"This is all my fault." I rolled onto my back, and stared at the ceiling. The guilt was becoming a constant friend, always waiting in the back of my mind to spring on me.

"He lied. There is still a lot for Gallion to tell you regarding my father. Don't blame his actions on yourself."

"If what Gallion had said is true and neither the Morthi and Alorian elves have played a part in this, why would he do it?"

Hadrian sat over the side of the bed, his back to me. I flushed hot when he stood and I noticed his lack of clothes.

"Browlin is leaving for Eldnol today. Gallion has suggested she asks permission for us to take shelter there."

"Do you think they will let us?" I asked.

"I hope so. We have only enough supplies to last us a few more days, and Gallion has something that may entice the Queen Kathine to accept our request."

"Is this another secret? Something else that is being kept from me?" I was frustrated. I saw the way everyone looked at each other.

"You know enough. For now. And I would like to catch Browlin before she leaves, I have an important message I need to be passed along."

∽

"IF YOU'RE HERE for my sister you've just missed her. The old bat is more impatient than me, and that is saying something," Gallion called, turning my attention from the never-ending view of the sea back to him. He was topless, and covered in muscles from his large chest to his defined stomach. We found him on the beach, the orange sun glowing in the open, blue sky above him. He was holding a pose on the sandy shore, his legs lunged before him and both his hands held high above his head.

"You can read minds too?" Hadrian said.

"I can do a lot of things," Gallion replied.

"I wanted her to pass along a message for me."

Gallion stood tall from his position and shook his arms beside him. "If we are given permission to go there, you will soon be able to pass as many messages as you want to. Zacriah, I must say I am glad to see you up and about. It will do you good to get some exercise in."

"I do feel much better today," I replied, kicking the sand from my toes.

"Well since you came all this way, stay. I'm meditating, it helps still my emotions and has incredible results on one's endurance. You *both* might benefit from it."

"Should we be preparing for the possibility of my father finding us?" Hadrian pointed out toward the horizon.

"Unless you are really a spy and you're feeding your father our location, then we have nothing to worry about. Spread out and copy me."

Gallion guided us through numerous stretches, moving from one to the next. Arms raised, legs apart, making us hold positions that pulled on every muscle.

"How are you so sure King Dalior won't find us here?" I asked, my eyes trained to the sea as I moved from one position to the next.

"A shield surrounds this island, think of it as a barrier between ourselves and the world beyond. No one can see in and we cannot see out," Gallion said, gesturing wide with his arms. "Do you forget the magick the Alorian elves possess?"

My stomach grumbled in response.

Gallion turned to face Hadrian who was stretching on the sand. "Hadrian, be a good boy and fetch us some food."

"I'd rather stay with him." Hadrian gestured my way.

"He'll be fine..."

"I will only go if Zacriah says so."

"Just go, I'll be fine."

"See! Now run along." Gallion pushed Hadrian back in the direction of the tree line. We didn't talk until Hadrian was out of view.

Gallion questioned me first. Sitting down on the sand and patting the space next to him.

"Have you worked out where you remember me from?" he asked.

"I have my suspicions."

He smiled, "Tell me."

"During the first visit to Olderim with Fa, we stayed with an empath. You are originally from Olderim so I could only guess that it must have been you."

"Ah, Stevun. It's been a while since I have last heard from him. How is he?"

"So, it was you..." Not many knew Fa's birth name. Not even I used it.

He nodded, "And do you remember why you came?"

"I think you know the answer to that. Why is it I can't remember you?"

"When Stevun brought you to see me, it was because he and Marina were very worried about you. Your powers scared them. I've known Stevun for years and he decided it best to see me for answers..." Hearing Gallion speak of my parents was unbearable. I missed them. "And answers are what I gave them, even if it was not what they wanted to hear."

Gallion leaned over to me and poked my chest. "It is funny how both you and Hadrian had such a similar experience. The only difference is his mother didn't beg for me to suppress his abilities. She understood what it meant, whereas Stevun couldn't grasp that."

My mind raced to catch up with what he was saying.

Gallion reached a hand to mine. "I know you've been learning about Dragori history thanks to Hadrian but there is a lot that the book will not explain."

"I'm just confused as to what this all means…"

"You know what I'm saying."

"Well whatever it is you think I am, I am not anymore. My magick left me in Olderim, it's gone." As I said the words relief flooded over me.

I can't be.

"It is not gone, Zacriah, you're just looking for it in the wrong place."

THIRTY-FOUR

IN THE WRONG place? I shook my head, trying to still my frustration.

"Let me explain." He tapped my chest again. "You've kept your magick in a hold for years. I can feel the empty space within you, deep down. The difference between a Dragori and an Elemental is that an Elemental has limited abilities and their power comes from within. What makes a Dragori more powerful is their abilities come from around them. So, you *are* looking in the wrong place, you should be looking around you; now it is *free.*"

Free. I reached for it again, this time closing my eyes to block out the world of distractions. I reached and pushed but still did not connect with anything within me, but emptiness. "I don't feel it anywhere. How can it be free?"

"Because I made it so."

"I'm not a Dragori. It's impossible! I've seen what Hadrian is capable of and I've never experienced anything like that. Wherever my magick comes from, being a Dragori is not the answer!"

Gallion took both of my hands in his and lifted me to stand. "I want you to focus, take a deep breath and really think about connecting with the air around you. Think about the way it feels against your skin, how it sounds in your ears. I will filter emotions into you until we see what the catalyst for your connection with it is. Each Dragori's abilities are linked to their element through an emotion. It is just a case of figuring what that is for you."

"But I'm not a Drag—"

"Yes, yes, you are. Believe me, I would know. I know as well as your father knows and your mother. You have me to thank for your lack of belief in what you are," Gallion interrupted, "Now, give me your hand so I can show you. I'm better at showing what I mean than explaining."

I had no choice. His hands glowed bright and forced emotions filled me.

I began to laugh, uncontrollably. I was being dragged along in the cascading river of emotions that Gallion pushed into me. Lost to his control.

The laughter soon turned into tears. My heart sank and the sadness gripped me. Tears filled my eyes and spilled down my cheeks, landing on the sand. I couldn't catch my breath.

Different emotions washed over me in quick succession, taking the place of the one before it, messing with my mind. Happiness, sadness, hate and love. I was drowning in Gallion's power.

I had the sudden urge to reach out and scratch at Gallion's face.

The strong emotion shocked me, but soon I lost all concentration and only felt *anger*.

A burning, intense rage.

I'd felt this anger before. And with it, memories of Olderim clouded my vision and I was no longer on the beach.

I knocked Illera's feline body away, she was no match for me.
Alina smiled.
I hated it, I hated her.
The power surged around me, following my every move, snatching the life from the survivors that attempted to escape my fury.

No one was going to survive this time.

Someone called my name.

No.

I threw more power behind my magick. I was unstoppable. A monster of their creation. A demon of their actions.

I was stopped before, I wouldn't be stopped again.

They would pay.

My name. Over and over, I heard it.

Someone was holding me.

I looked down.

No.

No.

No.

∽

THE SCENE OF the blood-stained palace melted before my eyes. Dissipating, until I was left, staring into Gallion's beet red face.

Sand scratched at my arms and legs, the wind tunnelling around us. My magick. I felt it, but it was different. It'd changed. I tried to pull it back, to stop the cyclone of air and sand around us, but I couldn't. It was out of reach.

Gallion was shouting something, but I couldn't hear him over the roar of wind. His hand gripped onto my arm and I watched his pulsing light spreading beneath his touch.

"Let me in!"

I couldn't. Panicking, I shook my head.

"Stop resisting, let me in!"

I heard him this time. As clear as day. I felt the barrier, it was in my mind blocking Gallion's magick from entering. I closed my eyes and threw my mind's fists at it, trying to break it. Pleading until it finally listened.

Gallion's power filled me once again, destroying the anger and draining it away.

I felt every inch of my surroundings and watched the air begin to still and the sand fall back to the ground. Sweat covered Gallion's scarred forehead, he was panting.

Hadrian stood, windswept and covered in sand beyond the barrier of wind as it broke down. Flames licked across his hands and his golden eyes were burning.

"What the fuck happened?!" Hadrian shouted. The food he'd collected was scattered across the beach, ruined.

"It had to happen, Hadrian, you know it better than anyone. We've wasted enough time not telling him."

"But he is still not ready. It has not even been a week. We need to take our time." Hadrian turned to me and cupped my face, "Are you hurt?"

"Why didn't you tell me…?" I replied, not able to take my eyes off Gallion.

"I'll be around later to explain this to you…" Gallion coughed. "For now, I need a moment."

"I didn't hurt you, did I?" I asked, panicked.

"No, my son. I'm not as in control of my powers as I once was. Let me rest, I will see you soon."

∽

AFTER HADRIAN HAD calmed down and Gallion slept, we all sat in the room and pieced together the puzzle that was me. Gallion explained that the only way for Browlin to bring me back from death's clutches was to reach a side of me that had been buried for a long time. Buried by Gallion himself thanks to my Fa's request.

"When Stevun brought you to me, he had a choice. To leave you to grow as a Dragori or to suppress it, and I am sure by now you can work out which path he chose for you,"

Gallion said from the side of my bed. "No matter what I thought, I did it for him. It took a lot out of me. He was more than disappointed when I could only block the physical traits of a Dragori. Your power, being linked to an important emotion, was harder for me to block. If I'd blocked that, you would never have been the same again. So, when my sister tried to heal you, and found that side of you, she used it as an anchor to bring you back."

I didn't interrupt him, instead I paced the room, trying not to look at Nyah, or Hadrian who sat listening.

"And that is why my hearing is stronger? Why I can smell every little thing?"

"Correct. A Dragori's senses are much stronger than any elf," Hadrian responded.

"So, any moment now I will be sprouting wings and horns?" As I asked it, it didn't sound so terrible. If I would be anything like Hadrian, it excited me.

"Not yet. It is going to take more than an old witch and a retired empath to unlock that part of you. I'm afraid my powers are not the same these days."

"It's what he's been training me for!" Nyah interrupted, "I can tell him that, right?"

"It is going to take more than you and me to complete the ritual. Turns out I was better at doing my job than I was supposed to be. It's why we are headed to Eldnol, we are going to need an entire coven of empaths to help."

"I still believe we need to take our time with this," Hadrian added from the corner of the room. "What is the rush? The Dragori are not needed like they used to. Without the druids, we have no purpose."

"My boy, an ancient evil is stirring. The Goddess wouldn't have brought you both together otherwise. There's been a prophecy, an Alorian seer has foreseen the return of the druids. It might explain what has been occurring across Thessolina in the recent months."

It couldn't be true. The druids died out centuries ago, how could they return?

"Ridiculous," Hadrian said. "You really believe the druids are behind this? It is impossible. It is my Father who is the threat. He has deployed twice the number of ships in the past day. It is only a matter of time before they find us."

"But you said he wouldn't find the island. You said we are safe." I turned to Gallion, shocked he would lie to me.

"No one is ever safe, boy. War is brewing, and it is over something the Alorian and Morthi elves have no control over. This island *is* shrouded, but it only takes luck for a boat to pass through the barrier. And with the number of ships Dalior has between here and Olderim, it is evident that time is coming." Gallion pushed off the cabinet he leaned on and called for Nyah to follow him. "I think it's time we leave these two alone, you and I have some training to resume."

Before he left the room, he turned to face us once more. "Browlin is to return by nightfall. We will talk then and plan our next move. Pray to the Goddess that we've been granted passage to Eldnol. I worry it's our only chance of survival."

∽

IT WASN'T LONG until sundown. Beyond the open window, the sky was beginning to darken, a light shadow of dusk resting across the tops of the trees.

Hadrian passed me a piece of spiked, orange fruit from a bowl and I bit into it. Glad to finally eat after the day I'd had.

"If you don't want to go through with the ritual in Eldnol, I will tell Gallion to stop wasting his time," he said, picking at his strange looking fruit.

"I want to do it, Hadrian. I finally feel like the answers I have longed for are in my grasp. I will not waste this opportunity."

Hadrian patted the space on the bed beside him and I moved to sit. "I have asked Gallion and he doesn't know much about the ritual, but it will not be easy. It may be painful, it might not even work. But if you are willing to take that risk, I will be there with you."

I tried to smile. "How is it Nyah can leave the island and find it again? I've been wondering about that."

"You truly have a question for everything." He chuckled, brushing a silver strand of my hair and planting a quick kiss on my forehead. "I am not sure how it works, and I worry that if I ask Nyah, she may talk me to death when explaining. But, Gallion acts as some sort of beacon to her. My guess is there is a link between them both, being empaths and all. In terms of her being followed, I trust that she is clever with her choices when scouting and can avoid that, we have not had an issue yet and she has been going out every day since we arrived."

I felt like I knew her well enough to trust her ability to stay hidden, but being so safe didn't sit well with me. I half expected an army to burst through the island at any moment, driven by King Dalior's need to punish me for what I'd done.

"And you promise my parents are safe?" I asked. Gallion had reassured me that he has someone keeping an eye on them

"Trust in Gallion's words. He would not tell you something that is not true."

"I am sorry for doing this to you, Hadrian, I never wanted you to go against your own family."

He frowned, taking my face in both of his large hands and pulling me inches from his own. I wanted to look away from his intense gaze, but at the same time get lost within it.

"You need to stop this. Apologizing for something that has been out of your hands since the day my father called for you and the other shifters to attend the feast. None of this has been your fault. My father has not cared for me, despite how he acts in front of the kingdom. Since my mother died, he hasn't been the same."

"You truly believe the answers will be found in Eldnol?" I asked.

"I do hope so."

If we don't find out there, I will make it my mission to find out for you, I silently promised him.

I had nothing to lose, where Hadrian had a whole kingdom to protect.

Hadrian held my face in his hands and kissed me, this time on my lips. We melted into each other, disconnecting from the worries and world around us. His mouth tasted like sweet oranges. He ran a hand down the back of my scalp and brought me closer to him. We sat there, lost in each other's lust.

I'd never felt like this. Never found it so natural to lose myself with someone. I felt whole with Hadrian.

Petrer.

I pulled away.

"What's wrong?" Hadrian asked, his eyes pinched with alarm.

"I've left him."

Hadrian went to wrap his arms around my back, but I shrugged him off.

"Who?" he asked.

"Petrer," I snapped, standing from the bed. "I've left him there. What is he going to think of me? What if Dalior uses him against me, that's what villains do in the stories you read right? I can't fathom what I would do if he was hurt."

With the rush of anger, my magick stirred to life. Gallion was right, it was no longer within me. I felt it pulsing in the room around me. I clenched my hands into fists, trying to catch my breath.

"You are going to need to calm down. Worrying will not change anything."

"If he is hurt—"

"I know, Goddess help who ever touches him. But father will be too focused on you to even look his way. Please, just calm down."

If you tell me to calm down one more time, you'll regret it.

I didn't recognize the voice in my head.

I moved for the door and flung my hands forward, sending the wind to swing it open. I walked onto the pathway beyond and threw my hand back, slamming the door closed.

I ran down the spiralling pathway away from the raised huts. The wind silenced my footfall without my need to ask it. My magick played off my own thoughts, it felt like a large extension of my own body and mind.

I kept going, not stopping until I was deep in the belly of the island. Not until I knew no one would hear me scream.

CHAPTER

Thirty-five

THE AIR WAS thick, heavy, and wet. This far into the island, the trees towered above me, twice the height of any on the island. Each were monstrous, it made sense for the Alorian elves to build homes above ground.

Strong, vine-like flowers blossomed up every possible surface until it disappeared into the dense foliage that blocked any sky light above. I used my magick to guide me through the darkness of the forest.

I kept running until my head spun and sweat coated my skin. I was glad to be away from them all, away from their internal judging.

My back jarred when I landed on the forest floor, exhausted from the run. I had no clue how far I was away from camp and part of me didn't care.

I could see Petrer's face everywhere. In the darkness when I closed my eyes to the shapes in the leaves and bark. I hated myself for forgetting him. No matter what he'd done to me I should've requested for his safety as well as my family's.

He was my best friend, my confidant, and I'd left him like he was nothing more than a stranger. I only hoped Hadrian was right and he was not in King Dalior's line of sight.

I sat there, amid the forest, for a long time. I screamed until my voice stung. I cried until my head ached. I was aware that the sounds of birds and insects had died down, leaving me with only silence as a companion. Night had fallen and Browlin would've returned, but I was still not ready to return to them.

I held a latch on my magick, getting used to how different it felt. I toyed with it, sending leaves from the ground, testing my new control. It was the only distraction I had from my thoughts.

I heard footsteps.

I stilled my magick and listened. Whoever it was seemed to be running, I could hear every rushed footfall.

Nyah burst through the tree line, red faced and out of breath.

"I've been looking for you for a while." She tried to catch her breath. "What good do you think running off has done? Hadrian is worried sick, Gallion's blaming himself for your disappearance and all I can think about is how selfish you are acting." She wiped her hand across her forehead to clear the damp layer of sweat.

"I'm not acting selfish."

"You most certainly are! You're my friend, and I will only ever be honest with you. So, I'm telling you, you are. Stopping running off and acting like the world is against you and help us sort this out. I swear if we weren't friends, I would have punched you by now!"

"Goddess, I am. I'm so stupid."

Nyah laughed. "Zac, you're doing it again. Honestly, you drive me nuts."

"You're right. I should get back," I said, overly aware of how I responded.

"Well, hold on. I've just got here, let me at least catch my breath," Nyah replied.

I caught the glint of the gold band wrapped around her wrist whilst she rubbed at her legs. She caught my stare, and made a face at the band.

"It's funny how this silly thing meant so much to me. Now when I look at it all I feel is dread. I've tried taking it off, but Gallion seems to think that it was never supposed to be removed. He also told me not to bring it close to Hadrian or you. Something about it being painful to a *Dragoreee*."

"Dragori," I corrected her, "Maybe that's what Dalior wanted. Seems odd that after Nasamel he started handing out gold all over the palace."

"Gallion has promised to help me remove it when we reach Eldnol. If we get to go. Browlin still hasn't returned."

"How is it, training with Gallion?" I asked.

She made another face.

"Not all it's cracked up to be?"

"Not really. Gallion's abilities have faltered over the years, he hardly knows what he is doing. The only thing getting me through is the promise of joining the coven in Eldnol," she said.

"If we can go…" I reminded her.

"Yes. If we can go. And plus, they might not even want me to join them. He told me they are pretty strict—"

There was a loud scream above us. Nyah stopped talking mid-sentence and we both looked up.

"What is that?"

The piercing scream stabbed into my ears and I threw my hands to block out the unnatural noise.

Nyah was up, pulling me to my feet.

Everything stopped again. We looked at each other and Nyah's next words set my world on fire.

"He's found us."

We ran for the camp, hoping that the trees still covered our movements from the shadows that passed overhead. I tried to get a glance at what they were, but couldn't make them out.

I reached out my hearing for Hadrian, trying to distinguish him from the other noises around us. Nyah ran ahead, and I followed, trying not to fall over the large roots beneath our feet.

When we reached the pathway, everything was dark. The firelights that usually lined the walkway had been extinguished and there was no sign of Hadrian or Gallion.

"They're on the beach. Gallion is reaching for me," Nyah whispered, pointing in the direction.

"Is it a trap? Has King Dalior got them?" I asked, looking up at the cluster of shadows flying off into the distance.

"We need to hurry."

I followed Nyah who was using her power to guide us to Gallion. I spotted them first, both men pulling a long object towards the sea.

It was a boat, a small vessel.

We stopped running when we reached them and began to help them drag the vessel to the water.

Gallion shouted to Hadrian who at some point had already shifted into his Dragori form. His wings were kept close to his back and the horns made him look like a demon in the dark. He growled and pointed a clawed finger into the distance. I followed it and spotted the ships.

The world slowed and all I heard was my own rushed breathing.

The dark night only illuminated the large shape of the ship. Fire light shone from the many windows on its side, and illumined the large mast with their orange glows. The King's emblem was hard to miss. So was the cloud of moving shadow that hung above the ship, flying around it.

"What are those things?" I asked, squinting to get a look at the shadows but no one answered.

"How did they find us?" Nyah said.

"Browlin. She's on the ship, I can feel her from here. She's been captured," Gallion replied, his voice cold.

My heart sank.

"Get in the boat, Zacriah," Gallion hissed.

I waded out in the shallow of the water and jumped inside, reaching for an oar, my trousers drenched, muscles tense from the cold.

Nyah had shifted and fluttered beside my head. I turned to see Hadrian, who threw Gallion into the boat beside me.

"You are going to need to help, Zacriah, use your power and get us the hell out of here. Push it behind us, it should create enough force to push us forward. Hadrian will help push the boat, we need to create distance between us and Dalior." Gallion was already rowing.

I closed my eyes, reaching for the air around me. It took a moment to grasp it, but once I did I could feel its excitement. I turned to the back of the boat and pushed my hands forward sending the air into the water. *I did it.* The boat pushed forward and I watched the water spray beneath my torrent of wind.

"More, boy, more!" Gallion shouted above my roaring wind. His panic motivated me. I looked to Hadrian who kept up pace with the boat whilst he flew beside it. His wings a blur, keeping him in the air.

Nyah was nowhere to be seen, she'd already faded into the night. I looked around for her, but it was impossible. She'd be safe, I knew she would.

I jolted forward, the boat slipping over the water with great speed.

"We cannot leave Browlin," Hadrian growled.

"No!" Gallion shouted across the scream of the wind. "That is what he wants. We need to get out of here now!"

"She is your sister, we cannot leave her behind!"

Hadrian was right. She'd saved me, I wouldn't let this happen to her.

Water sprayed around us, hitting my eyes and face. I spun my arms around, not thinking about anything, but turning our boats direction.

"What are you playing at, boy? Turn this boat back around." Gallion was reaching for my shoulder.

I glanced back to him. "We are not leaving her behind!"

Hadrian purred in agreement.

"No. Stupid boy, stop!" Gallion smacked out, hitting me in the back. I stumbled forward, my wrists screaming when I landed on them.

I turned back to shout at him, but Hadrian beat me to it. With his foot extended he flew and kicked Gallion in the stomach. Gallion dropped to the boat, moaning.

"What are you playing at?!" I screamed at Hadrian who was flying beside the boat again.

He growled.

Something landed in the boat beside my feet. I peered down to the creature and its bent wings. In the darkness, I couldn't make out what it was as it withered and twisted. It made a sound, a mix between a scream and a screech. I first thought it was a bird, until another smashed into my back.

My magick faltered and Hadrian roared.

Half formed shadows pelted from the sky around us and we drowned in their embrace.

CHAPTER

Thirty-Six

CLAWS TORE INTO me. I threw my hands up only seconds before the cloud of beasts overpowered us.

Frantically, I pushed and slapped at the creatures, trying to break free of their hold. They were everywhere, but still I couldn't make out what they were.

I couldn't see anything. Not Hadrian or Gallion. I didn't risk removing my arms from shielding my face. The boat rocked beneath us and I lost my balance, falling to the ground. I could hear Hadrian from somewhere above me, his roar breaking through the cloud of darkness. Heat exploded, searing the hairs on my arms, which covered my head. Gallion shouted and then all I heard was a splash in the water. I knew without looking that he'd fallen from the boat.

The shadow creatures distracted me from using my magick. Every time I reached for it another creature starched, bit, and clawed at me.

Another burst of heat came from above me and the attacks started to falter. The smell of cooked flesh made me gag and small bodies rained down around me. I looked up to see the half-shadow creature's fall into the sea after they clashed with ribbons of flame.

"They are retreating!" Hadrian shouted.

He was right. They were flying back towards the ship. I scanned the sea looking for Gallion but was unable to spot him. Hadrian landed behind me, his wings held high as he stomped on one of the creatures.

"What are they?" I asked.

It looked like a ball of bone and fur. It was midnight black, and whips of black shadow swirled around it.

"I do not know," Hadrian replied.

A noise sounded from the side of the boat and Gallion's hands reached over the side. I scrambled for him and grabbed on, trying everything to pull him back inside. His face was covered in blood, gold blood.

Hadrian wasted no time in helping me pull him into the boat. Gallion sagged to the floor and laid there pointing in the direction we'd been heading. "We must leave Browlin, go…" His voice was weak, his eyes remained shut.

Hadrian jumped back into the air and I reached for my magick. I latched onto it as much as I could muster and built off a pressure behind the boat. We agreed to follow Gallion's plea, it was our only choice. Browlin was gone.

"Where are we even headed?" I questioned, defeated. Gallion lay before me and Hadrian was somewhere above us in the air.

"I don't know. Just pray we gain some distance before those *things* come back," Hadrian replied.

On cue, the cloud of beasts called out again, filling the night sky with their howls.

They were coming back.

Before I could shout, Hadrian doubled back around and flew at them. I shouted for him to stop, but it was wasted.

Hadrian shot for them and in the last moment before colliding he changed his direction. He flew up, distracting them enough to follow him. Up and up they went until he was nothing more than a dot in the distance. He was closing in on the ship.

I pushed my magic, urging the boat after him. I kept my eyes trained on him, not losing his location for a moment.

Hadrian opened his wings and stopped dead in the air. Then beasts crashed into him and he was swallowed whole.

I didn't see him, only heard the screams of the shadow beasts. They pulsed around him, spinning and twisting until he was trapped within their hold.

I saw a flash of light burn through the beasts. It was small at first but soon the entire night sky above the skip was bathed in fire. Like falling stars, the beasts fell into the sea, leaving Hadrian alone in the sky once more.

I ignored Gallion who groaned on the floor beside me and kept up my pursuit for the ship. Hadrian rained fire down on it, flying above. Balls of blue flame shot in quick succession, illuminating the many bodies that jumped overboard. The night was alight with Hadrian's fire. Reds, oranges and blues danced across the sky, spilling onto the ship.

Hadrian was too preoccupied to see the gleaming net shoot at him. I was too far to hear him when it tangled around his body. He dropped onto the ship and didn't return to the sky.

"NOO!" I screamed, my power pushing our boat closer, faster.

I was gaining on the ship, not thinking about what would happen when I got there. I needed Hadrian back.

Gallion's cold fingers wrapped around my ankle and my anger burst into ash. My body became heavy and I fell in the boat in a heap. I kicked back at him, not caring if I hurt him.

My foot connected with his face, but he still didn't let go. "We can't help him alone."

"We have to try, we have to," I cried. I could feel the boat slowing. I looked up only to see the ship towering above us. I'd made it. I had to get him off me.

Gallion thrust his power into me, blocking my ability to reach my magick.

"Listen to me, Zacriah! Any moment now they are going to take us both. It is up to Nyah now to call for help. It is best for us both if you don't fight them." His words were nothing more than a whisper. The world was fading away.

"You are going to thank me for this when we get out but for now you are going to need to be calm. May the Goddess watch over you, Zacriah, I am sorry."

Our boat slammed into the side of King Dalior's ship and my eyes closed.

∽

MY MIND WAS awake, but my body did not respond.

Time passed, how much I wasn't sure.

I heard the ropes falling against the side of the ship and a thud when unknown bodies landed within ours. Hands lifted me and fumbled around my waist.

They were talking above me, about me, but their words were not clear.

Something collided with the back of my head and my mind burst in a flash of white.

CHAPTER

TbIRTY-SEVEN

I WOKE TO a splitting pain lacing the back of my skull. It throbbed, pulling me from a deep oblivion. I reached a hand behind my head and felt for the pain. My fingers ran across a bump and when I pulled them back, they were soaked in blood.

I opened my eyes, the memories of the ship, the attack, and the shadow creatures coming back to me all at once. *Where am I?* Panic raced through me and I forgot all about the pain.

I swayed, my stomach turning. I faced a wood panelled wall, a weathered brown colour. I knew where I was.

I was on the ship. King Dalior's ship.

Turning my head, I looked to the other side of the room. My heart sank when I spotted the two guards standing above me. They whispered to each other. One held something metal above my head and smiled before tipping it.

Water splashed over my face. I coughed and spat, the smell of stale water enough to make me vomit.

"You can piss in that," one of them said. His voice was dark, raspy. I looked back towards him, to the shadows that spilled from his body. I blinked but they were still there. I looked to the second guard, who also was covered in ribbons of black shadow.

They looked like the creatures that had attacked our boat.

Hadrian. Gallion. Nyah.

My vision swam for a moment. I blinked through the panic to see the two guards passing through a door and slamming it shut. I was left alone.

I waited, listening to make sure their footsteps had faded away before I tried to move. Chains were clamped around my ankles, holding me to the floor. I yanked at my legs, but they wouldn't budge.

I looked around for something, anything to break them. But beside the dented tankard the guards had dropped, there was nothing.

I pulled myself up to the closest wall, pressing my back against it and sat staring at the door. The swaying of the ship and the pain in my skull made me dizzy.

I wouldn't cry. I had to be ready.

It took a while for the rock of the boat to finally lull me to sleep. I fought against the urge, not wanting to let my guard down.

But when no one came back for me, I gave into its song.

$$\backsim$$

MY THROAT STUNG. Every time I risked swallowing my own spit, it felt like knives cutting into me. That was until I had no spit left. The lack of water dehydrating my body to the point of weakness.

The lids of my eyes had crusted together. A single beam of light streamed onto my face from a small hole in the side of the wall. Two nights had passed and the sun had raised to greet me the third day.

I sat up, using my remaining strength and adjusted myself to peek through the hole. My palm's caught splinters whilst I half dragged myself across the rough wooden floor. I ignored the bit of wood that cut into me.

The view was limited but I saw no sign of land. All I could hear beyond the ship's wall was the splash of water against wood and the call of seagulls that cut through the sky beside us. No ports, no Olderim.

I slumped back to the floor, smacking my dry tongue against the top of my mouth to try and create some spit. But it was pointless.

There was a shuffle of noise outside of my cell.

I hadn't noticed the presence, or heard the door open and close since I'd been awake. Whoever it was had been in here, watching me sleep.

I squinted in the direction of the figure, not believing who stood before me, leaning up against the closed door.

"Petrer…" His name sounded harsh from my mouth.

I looked him up and down, surprised at how healthy he looked. His skin was flush with life and he wore a guard's uniform, the same I'd seen many times before.

It was his face that looked different.

He didn't move. He just stood there, watching.

"Please help me out of here, Petrer. You've got to help me." I was pleading with him. Begging. He didn't respond, he only looked at me, turning his head from side to side like a puppy.

He smiled and pushed off the door, "And why would I do that?"

"You must. I'm in pain, Petrer, please."

I looked over him for any signs of the shadows. But there was nothing, not a single sliver of darkness.

"Well I'm fine. More than fine." He kneeled beside me, his breath hot on my face. "I haven't felt this good in a while."

I reached a hand for him, but he slapped it away. I recoiled in shock, "Please, Petrer…"

He laughed, a slow, deep laugh. "King Dalior has sent me in here to give you this." He pulled a gold band behind him. "A gift."

I recoiled from it. It pulsed, like a mirage. "I don't want it."

"You can either put it on, or I will do it for you. Either way, I'm not leaving till it's wrapped around that pretty little wrist of yours."

"Why are you doing this? Whatever King Dalior has done to you…"

"It's what *you've* done to me. I've seen you with him, that pathetic excuse for a Prince. Did you think I wouldn't notice? You were mine, *are* mine. King Dalior has promised you to me, my own gift for keeping you controlled."

This wasn't the Petrer I knew.

I looked him in his eyes, those beautiful brown eyes and shook my head.

"I'm not yours." My words were nothing more than a whisper.

Petrer lunged for me and gripped onto my forearm.

"You're hurting me Petrer!" I sobbed, failing to pull myself from his hold.

"You are a monster, you need to be cleansed. This will help you. It will. It will. He told me…"

I watched in frozen horror whilst Petrer pushed the band onto my hand. The instant it touched my skin the burning sensation sent spasms up my arm and into my body.

"Stop!" I screamed, trying everything in my power to get away. "Please, Petrer, stop!"

But he didn't. He giggled like a child, tightening his grip and pushing harder on the band.

There was a loud crack.

I screamed.

My hand was broken. I looked down to it whilst it hung, mangled, red and swollen.

Petrer was laughing, his wide dark eyes burning with glee. The band was on.

I clutched my broken hand to my chest, sobbing as Petrer watched me. With every second the pain intensified until I couldn't take it anymore.

"Look at you…" It was not Petrer's voice. "Pathetic."

I looked up and saw that Petrer's eyes had rolled back into his head, but his mouth was moving.

"You underestimated me. You thought you could escape, but now you're mine. I am only going to warn you once. That band is going to stop you from accessing your powers and shortly I will need to speak to you. If you think of making a single wrong move I will have Hadrian killed."

"What have you done with him?" I shouted, spit and blood flew from my mouth. I'd bitten into my tongue, trying anything to stop the pain.

"You will see soon enough."

The burning beneath the gold band had stopped, but my broken hand still screamed in agony. Petrer choked and his eyes returned to normal. He looked at me in a daze and turned for the door.

I didn't call for him to stop. I couldn't stand the sight of him.

Dread mixed with panic and anger in my mind. I risked reaching for my magick, but the band lit up and burned with intensity.

It was clear that King Dalior possessed magick. A dark, evil magick.

CHAPTER
TbIRTY-EIGbT

MY BODY CRAMPED. I retched on the floor until all that came out of me was rasping breaths. I longed for water, the sound of it beyond the ship teased me to the point of madness. It'd been hours, days, years since Petrer left me. I was, at first, thankful for the peace. I flinched at every sound outside of the door, hoping to be left alone. But that soon changed. It was hard to grasp the concept of time whilst the gold band sapped all energy from my body. I would do anything for him to return, for King Dalior to return. Anyone.

The cell smelled of dried piss. The warmth of the sun penetrated the panelled walls, warming the cell and intensifying the smell. It was hard to tell the difference between my own scent and that of the room. Everything blended into one.

My broken hand was wrapped up in a strip of material I'd torn from my slacks. The burns beneath the bandage had also dried and crusted. I picked at them, allowing rivulets of red to run down onto the floor. The pain beneath the band was not as bad as it first was. I'd grown used to it, and stayed away from my magick which seemed to be the only time it created pain for me.

Being left alone was going to be the end of me.

I tried begging for someone to return.

"Please."

I repeated it over until it was nothing more than a wheeze. My voice no longer sounded familiar to me.

I couldn't cry. My eyes would burn, but tears never followed.

I was alone. All I could do was gaze at the four walls. My four walls.

Until sleep became my only saviour.

The door opened. Footsteps. They took me...

Hands pinched my sides, my feet dragged on the floor. I blinked, crust scratching beneath my eyelids. I no longer cared to see...

Wood creaked, a door slammed and voices hushed around me...

I was submissive to the pain...

Water splashed over my face. I woke gasping, driven by the need to drink it. My body moved before my mind would focus, my tongue lapping the water that dribbled down my face.

I groaned with pleasure, the liquid slipping down into my mouth, cooling my dry throat. Once my mind caught up, I stopped dead. Someone held a jewelled chalice before my face. I took it and downed its contents. I gulped the water down until I needed to breathe.

My head spun, and with it so did the room. I looked over the rim of the chalice, dread settling over me.

My hand relaxed and the chalice clashed to the floor, spilling precious water.

King Dalior smiled at me from where he stood, his head cocked in amusement.

"It's good to see you." His voice dripped with malice.

I recoiled back.

"I am not going to hurt you, Zacriah, I merely want to talk."

I landed back on both hands and regretted it. Pain shot up my arm, my broken hand cramped. I brought it to my chest, aware of the incessant throbbing.

"I am very sorry about your hand. I am sure we can come to an arrangement to fix that for you."

I brought my legs up and wrapped my good arm around them, ignoring him.

I dropped King Dalior's gaze to get a look around the room for anything I could use against him.

The room dripped in red velvet. Behind where King Dalior stood was a wall of windows, looking out over the sea and endless view. Before it was a desk, covered in what looked to be a faded map.

Beneath me, the carpet of purple, silver and red looked new. Untouched. Papers scattered the floor beneath the desk, covered in drawings and marks that I'd never seen before. There was a strange smell that hung in the air of the room. I couldn't place what it was, but I was sure I'd smelled it before.

To the left, beside the wall, was a strange shaped table covered in a ruby red sheet. The smell was coming from there. But nothing was on it and I couldn't see what was beneath it. I looked back to King Dalior who pushed off the desk and walked over to me.

"Fetch him more water," he said to someone behind me. I wanted to turn around and see who it was, but I couldn't take my eyes of off King Dalior. I wouldn't drop my guard.

He bent down before me and picked the chalice that I'd dropped. He passed it to the hand that reached over my shoulder. I flinched at the stranger's closeness.

The chalice was back in King Dalior's hands and he held it out for me. I was reluctant to take it, but my burning thirst was too much to ignore.

"It is only water. Drink."

I took it and drank.

"It saddens me to see you in such a state, but you must understand it is what you deserve. If you had listened to me and not spoken to Hadrian, then we would never be in this situation."

He looked sad when he spoke. Like he believed his own words.

"Leave us," he said to the faceless guard behind me.

Boots clapped against the floor boards and a door closed behind me.

King Dalior was still inches in front of me.

"It pains me to see such a beautiful creation such as yourself wasted. I know your power and its capabilities and when Alina told me about your power it only excited me. The God has been looking down on me, blessing me with luck. Imagine my surprise when she told me about Hadrian. Two here, in my city. What are the chances?"

King Dalior stood and walked behind me. I followed him with my eyes and watched him place a wooden panel across the door. The *only* door. He was locking me in.

"My plan was to wait and watch. Something I've become quite good at. I've had *years* to perfect it." I watched Dalior walk from the door to the desk, and he reached for a book. I knew what it was before he even turned back around.

"Recognize this?" He held it open on a page I'd studied before. He pointed with a black-painted nail towards the drawing of the Dragori, a smile plastered across his face.

"It has been a long time since I've heard of these creatures. A long time since my people created them. A long time since they were stolen from me. But now, you are mine. If only my brethren could see me."

I shook my head, holding tight onto my arm and stared at him. He couldn't be.

"You and Hadrian have both caused me a lot of strife," he spat, slamming the book closed, "but I am willing to forgive you for it, if you consider my request. Join me, fight by my side against my enemies and your crimes will be forgotten."

"Why?" I croaked.

I fell backwards the moment he turned to me. His face was contorted in anger and he spat whilst he screamed in my face.

"You have no idea what *they* have done to me. What pain *they* have caused. It is my time to get my revenge, I've waited long enough and you will either help me or face the consequences. The elven continents must pay for what they have done."

"Where is Hadrian?" I snarled, pushing my face closer to his. I would not let him scare me.

"Wouldn't you like to know? I never did thank you for saving him. If Alina succeeded in killing him I would have been one Dragori short."

My arms shook, "You wanted him dead! How could you do that? He is your son, your blood."

He laughed. A slow, deranged noise and smiled.

"You silly, silly boy. You still know so little."

"You tried to kill him and blame the Morthi, you wanted to use him to start a war for your benefit."

"True, but in the end, I didn't need to spill blood to get what I wanted. Now the whole of Thessolina has answered my call. There will be war. And you will be a part of it."

"No," I spat, attempting to stand.

"You will."

He walked to the left of the room, right towards the covered table. His jewelled hand gripped onto the material and with a great tug, he pulled it off.

It wasn't a table at all. Beneath the sheet was a cage. Sunlight danced across the golden bars and inside it, was a body. Blood covered every inch of his naked skin, cuts and burns like runes etched into him.

I couldn't tear my eyes off him. I stood from the floor, arm still clasped to my chest, and walked over. The smell I'd noticed before was stronger since the material had been taken off. I knew what it was. Burning flesh.

I didn't want to believe it.

I could see King Dalior out of the corner of my eye, but I didn't look to him. I didn't need to.

The body was curled into a ball, rocking back and forth on the base of the cage.

"Hadrian?" I whispered.

The elfin looked up and golden eyes looked through me.

"Hadrian…"

CHAPTER
TҺIRTY-NINE

I LOST ALL grasp on reality and forgot about the pain beneath *my* gold band.

The smell of burned flesh stung my nose, but didn't stop me from trying to reach for him.

I ignored the burns off the gold bars when they knocked against me. I just needed to reach him, touch him.

I called his name, but he didn't say a word in response. He just looked through me, emotionless and detached.

It was clear to see just how much he'd been through. His hair had been burned away in certain parts of his head, clumps laying around him. Lacerations covered his arms and legs, his chest dirtied and covered in blood. He looked like a little boy, a scared child.

"When my people created you, we needed a way to control your powers. So, during the ritual we made sure we gave you a weakness. Gold," King Dalior's voice sang from behind me.

I turned and growled, every part of my body wanting to hurt him. The band burned the moment my anger took over and I willed for my magick to listen. It ignored me, refusing to answer my call.

I threw myself at Dalior. I reached where he stood and launched a back handed slap to his face. He caught it.

He clenched his large hand around my wrist. In the next moment, I was launched in the air. My back slammed against the edge of the desk and I slumped to the ground. The energy that had flooded my body was dwindling rapidly.

King Dalior ran at me. I had seconds to get up before his steel boot would've connected with my jaw. Something crashed to the side of my face. I saw Dalior's foot had connected with the leg of the desk.

"You dare try and attack me!" he screamed, swinging for my face. I was still on the floor, dragging myself backwards until my back knocked against the locked door. I pulled myself up, one handed, and threw myself to the side as a fist came for my face.

I kicked out. It connected with his leg.

King Dalior roared and grabbed a hold of my shoulders. The wind was snatched from my lungs when his knee connected with my stomach.

I gasped, the world slowing down. His fist came right at my face. Before it reached its mark, the boat rocked and we were both sent toppling to the floor.

My head missed a side cabinet by inches as I rolled across the floor. I could hear King Dalior's frustration from the opposite side of the room.

The ship had been hit.

I heard shouts beyond the room. I looked at Dalior who lay dazed on the floor and to Hadrian whose cage had shifted. He was sprawled out on the base of the cage not moving. I needed to get him out.

My broken hand throbbed from where I'd landed on it. I pulled myself up and stumbled towards Hadrian, but caught movement out the corner of my eye. Beyond the window, ivory-white ships covered the sea line. The masts of the ships had a single symbol on them. The burning feather of the Alorian elves.

They'd come for us. The realization gave me enough energy to reach the cage. I turned back to check on King Dalior, but he was no longer on the ground.

Something heavy connected with the side of my head and I lost focus. For a moment, I saw nothing but black.

"I will not let them take you. You are mine." I felt his presence grasp me from behind. Slapping my good hand against his arms, I tried to claw my way out of his grasp, but he didn't let go.

I screamed as loud as I could. If they had come for us, I needed them to find us.

The ship rocked again, but I was still stuck in his embrace. He wouldn't let me go.

I threw my head back until it cracked against King Dalior's jaw. He screeched and spun me around, grasping my broken hand and squeezed.

I opened my mouth to scream, but I choked on the pain. My legs gave way beneath me and I dropped to the floor. It was over. I couldn't fight any more. I peered at my broken hand, the skin already bruised in purple and yellow.

There was a sound beyond the door.

The noise came again, and I noticed King Dalior's focus was also directed towards it.

There was a final shudder and the door burst open. Wood and water exploded across the room. I turned my head to Hadrian as the water rushed over me. I cried out and covered my head in shock.

My mind raced to catch up. I scrambled from the ground, water up to my ankles. We were sinking. Then the water started to pull backwards towards the door.

I followed it, turning for the door to see a woman. She stood in the entrance of the room, arms raised, and water spinning in the air around her. She lunged forward, her right hand striking out with a silver sword. Right towards Dalior.

He dodged her attack, but didn't take notice of the snakes of water that shot out from behind her. He flew across the room and landed against the wall of windows, trapped in the hold of the woman's water. Cracks spread across the panes of glass beneath him. They were going to break. The woman didn't stop. King Dalior struggled to break free from the waters grasp. He howled and thrashed, only urging the glass under him to break.

I tuned back to the woman who walked, hands raised, towards him. With every step she took, the water beneath her boots joined the hanging wave behind her. More tendrils of water reached for King Dalior and held him pinned to the glass.

I couldn't speak.

The room darkened. King Dalior's laugh was loud, clear as a bell over the rushing water. The hairs on my arms stood on end and I turned back towards him in horror.

His eyes faded black and his skin began to melt, dripping from his face like molten liquid. Like a snake shedding its skin, he no longer looked like the King. Shadows spilled from his body and wrapped around the woman's water, merging with it.

Dark runes covered his skin beneath his black eyes. His hair fell from his head, disintegrating in the air around him. A deep, earthy laugh fell from his stained black mouth and he raised a hand, pointing at her. "You."

It was the only thing he could say. The woman jumped on the desk without effort and the hood on her head tumbled off.

"Fuck you, druid!" she screamed. Her water exploded towards him.

It happened so fast. The glass of the windows smashed and the water dragged Dalior beyond into the sea.

She turned to me and shouted above the ruckus, "Stand back!"

She raised her palms and sliced them at the cage, water flowed and smashed into the bars. It took four attempts for the water to cut right through, and the bars to fall to the floor.

Hadrian groaned when the water lifted him from the base of the cage, cradling him and pulling him from the gap she had made. He rolled over in it until the water placed him on the floor before pulling back to the woman.

I threw myself beside him. "Hadrian, wake up!" I brushed my hand against his face, but he didn't open his eyes.

The woman reached down and grabbed my arm. "We need to go. The druid is not dead and this ship is minutes away from being under the water. Help me."

She scooped Hadrian's body into her arms and ran for what was left of the door. She was so tall she had to duck beneath it when she ran through.

I stumbled after, struggling to find energy.

Smoke filled the corridor beyond the room. The smell of burning wood made me cough and struggle to catch my breath.

I followed her up the steps until we reached the deck of the ship. It was an all-out war, purple and silver clashed together in battle. I watched the taller beings overpower the guards who tried to fight back, smashing them to the bloodied ground of the deck and moving onto the next. The woman moved through the crowd, signalling a group of her elves to surround us. Within the circle of Alorian soldiers I noticed animals all around the deck. Birds flew around the ship, trying to circle and break the soldiers. I looked around for them but there was no sign of the shadowed beasts.

I tripped over a fallen sword and of the Alorian soldiers grasped a hold of me. I looked up to thank whoever it was, but caught a blur of red hair ahead.

Nyah.

She moved through the Niraen guards, slicing at them. She was a beast, an animal. She wailed as she battled through oncoming attacks, overpowering each one. She was unstoppable.

"Zac!" Her scream lit up the sky when she caught my stare. Her attacks and movement sped up, and she made a path for the protected circle around me. We'd reached the edge of the ship and the woman passed Hadrian to a waiting Alorian solider.

I watched in awe as wings of white ivory grew from shadows that spilled from the woman. The wings were covered in thick feather. Dragori.

"Emaline!" the guard holding Hadrian shouted and she turned to face him. "Take him with you!"

She plucked Hadrian back into her grasp, flew across the side and disappeared.

There was a thud and I was dropped on the deck. I turned back to see a spear piercing through the head of the Alorian solider that had held me. Blood gurgled from his mouth and his eyes rolled back as he fell forward.

I looked in the direction the spear had come from to see Petrer, his arm still raised in a throwing position. He was looking at me, pulling a short dagger from his belt and holding it ready. A shrill cry distracted him. It was Browlin. She was covered in blood, her white dress flowing around her. Opal Light swirled around her as she materialized between two dead Niraen guards, and she ran for Petrer. She moved like a ghost. A burst of light shot for Petrer's hand sending the dagger skirting across the floor away from him.

I wanted to scream for her not to kill him. She reached her hands for his face, but he ducked and weaved under her open arms. In seconds he was behind her, his hands gripped around her neck.

Her face was turning blue. They both faced me, Browlin trapped in his hold. Their expressions were different. I was certain I saw her smile at me. Petrer turned his body sharp and the sound of her neck snapping stood out above every noise on the ship.

I ran for him. I hated him.

Browlin was thrown carelessly to the ground and Petrer smiled. Before I reached him, I was off the deck of the ship and in the sky.

"It's done," the Dragori woman, Emaline, growled in my ear. Her arms held my own and we flew up into the sky. I didn't take my eyes of Petrer who watched me from below.

Emaline changed direction and flew away from the battle. I noticed a small vessel in the sea below and she aimed for it.

I saw Gallion first, waving for us. Beneath him, Hadrian was splayed out on the floor.

"Get to our boat!" Emeline hovered above us, pointing at the grand Alorian ship that hung in the distance.

"I will give word to the rest on the ship to retreat. Then I will finish this," she said, dropping me beside Gallion. I turned to thank her but she pushed her hands out controlling the water beneath our boat to move us forward. The boat flew across the water and Emaline flew back to the battle.

"You're fine, boy, you're fine!" Gallion hushed in my ear.

I looked into his eyes, my own a blur with tears. I had to tell him.

"I know, Zacriah. I felt her go…" He touched his chest above his heart and nodded, "She will be with the Goddess now."

His words broke me.

EPILOGUE

IT'D BEEN TWO long weeks since we first arrived in the city outside of the capital of Lilioira and I still got lost. Unlike the small cluster of buildings on the island we'd stayed at, Kandilin was large and levelled, confusing to follow. I'd dismissed the guide that was given to me days ago, a mistake I regretted whilst I walked past houses.

Every Alorian, solider, or civilian I passed bowed their head and murmured beneath their breath. I was *not* used to so much attention. I always felt eyes on me, never once having a moment to myself. So, I focused on my scarred hand and clicked my fingers when I passed their stares and moved into the belly of the treetop city.

I peered over the elaborately carved walkway, staring down at the vein-like river ways that ran through the monstrous trees Kandilin was built on. Boats and ships moved across the water beneath, they looked miniature from up above.

I didn't remember much of the journey to Eldnol, or what happened when we arrived. I was thankful for the missing memories.

I'd also not seen Gallion for days. Word was he was preoccupied with days of meetings in Lilioira with the Queens regarding the attack. He'd promised to come back for me once Hadrian was better. But in the two weeks since, there was still no improvement in his health.

A large, amber griffin chirped when I walked past it, the saddle on its back shifting. I reached across and ran a hand down its feathered head. They were the most beautiful creatures I'd ever seen. It had been sent to guard me and had followed me to and from Hadrian's room every day. Its sandy tail twisted in pleasure when I scratched behind its ear. I was getting used to his company. He was one of many that filled the tree-top city. I could see them flying amongst the trees, an Alorian rider guarding the city. Everyone was still on high alert.

I walked ahead, beginning to recognize the buildings close to me. I was near.

To my right, I waved at the Elementist who had removed my gold band when I first arrived. He smiled and waved back. He was a gentle man, and someone I owed a lot to. He'd worked hard on Hadrian, extracting the poison from his blood.

I rounded the corner, stepping through the silk curtain into Hadrian's room.

"How are you feeling today?" I asked, moving straight to the side of his bed and dipping a clean cloth into the silver bowl of water on the bedside table.

"Better," Hadrian grumbled, his eyes close. "I was having a dream, a nice one."

"Dreams. It's been a while since I've had one of those," I replied, running the damp cloth down his face. It had taken a lot for the healers to bring him from the state he arrived in. The burns from the gold cage had become infected, they still looked raised and sore. They said it would take a long while for it to be out of his system. Time, I worried, we didn't have.

"You are later than usual," Hadrian said.

"I slept in. I was with Nyah last night, she's been preparing me for today. So, as you could imagine, I didn't get to bed until late."

I dropped the cloth back into the silver bowl and picked up a chalice of water. Hadrian sat up on his own, wincing, and I helped tip the water into his mouth.

"Is there any news on Browlin's burial?" Hadrian asked.

The mention of her name sent an uncomfortable twisted feeling in my chest. "No. I haven't heard from Gallion still."

"I hope he returns soon. I would have thought he would be back for your ritual today."

I leaned into his hand, thankful for his touch. "Did I…"

"I am feeling much better, let me come with you. I want to be there for you."

I shook my head. "I'll be fine. And you still need the rest."

"Is that woman going?"

"If you're talking about Emaline, then no," I replied.

Emaline had not spoken a word to me or anyone since the incident on King Dalior's ship. I'd asked after her daily, but I got the same response. She didn't want anything to do with us.

He tutted in response, grimacing when he led back down. "At least you have Nyah."

"I know. I'll come and find you after, fill you in with all the details."

I could tell that Hadrian's smile was forced.

We hadn't spoken about what happened on the ship. That was Gallion's only suggestion before he left. From what I understood Hadrian didn't remember much of what occurred. But I did. I replayed it over in my mind every spare moment I had. I saw King Dalior's face melt until it was no longer him. It had never been him. My heart broke every time I thought of it. Hadrian still believed his father was out there. It'd never been King Dalior.

I remembered the burning of the gold, the pain. I remember his threats. Petrer, Browlin, everything.

"Will you stay with me till I fall asleep?" Hadrian asked.

"Of course."

I began to trace my fingers across his bald head. I traced patterns and designs with my nail. I felt the slight pricks of new hair growth beneath my fingertips when I ran circles around his skull.

We were silent for a while, the only connection between us was my hands caressing his head. I moved down his neck every now and then until the hairs on his arms stood on end and his skin was covered in goose bumps.

A deep horn sounded beyond the room. I dropped my hand from his head and he looked up at me.

"I have to go," I said, knowing that the horn was my signal. The ritual would start soon. I placed a longing kiss on his forehead and moved for the door.

"They say that fire is nothing without the air that fuels it. You are my air, without you I would just stop. I need you, I want you and I will get better and be there for you."

I swallowed back the lump in my throat and looked at him from the side of the room, wishing I could jump into his arms and have him hold me.

"Sleep well," I said, biting back the tears that wanted to release.

∽

THE AIR PRESSED in on me. I was frozen to the stone floor inside the pentagram that'd been etched beneath me in white chalk. The room was bathed in darkness.

Around me, the hooded figures of empaths swayed and chanted in a language I'd not heard before. They each held a single candle, illuminating their faces beneath their hoods. Although their song was beautiful, it didn't distract me from the building feeling within me.

As their song grew, I watched the smoke from the candles build into a cloud of shadow above me. It swirled in circles, darkening in colour until it was hard to make out in the black of the room. Everything began to melt away, the empaths disappearing, but their chants still audible. I was pinned to the floor, staring at the ceiling of a shadow. It spun faster, the bubbling sensation building within me until I couldn't take the pressure any more.

I opened my mouth to scream and the shadows stilled.

They hung in the air for a moment, then shot towards me, filling my mouth.

The pressure built within me.

Then my world exploded in light.

❦ THE END ❦

Acknowledgements

First, I want to thank all those who said I couldn't do this. That I would never be able to write a book, that it was stupid for me to try... jokes on you.

I want to thank these incredible supports of Cloaked in Shadow before the book even came out. Thank you for giving it a chance and reading it. Jo Painter, Emily R. King, Kathryn Purdie, Danielle Paige, Gabriella Lepore, Rachel E. Carter, Emily Sowden, Hannah Quinn and Kirsty Bonnick, Mum, Dad and Sarah.

Harry, my Hadrian. I love you so much. Thank you for supporting me and being so patient when I needed to write. I love how interested you are even if you don't read. You will always be my love, first and foremost. Thank you for just being you. DI LOVSIES YOUSIES. And to Hannah and Debbie for making me smile and laugh.

Jasmine, my Nyah. Thank you, thank you, thank you. You have been my best friend for a very long time and your honest, loving heart is what has helped me through writing this. You have spent hours reading this story and helping me fine tune it. You have taken my characters into your heart and I am blessed to have you as my friend.

Gwenn, my amazing cover artist. You brought Zacriah to life and I am honored to work with such a talented, TALENTED human.

Oftomes. To all those Oftomes authors whose hard work has inspired me. You each are a shining example of incredible talent. Thank you for just being you.

Christine. I will forever be your bush pig. You will NEVER be my troll. Thank you for supporting me and getting excited with me. I love chatting with you and I can say with my hand on my heart you are the best thing to come out of 2017. CHUCKEN.

Olivia, my amazing editor. Without you, this book would only be a string of words. You made this a story. I adore you. You have worked endlessly on this story and I am so lucky to have found someone who loves it just as much as me.

Jill, thank you. Thank you for taking this book into your heart and proofreading it like a Goddess. Your skill and love for the craft is wonderful and inspiring.

Claire & Chris. You have supported me from the start. I am so happy that I can call you both friends. Your phone calls, calming me down from my freak outs and helping me when I needed it the most is just a couple of examples of why you are so important.

Sasha. Thank you. You have inspired me, encouraged me and been someone I LOVE dearly for years. You have pumped excitement, encouragement, and understanding into me. I appreciate you more than words can say.

COMING SOON
THE OFTOMES 2018 DEBUTS

Colliding Skies by Debbie Zaken

"Brilliant pacing, sizzling romance and a storyline I absolutely devoured." **Victoria Scott**,
author of Fire & Flood.

COMING MARCH 2018

Catching Stars by Cayla Keenan

"Magnetizing—an intricate, brutal world of sorcery, betrayal, and mystery that will captivate and entice until the very last page." **Emily R. King**,
author of The Hundredth Queen Series.

COMING JUNE 2018

Revived by Jenna Morland

"A fast-paced, mystical adventure mixed with heartbreak and hope that will keep you turning the page well into the night." **Brenda Drake**,
New York Times bestselling author.

COMING AUGUST 2018

Saving Death by R. L. Endean

"A heart-pounding romance you'll love curling up with on a dark, chilly night!" **Lorie Langdon**,
author of the Doon Series and Olivia Twist.

COMING OCTOBER 2018

CPSIA information can be obtained
at www.ICGtesting.com
Printed in the USA
LVHW021010240119
605077LV00003BA/219/P